Fifty Handfuls

By

Michael Aloisi

authorHOUSE™

1663 LIBERTY DRIVE, SUITE 200
BLOOMINGTON, INDIANA 47403
(800) 839-8640
WWW.AUTHORHOUSE.COM

First published by AuthorHouse 01/13/05

ISBN: 1-4208-2443-0 (sc)

Library of Congress Control Number: 2005900016

Printed in the United States of America
Bloomington, Indiana

This book is printed on acid-free paper.

To
J.Anna
For being my constant Cheerleader
And
To
Geri for doing more work than me.

1

Lying on her side, she stared blankly at the creamy blue silk she was sliding under her French manicured nails. Kat still had no clue how or when she acquired this odd fetish. She just knew it calmed her. It had gotten to the point lately that she even carried a small satchel of silk around with her at all times. Secretly keeping a hand in her pocket, she would slowly pull the silk back and forth under one nail at a time to feel the soothing threads tickle the all too sensitive flesh.

Hearing the downstairs door open she peered over at the glowing green-neon clock: 11:13. She smiled a little as she anticipated the upcoming routine. Listening to the footsteps, she prepared herself for the smell she loved, yet made her gag at the same time. Jasper walked by the open door to the bedroom, allowing a large gust of over-used cooking oil, onion, garlic and a whole ocean full of seafood to float to Kat's nose. Trying not to breathe in the toxic fume while at the same time savoring it, Kat listened to the shower.

She knew in a few moments the hamper would conceal the stench and the rest of it would be washed down the drain, leaving her to wait for tomorrow at 11:13 to play the same nostril game.

As usual, when she heard the shower shut off she turned on the television to the nightly news for Jasper to watch, which he never did. Kat watched the door waiting for her clue to what would happen tonight. After four years of this routine she'd learned that if Jasper walked in with his towel, he wanted to make love.

On cue, Jasper walked into the room wearing his small blue sleeping shorts and a damp yellow Egyptian cotton towel over his shoulders. He bent down and kissed his wife on the forehead like always. No matter how many good-bye, good-night, hello, or I love you kisses, the last one always landed on her head.

As Jasper walked around to the other side of the queen-size bed, Kat noticed a new bandage on his left forearm.

"Alright let me guess." she said, putting on a quizative look.

"You'll never get this one Hun!" Jasper smiled back. This was the only up side to getting hurt at work. Every time he got a cut or burn he would look forward to this "guessing game", the thought of it always eased the pain a little.

As Jasper placed the towel strategically next to the bed, Kat said,

"Well I'm just going to have to have a look at it now ain't I?" Jasper hopped on the bed next to her.

"It's really not that bad, don't get your hopes up."

He always liked to downplay it so her reaction would be stronger. Kat carefully pulled back the bandage to reveal a half-dollar sized patch of white shriveled skin ready to fall off. She grimaced but quickly changed her face.

2

"Dang it! I wanted to see bone." Carefully she looked at it from all sides as if inspecting a rare diamond.

"Well it's definitely not a cut…I'm going to say a sauce splatter from a Chicken Marsala gone wrong?"

"You're getting too good at this, but you're still wrong." Kat carefully placed the bandage back.

"One of the new dishwashers didn't dry the frying pans good enough so the water dripped down into one of my pans of oil." He confessed.

"Always blaming someone else! Hey, how come Emeril doesn't have arms that look like they've been through a war?" Just before Jasper could answer, Kat lightly poked the burn. He yelped in pain and laughter.

"So that's the way it's going to be." He quickly jumped on Kat, tossing her around playfully until the laughing stopped and the kissing began. As their tongues danced the elaborate chorography that they both knew so well Kat thought to herself, "Right back on schedule."

Without unlocking their wet lips, Jasper skillfully removed his small blue shorts and tossed them on the chair next to the bed before removing the goose feather comforter between them that separated their two naked bodies. As if on autopilot, Kat reached down to help guide him in. They began to make love.

The two of them never talked about how routine their making love was (probably because it wasn't a problem). They both climaxed together ninety-six point three percent of the time, something they'd mastered nine months before getting married.

Jasper on top was always the starting position for the first several minutes. At this point Kat was never really into it (usually she planned out what she had to do the next day). Jasper on the other hand would always be thinking of her skin at this point. Ever since the first time they were intimate he loved how soft and smooth it was. Of course it only felt softer than most women's because he was totally infatuated with her. When Jasper's calloused hands started to gently glide down to her thighs, Kat knew it was time for position two.

They only accomplished this complicated movement successfully about half the time, and tonight was one of them. He lifted her thighs up in the air and she would then wrap her legs and arms around his back. With difficulty, he would shimmy up on his knees and in one combined effort they would thrust up and land in a sitting position facing each other. They smiled proudly at each other, since the last two times he'd slipped out of her.

This was when Kat's mind would go from planning to lust — it was the one position in their routine that Kat controlled. She would slide him in and out at her pleasure. Jasper also loved this part; it was exciting for him not to control the motion. It took him a long time to get used to letting her do it. For the entire time in this position they would refrain from kissing and just stare into each other's eyes (something Jasper had learned from reading the dust jacket of a book on Tantric sex). The clue that they were ready for the final position was when the sensation of wanting to come became so intense that they would lose eye contact (Jasper usually looked away first).

Final position - Jasper would pull her close and push her back onto her back only for a second, untangle their legs and then carefully roll over so Kat was on top. At this point the thrusting would stop and a deep lustful kiss would begin. This originally came about when Jasper needed to take a break so he could hold off on coming. He no longer needed to do that, yet the kiss remained out of habit.

4

Jasper, now back in control, would start a slow-motion thrust. The kiss would now end so Kat could nestle her head in his neck (for concentration purposes).

Kat had always had a hard time orgasming with other men. Her first one didn't come until she was twenty-one with a little help of several Long Island Iced Teas and a man she thought she was in love with. After that night it was several more years until she met Jasper that she had her second, and third. Kat had always blamed herself for not being able to finish (thanks in part to a naive high school boyfriend who told her "She must have a problem down there."). When she met Jasper she learned it was the men. Not one of them took the time or cared enough to see what she liked or needed. Jasper did. After only several months of their lovemaking routine her regular orgasms began.

Now in the third and final position both their minds would be thinking of nothing except for pleasuring the other. Jasper liked to vary this last part, even though his idea of vary was fast or slow thrusting. Kat actually preferred the nights like this one when he would never go faster than a snail crawling across a branch. It would build up the intensity within them, knowing that three quick thrusts would make them both explode. But they knew that if they could hold off and keep the pace that it would take an extra fifteen seconds for their toes to uncurl.

Listening to the pace of Kat's breathing in his ear, Jasper would know how long to hold off. Usually around this time one phrase would repeat over and over in his mind "Come on Kat hurry, come on." Kat's body started to clench as the visuals of Jasper's body in her mind turned to a blank canvas of picture-less sensation. Knowing she was on the verge she muttered "Jas...pr" which gave him the signal to do the move that pushed her over the edge and into her

5

climax. He quickly grabbed both of her rear cheeks applying pressure, making the seal between him and her tighter. The extra sensation always began her orgasm. Knowing that Kat started Jasper would release everything he had deep into her body. Feeling the rush of semen pound her insides peaked the orgasm. Squeezing each other as if to not fall off a cliff they remained breathless and silent for a long few minutes.

Finally Kat would kiss Jasper on the chin and carefully slide him out of her while he let out a few moans of sensitivity. Lying next to each other staring at the ceiling Jasper asked.

"Well?"

Kat pondered for a second before responding.

"Seven point five, you?"

"Definitely an eight." Jasper responded while blindly reaching for the towel next to the bed. He'd wipe his groin dry of their juices while Kat shut off the TV. Holding the towel in the air Kat took it from him and did the same before tossing it on the floor.

"Goodnight, my doll" Jasper whispered before giving her one quick kiss on the lips and two on the forehead.

"Night." Kat replied, pulling the sheet up tight around her and rolling on her side, allowing Jasper to spoon her to sleep like always. Before closing her eyes she checked the clock-12:21 exactly twenty-seven minutes of lovemaking, their average.

By 12:51 Kat was officially pregnant.

2

"I'm telling ya Misses C, I swear the guy hates me."

Jack slumped in the chair but quickly sat up when his hair touched the high back. The last thing he wanted was to mess up his perfect spike. It took the sixteen-year-old over forty minutes and one regular size bottle of Elmer's glue to get it just right.

"Jack, Mr. Files doesn't hate you." Kat answered with complete "cut it out" tone.

"Look, he's old fashioned. When he started here guys like you had to wear ties. He's just not up to times. Mr. Files can't appreciate a cool collar like that".

Jack smiled as he touched the multi-colored dog collar around his neck.

"You really like this?"

"Are you kidding? That goes perfect with your hair."

They both giggled a little.

"Look you just have to give him some slack, just do your work and don't goof off. That way he doesn't have a reason to send you down here." Jack couldn't stop smiling at Kat. He'd rather be in her office any day than have to listen about history from a seventy-year-old man. In truth, Mr. Files never really bothered Jack, he just needed excuses to see Kat.

"Now go back to class, and make sure Mrs. Albro stamps your pass." Jack got up and walked to the frosted glass door and turned around.

"Thanks Misses C."

"You're welcome Jack."

As the door shut Kat smiled as she remembered how she'd had a crush on her gym teacher in High School. She stared across the tiny barren, cold green room, pondering how the teen mind worked. She laughed at how she used to put on extra makeup before gym class hoping Mr. Kay would notice her more. As she started to replay a particular dodge ball game, a knock came upon the door snapping her out of her reminiscing.

"Yes?" Kat answered, picking up a pen, pretending to be working.

The door opened only a few inches. Instantly she knew who it was. Only Thomas Kidd would hesitantly open the door as if she might be changing.

"Come in Mr. Kidd."

A short scrawny man with pockmarks and a nose so big that it made it hard to look him in the eye, stutter stepped his way into the room. Kat was amazed how this shy awkward man ruled with an iron fist when it came to the kids, yet could hardly speak a full sentence to her.

Every time Mr. Kidd came in this room or anywhere near Mrs. Cutter, his heart started to race. He knew that being twenty years her senior meant he had no chance with her, let alone the fact that she was married. But never had as beautiful a woman treated him as nicely as she did. It was always hard for him to speak for the first few seconds he saw her. He needed to take a breath and absorb her face and the way her straight sandy hair lightly brushed her shoulders when she moved. The way her green eyes changed color ever so slightly depending on what she wore. She wasn't the most beautiful woman he had ever seen but she was the nicest.

"Mr. Kidd?" Kat asked after he stood there for few seconds, which she was used to.

"Oh, uh… Mrs. Cutter, I uh, well the school board and I need to have a talk with you." he said without making eye contact.

"Is something wrong?" Kat asked as she noticed Mrs. Albro peeking in from her desk outside the room.

"On no no no… the opposite actually, well I, the school wants to… well you've been wonderful. A lot of parents call and thank you for the, the help with the students. So the school board wants to offer you, well."

Mr. Kidd's rambling always drove Kat crazy but she never showed it.

"Well you know how Mrs. Lech passed away?"

Kat nodded.

"Well you're being offered to be the Head of Guidance at the Junior High School. Well you'd have to apply of course, school policy. But they already decided they want you. That is if you want it." He finally spit out. Offering her the job was like a knife to the gut. He couldn't stand the thought of not being able to see her every day.

Kat sat in silence for a moment, with a huge smile on her face.

"Well I'm flattered. When do I need to let you know by?" Mr. Kidd was ecstatic that there was a chance of a No.

"Not right away, a day or so. I'll go get you all of the paperwork to look at, but I, I don't want you to feel obligated to take the job." He said finally looking her in the eye.

"Thank you Thomas." His heart almost stopped, hearing his name come out of her mouth.

Kat was so caught off guard by the offer that she hardly noticed the beads of sweat accumulating on Mr. Kidd's forehead. Actually her mind started wandering to so many places she almost forgot he was in the room. She never thought she would even be considered for the job since she was the youngest counselor and only worked three days a week because of the school budget. Mr. Kidd noticed her daze and quietly excused himself from the room. Kat didn't even notice him leave, she had too much to think about.

3

Kat was sitting at the regulation school lunch table moving around her mashed potatoes. The small beige shellacked brick room always made Kat feel a little uneasy. The room had no windows and only two solid wooden doors and always made her feel like she was in a waiting room of some mental institution. The fact that she was always first in the room was the oddest part. She could hear the subdued murmurs of the much larger student cafeteria on the opposite side of the wall. The sounds reminded her of an inmate pen. Finally the bell rang, two minutes later the door swung open with a flood of complaining teachers. Quickly the room filled like the bottom of an hourglass running out of time.

In the middle of all the somber colors, Kat could see a flash of red bouncing around. She smiled, knowing it was Tina, or Mrs. Monroe, as the Superintendent- after three weeks of debates-determined the students must call her. With all the energy of a lab rat on caffeine (and the looks to match) Tina sat down across from Kat.

"Soooo? Are you leaving me?" The eccentric forty-two year old asked.

"How could I ever leave you here all by yourself?"

The lab rat's eyes widened as if she'd caught the sight of food.

"Are you kidding me? I'd leave you behind like a dirty tampon if I had the chance!" They both chuckled at her vulgar comment but laughed even harder at the dirty looks it received by the older teachers (or at least the teachers who acted older) who were within earshot.

"How the hell did you hear about this already anyway?"

"Well you know me, I bought stock in the Whisper 2000 all those years ago!" Kat really never expected a straight answer out of her. Only once after a few drinks (during one of the two times they'd hung out outside of school) did she really open up. During the long car ride home Kat had learned that under the bubbly exterior lay a tortured past.

"I really have to talk it over with Jasper first."

Kat replied with a sigh.

"Man, are you ever cock-whipped!" Of course "cock whipped" was said louder than the other words just to annoy people. Kat rolled her eyes, looking less than amused.

"Yeah well if you ever had a relationship that lasted longer than an orgasm maybe you'd understand." Kat's face turned cherry-red before the last word of the sentence came out of her mouth. She was so shocked at herself for using such language and saying it so hatefully. Obviously she was used to Tina mouthing off, but to hear herself talk like that was more than embarrassing.

"Well I must say you have been hanging out with me too long!" Tina looked pleased with Kat's quip.

"Look honey, all I'm saying is you better not let this opportunity pass you by. I've worked in this town for almost ten years now and I've never seen them make an offer like this before. And sweetie, when someone says no to the committee that's something they don't forget. You'll be bottom on the totem poll for the next twenty years."

4

Holding a red marker as if it were a torch Jasper stood in the middle of their home office (or at least what they called their office, which was really just an extra room with a desk and a few knick knacks.). His chef uniform only had a few spats of food on it being that it was before the dinner rush. He usually never went home on his afternoon break but today he was in a panic, the hostess had quit and taken two busgirls with her.

The calendar that was in front of him was Kat's daily activity bible. It looked more like a child's easel than a day planner, oversized and marked up with five different colors.

Jasper's eyes scanned back and forth over the calendar. He never understood her method of markings, in fact he was actually pretty amazed by it. Instead of writing down words she used an elaborate system of shapes and color lines to plot out events. He looked back and forth from the calendar to the marker in his hand.

"Damn it," He thought to himself. The last time he'd marked her calendar with the wrong color he'd never heard the end of it. Defeated, he put back the marker in the hanging rack. Instead he opted for a pen and pad of florescent purple sticky notes. At first he hated the fact that she'd bought a whole case of the purple ones but quickly changed his mind when he realized how much they stood out, when you're trying to get someone's attention.

Just as the pen touched the paper he heard a key enter the front door and the knob turn.

"Jasper?"

"Up here Hun."

He waited for her at the top of the stairs. Looking up at him, she could tell he was stressed out. His eyes were so expressive that she could instantly tell what mood he was in no matter how hard he tried to hide it.

"What is it?" Kat said in a joking manner hoping to ease him.

"I still can't figure out your crazy color system!" he replied. Finally at the top of the stairs Kat smiled at him with a raised eyebrow until he finally spread his arms in the air, for a smell inspection. As Kat leaned in and carefully sniffed each part of his upper torso he mused about how she could instantly put him in a good mood even after all these years.

"Well do I pass ma'am?"

"You're on the border but I guess I'll let it slide this time." Like two magnets they quickly sucked together, wrapping their arms tightly behind the others back. With her face squished tightly in his armpit she asked,

"Well what is the bad news?"

5

As Jasper left the house Kat sat on the stairs in utter confusion. She had been on such a high coming home she was hardly able to wait to tell Jasper of her promotion. But now he needed her to work on all her days off for the next few weeks. That would be impossible. She had several committee meetings and would have to start full time next week if she took the job. Tears started to trickle down her cheek, which took her by surprise since she knew Jasper would understand. Not only understand, he would be ecstatic for her. Yes it would cause him more work and stress, but also he would try to hide it from her. So why was she crying? Roughly she wiped away the tears trying to laugh them off as she headed up stairs.

Being her anal self, Kat went to her calendar to make sure Jasper hadn't made marks that might confuse her. Pulling out her matching day planner from her pocketbook she carefully compared the two. No new marks were on the board, which made Kat happy. Her eyes were still a little moist, making her blink more than usual. In a slow circular motion Kat rubbed her eyes, slowly at first then a little faster as if speed would rub out the confusion in her head. When she finally stopped, it took a moment for her vision to refocus. When they did she was still looking at the calendar but this time she noticed something she'd forgotten about. A tiny purple "Q" was in the upper left hand corner of the box for yesterday. It took Kat a moment to straighten out the days in her head. That's when she realized that she should have gotten her period yesterday. She was never late.

Since she was eighteen, Kat had always marked when she was going to get her monthly visitor on the calendar so she could plan around it (like not going to the beach that week). At first a "P" was used as the marker but when one boyfriend figured it out, he embarrassed her by talking about it at a dinner party. That's when she changed it to a "Q". She could never really figure out why she'd picked that letter. But that didn't matter right now. The fact that she rarely was ever late did matter.

A small tremor of panic went through her body. It started as a gurgle in her stomach and moved it's way outward like a ripple through a pond. It finally exited through the tips of her digits. Quickly she told herself,

"Don't worry it's still early, I'll probably get it before bed." With her mind still swirling with too many things, she decided to lie down for a while.

6

Kat sat at her desk surrounded by a sea of diners. She looked around feeling awkward. She was the only one at a desk, yet no one seemed to even glance at her. The hundreds of patrons seemed to have no faces yet they crammed more and more food into their invisible mouths. Though she could see the forks hitting the plates she couldn't hear them. In fact she couldn't hear a thing.

Finally she looked at the desk in front of her. It was devoid of all her usual supplies and trinkets. The fake linoleum had hundreds of Q's etched into it. Every one was the same size and shape, all in neat rows as if on a letter chart in a second grade classroom. Suddenly, someone sitting across from her broke the silence. This face she could see, it was her own. The only problem with it was it had a spiked Mohawk and a dog collar on. The voice also wasn't hers; it was too high pitched and didn't make any sense.

With all this madness around her somehow she wasn't scared, until all the diners stopped eating and turned their blank faces towards her. The voice coming from her other self, got louder and louder. She could feel hundreds of eyes, though their faces didn't have them, staring at her as if waiting to see what she would do.

So she stood up, and when she did, three glowing doorways rose out of the ground behind her desk. Each one had a different hue to it, each a pleasant color yet constantly changing. Kat looked back at her alternative self; it was still talking and staring at the chair as if Kat were still sitting.

Each door looked welcoming to her, almost as if each one was calling to her with a separate soothing voice. The patrons, still staring, raised their arms in unison, all pointing to different doors. Just as Kat started to walk towards them to get a better look, she woke up.

7

The first thing she did after opening her eyes was grab her piece of silk, which was under her pillow. Quickly she eased it under her fingers. She didn't even bother trying to analyze her dream. Anytime she had the least bit of stress in her life she would have blatant dreams that would wake her up. It was something she got used to and was fine with since they would go away as soon as she worked things out.

Glancing at the clock shocked her; she wasn't at all tired when she'd lain down, yet she'd slept for 5 hours. It was now eight o'clock and she was starving. Not in the mood to cook, she ordered in a small pizza with everything on it. While she waited for it she kept herself busy by channel surfing, something she rarely did. Kat actually had a very active life: Wednesday, Thursday and Friday she worked at the school and Saturday and Sunday she was at the restaurant working for Jasper (which took her a long time to like). Then Monday and Tuesday were her days off with Jasper. The school nights were her time to hang out with her friends, which she did regularly. Being alone tonight was a rarity.

The doorbell rang a hollow ring. The pizza guy who looked more like a Jehovah's Witness took Kat by surprise. The man wore a tie under his red Pizza Palace coat and didn't speak a word except,

"Nine sixty-three."

Kat paid him, shut the door, and quickly locked it.

Eating in front of the TV made Kat feel horribly alone. That was something she hated. Kat went to great lengths to make sure someone was always around her even if she didn't like the person. There were times in her life she kept boyfriends around for months even though she hated them just so she didn't have to be alone. It most likely stemmed out of her childhood that she spent as a latch key kid. From ten years old she would come home after school to an empty house, make her own dinner, and tuck herself in. Around nine her mom would come home and kiss her goodnight, around eleven she could hear Dad come home. On most nights he would come in and sneak her a kiss goodnight.

Nowadays the only time she liked being alone was when she was in bed waiting for Jasper to come home. As she chewed on a large piece of sausage she wished that Valerie hadn't canceled their plans for tonight.

Swallowing the last bite of pizza she looked proudly at the empty box. She was impressed with herself that she could polish off a whole small pizza. But that pride quickly changed into self-loathing as she pinched her belly.

Kat cleaned up and went upstairs to get ready for bed. After brushing her teeth she checked to see if she had her period, which made her laugh since she knew she didn't.

But just to be safe and so Jasper wouldn't catch on that she didn't have it, she put on a pad and headed off for bed. (Jasper always knew when her period was, he looked forward to it actually since it was the one time a month he received oral) That night her dreams were worse.

8

Kat woke up the next morning before the sun at 5:52, which was the only thing she hated about the school job. The monthly Q still hadn't shown up. She got ready for work like usual, trying to keep a chipper mood. At 6:40, fifteen minutes before she left, she usually woke up Jasper for a quick chat. This morning she decided to let him sleep. Even though she wanted nothing more than to tell him about her promotion, she was too nervous.

Driving to work she called Val from her cell. Val was a college roommate and a fellow guidance counselor two towns over. The two of them shared every detail about everything in their lives. On average they talked several times a day and saw each other regularly. As the phone rang, Kat knew that Val would also be driving. This was one of the few laws that Kat didn't mind breaking. Val answered.

"So early my dear, it must be important!"

"Lunch is a must today."

"My school or yours?"

"Definitely yours!"

"Oh your luck today is taco pizzas"

They chatted for another moment, but about nothing serious. As Kat pulled into the parking lot she only hoped that she could hold off giving her decision until after lunch.

9

Val met Kat outside with a big hug. Security was higher at Val's school, so she always had to get escorted in. They both got the standard issue trays but went back to the office instead of the teacher's lounge so they could talk with more privacy. Val was at this job full time so her office was completely decorated right down to a Garfield welcome mat. Seeing how at home in her office Val was made Kat want to take the job offer more. They sat down at the cluttered desk across from each other.

"Spill it love." Val said, picking up her small Mexican pizza. Kat went on for five minutes about how she was offered the job, but Jasper really needed her now too and that she could only choose one. She did leave out the part about not getting her monthly visit yet, that was a subject that had to be handled separately.

"Not to be rude Hun, but this is really not a choice. You went to school for a long time, and put in several years of part time for this offer. Jasper can always hire someone." Kat knew that was the answer and that she was going to take the job, but for some reason decisions were always easier for her when passed through someone else.

"No, I know, it's just once I take a full time position I'll never see Jasper, he only has Mondays and Tuesdays off. I just really like seeing him four days in a row all day, and I can always get a full time position somewhere…"

"What's really bothering you?" Val cut her off.

The question didn't shock her; they were so close that sometimes they swore they could read each other's mind.

"I'm late." Val stopped eating.

"Well that really throws a wrench in things now don't it?" It was meant to lighten things but instead brought tears to Kat's eyes.

"Look Hun, immediately after school I'll come over with some tests, OK." With that they changed the subject and finished lunch on a high note, even though it was a false one.

10

Sitting on the toilet should have been an awkward experience for Kat but Val and her had been through much more embarrassing things. Including one night that happened their junior year in college, which they still had yet to talk about. Kat urinated on the little white stick and nervously handed it to Val.

"Gee thanks." She said, trying to break the silence. Kat finished on the toilet while Val carefully placed down the stick and set the timer.

"I guess it's a waiting game now."

"Why don't we go down stairs and have a drink while we wait?"

"It's a little early, but right now I need a double."

Kat rarely drank; she'd left those days behind her just like that night. In fact she couldn't remember the last time she'd gotten drunk. But that would change tonight regardless of the color the stick changed to.

Downstairs they mixed two rum and cokes. Val had brought the necessary ingredients along with the test. Sitting down they clinked the two glasses together with no enthusiasm. It was a tradition of theirs that had started freshman year. After both being dumped by the same guy they made a toast to live life to the fullest, and to always toast.

Val sipped, Kat gulped, as they sat in silence. Finally Kat spoke up.

"If I…This is just the worst possible time ever, I mean we always wanted kids but…" She stopped speaking and stared out the sliding door like a zombie. The back yard was well kept but empty. Only a picnic table and a new grill were in the small but comfortable yard.

Val herself had gone through this, more than once. As a teen she was a stoner, drinker, lawbreaker and pretty loose. By the time she was twenty she'd had two abortions, the third came only two years ago. After filing for divorce she found out she was two months pregnant. She never told her ex-husband, Kat was the only person who knew. Her life experiences made her a great counselor and friend.

"Look sweetie, you know I will always…" The timer rang cutting her off.

11

The bathroom door was shut tightly. The two of them sat on the floor in the hallway outside. The bottle of rum was in front of them; they didn't bother bringing up the coke. Kat carefully laid down and placed her head on Val's lap.

"Sugar, it's been an hour, we have to go in. For all we know there is probably some sort of time limit. And besides, I really have to pee." Val of course knew she could go to the bathroom downstairs but she was once again trying to make a joke for Kat, who was quickly approaching her alcohol limit.

"Before I know the results, I have to figure out my life. If I am pregnant then I can't take my dream job. Hell I'll probably lose the one I have now. Oh and that would be great at the restaurant a big blubbery pregno waddling you to your table." Val held back a laugh as she stroked Kat's hair.

"Alright that's some of the down-side let's look at the up-side. You and Jasper have always wanted a kid. A few years down the road you could get another job."

"No, no, no, I need to be established first, have a Head of Department title under my belt. Then I can take a leave and come back to the job without worrying."

The conversation went back and forth for so long that Val just wanted to yell, "Well then just get a damn abortion!" But she remembered how hard it had been for Kat just going with her. Also Jasper was a very big pro-lifer. She knew if the time was right she could talk to her about it, but as of right now Kat didn't even know if she was pregnant or not.

Kat kept rambling on and on. Finally Val had had enough.

"That's it!" She pushed Kat's head off her lap and stood up. With all the gusto of a general leading soldiers to war she marched into the bathroom.

Kat lay looking up at the ceiling they'd just painted a few weeks ago. Her breathing practically stopped as she prayed to hear she wasn't pregnant. After only four seconds of no noise Kat knew the result of the test.

12

It took a heroic amount of energy for Val to calm down the recently impregnated woman. Finally she got her into bed. Kat was more than drunk and under the covers when she screamed at the top of her lungs.

"Do you realize what I just did?"

"What are you talking about?"

Val said pushing her back down into a flat position.

"I'm pregnant and got drunk." Tears started flowing out of her already wet eyes. The thought also had not crossed Val's mind, she was pissed at herself for bringing over the rum, how could she be so stupid?

"It's only one time dear, no big deal ok? You just need to rest and tomorrow we'll talk more, ok? I'm going to take the bottle with me and leave a note for Jasper saying you got food poisoning alright?"

"What did I eat?"

Val didn't know if the question was asked to know her cover-up story or if she really thought she'd eaten some something, but it did make her realize that in fact they hadn't eaten all night. That put Kat in a worse situation for tomorrow morning.

"Just tell him we had left-over sushi." The thought of sushi made Kat's stomach do a flip. Her mind was getting foggier and foggier. She wanted nothing more than to sleep and to not be pregnant.

"Honey, don't tell Jasper a thing, we'll figure out what to do later, you and me like the old days. We'll get through this."

It took another fifteen minutes for Kat to pass out. Val made a note for Jasper, put a large glass of water and a puke bucket next to the bed, took all the evidence from the house and left Kat to sleep. Leaving the house she felt a little guilty, for wanting Kat to get an abortion.

13

Luckily for Kat the next day she didn't have to go into the restaurant until two, or so she thought. When Jasper came home last night he'd almost tripped over the half-full puke bucket. After reading the note he thought it was a bit odd since Kat didn't care for sushi, when he smelled the alcohol coming of her breath he knew the truth. That's why he didn't have a problem waking her up before his morning run.

"Hey Rum head" He whispered as if it was a love call. Kat stirred and opened her eyes to morning light that seemed brighter than ever.

"So what did you really do last night?"

"Hmmmm…Drunk."

Jasper giggled, he found it amusing that she got drunk. Amazingly he trusted her and suspected nothing more than a girl party at the house even though he couldn't remember the last time he'd seen her drunk.

"Val must have been pretty drunk too, she left a note saying you ate bad sushi." Kat's only response was to put a pillow over her head. Jasper did his stretches next to the bed instead of in the kitchen like he normally did. Running was one of the only passions in his life. He ran at least four days a week. Never collected anything, didn't care for books. Just running. It was his only hobby, he'd run anywhere from 4-12 miles depending on the day's work before.

"You know I was worried I was going to have to find someone to work for you today, which would have been impossible, but when I kissed you goodnight, well you smelled like a bar, still do actually. Bad sushi might keep you home, but a hangover, no way baby!" Kat rolled on her side with the pillow still over her head. Jasper finished his last stretch and got up off the floor.

"I'm going to do a long one today Hun. Do you want me to set the alarm so you can get up and ready for work?"

"Go…away…boss." Kat murmured through the pillow. Jasper kissed the tiny piece of exposed head and bounded out of the room.

After hearing the front door shut Kat took the pillow off her head. It took a while for her eyes to adjust but not as long as it took her throbbing head to remember she was pregnant. With the grace of a ninety-year-old she threw the sheets back and sat up. She looked down at the puke bucket, which was clean, she was confused and wondered if Jasper had cleaned it or if she hadn't vomited.

For every one step she took her head pounded three times. Finally reaching the bathroom, she opened the medicine cabinet with her eyes shut since this was the brightest room in the house. Five-pills went down her throat with the ease of razor blades.

As the water started to pour out of the five-speed showerhead the realization hit her again. A panic came over her as she worried about the aspirin she had just taken. Finally her eyes were open as she scanned the bottle's warning label. *"If pregnant or breast feeding consult medical professional before taking."* The panic slowed as she thought about how vague the stupid label was. The rush of adrenalin made her heart rate go up in return, making her headache worse. That was the deciding factor in whether to induce vomiting or not.

Sitting in the tub letting the water beat down on her she waited for the pain reliever to take affect. For the first time she was starting to think rationally about her situation. After about fifteen different schemes she finally decided to mix the truth with a few white lies.

By the time her fingers got a nice light wrinkle the drugs were working somewhat and she was almost ready to get out and face Jasper.

14

Sitting on the living room couch wearing the orange fluffy robe that Jasper bought her two Christmases ago she gulped coffee out of a jumbo Grab and Go coffee mug. She went over and over the half lie in her head just to be safe. Her bloodshot eyes were locked on the street in front of the house waiting for Jasper.

Her heart sank at the sight of him, not out of nerves but out of love. He was shirtless, covered in sweat, holding his yellow tank top, and wearing his favorite black shorts. Jasper always did a sprint for the last minute of his run. Kat only saw him for a few seconds as he zoomed by the window. But she knew he'd cool down and walk by twice more before coming back into the kitchen to stretch.

Twenty seconds later he reappeared, strolling this time with his hands on the top of his head. All the stress and bad thoughts left her mind as she stared at his skinny body. It made her think about how Jasper always joked that he was the only skinny chef in Massachusetts. She watched as he wiped sweat off his face, turned around and headed back. As he started to walk up the driveway and out of view Kat snapped out of her puppy dog trance.

Putting on a fake smile, she opened the kitchen door before he got up to it.

"Good morning my love and how was your run?"

Kat said with fake enthusiasm. Jasper laughed as he tossed his sweat-drenched shirt at her.

"Good thing you're not an actor. But I must say surprisingly you don't look too bad." They gave each other a quick peck on the lips, which Kat immediately wiped off. Jasper walked in and placed his right foot on the kitchen counter and with the grace of a ballerina put his head to his knee.

"So what was last night all about?"

"Well actually I have some terrific news, well for me at least, not the restaurant." She was impressed at how calm she was. Jasper switched legs with a grunt.

"Well, let's hear it then."

"I have been offered a job and accepted without your approval, but I was excited and couldn't help it. Anyway you are now looking at the new Head of Guidance at Craig Steinbeck Junior High School."

Jaspers leg dropped to the ground and he spun around with the gusto of jazz dancer.

"Are you serious!" With one giant step he engulfed her in a hug of sheer joy and sweat. Kat screamed with a disgusted laugher, not realizing what he was doing he let go. The smile, on Jasper's face was a sight that she would never forget. How could she have ever been worried about telling him? She wished she could have taken a picture of him standing there sweaty, half naked, and beaming. Kat couldn't tell if she saw tears start to form or if it was just sweat. Without saying another word Jasper just went in for another grizzly like hug and this time he wasn't letting go.

15

That night at work Jasper came out of the kitchen and made the whole restaurant toast her. She was a little embarrassed but excited at the same time. That evening at home a rarity happened. The second they walked through the door Jasper mauled her with kisses, stripped her of clothing and made love to her in the kitchen, living room, and finished on the stairs.

Through all of this Kat was happier then she had been in a long time. She kept lying to herself about the whole pregnancy thing, the test was wrong, it was a bad dream, it was something she'd eaten that made the stick pink. She even went to the extent of dodging Val's calls, which she knew she would get hell for later. Finally she made a deal with herself to take a few days before dealing with it, she just wanted to enjoy her promotion and Jasper's special congratulations.

It wasn't until six days later when Kat was shown her new office that it really sunk in. She was getting a tour by the Vice Principal Mrs. Tallery a short woman who dressed like a librarian and had an accent that no one could figure out (since she'd grown up in this town). The tour of the school took about twenty minutes. The way Mrs. Tallery explained everything made Kat feel like she was at a museum. She concluded the tour with the introduction to her new office. Kat's initial thought of it was "My office is bigger than Val's, I can't wait to rub it in her face!"

"I'll go get Mrs. Hillier. She'll be your secretary."

Kat couldn't hold in her excitement, the second the tiny woman left the room she jumped up and down. Calming herself she looked around the office, it was pretty much all furnished, it just needed a touch of home. With her back to the door Mrs. Tallery entered again.

"Mrs. Cutter let me introduce you to Mrs. Hillier. Unfortunately you won't be able to get to know her very well she only has a few weeks left." Kat turned around with a large smile that quickly faded at the sight of a young woman who was most likely more than eight months pregnant.

"Only three more weeks until she pops out!" She said, giddily offering her hand to Kat. They shook hands but Kat didn't say hi. Sensing something wrong Mrs. Tallery spoke trying to break the awkwardness.

"Mrs. Hillier will be on maternity leave for six months then it's up to her to come back or not."

Kat sat down in a green swivel chair with an ashen look on her face. The two women rushed to her. Kat just stared at the woman's stomach with the sentence playing over and over and over in her head "it's up to her to come back or not, back or not, or not, or… not."

16

Driving over to Val's after work she went over the situation in her head. She had worked her way out of it with a quick lie about not eating breakfast and being excited. Rumors must be flying around the school about her already. The embarrassment was killing her but she swore to wow them tomorrow. As for now she had a bigger issue to deal with.

She arrived at Val's house that was won in her divorce. It was rather large. People who didn't know about her past wondered how she could ever afford a half million-dollar home on her own. Val actually despised it but acted the opposite. Three bedrooms, two baths, and five other rooms were too much for her. She longed to move into a small apartment but was afraid to ruin her Martha Stuart appearance (minus the whole jail thing). Though Kat wouldn't be surprised if one day they ended up sharing a cell.

Kat didn't bother to knock since she had her own key and the code to the alarm. They were actually given to her in an attempt to get her and Jasper to move in with her. But the hints were too vague and Kat never realized it.

Sitting at the computer Val heard the alarm beep alerting her of Kat's arrival, she didn't bother to get up. A moment later Kat silently took a seat next to her. Hitting the print button Val swiveled the nine hundred thirty-three dollar leather chair that her once rich ex-husband bought himself, towards Kat. The laser printer silently spit out several pieces of paper.

"Well my dear, I've went to the trouble of making you a pro's and con's list, and I printed up a list of abortion sites so you can learn facts on it."

Kat's heart dropped and she felt slightly sick hearing the word abortion. Up until this moment neither of them actually had said the word, they both just hinted around it. Noticing the sick look on her face Val rolled the chair up to Kat and placed her hands on Kat's.

"Sweetie we've known for a week now, it's time we actually start talking seriously."

Kat's lips tightened and she nodded her head. She was getting used to avoiding thinking about it, which maybe wasn't such a good idea because now everything seemed too real.

The two adjourned to the living room where Val had already placed out a spread of junk food. Kat was kind of weirded out at first sight because it felt like they were going to have a cocktail party to decide whether or not to kill a baby. Even though Kat was not against abortion that was still how she thought of it.

It took an hour of talking until Kat really started to feel at ease discussing the pros and cons. The second hour was even more productive as they talked about procedures of extraction. The third hour was less talk and more dessert of Kit Kats and Milky Ways along with lots of milk. Kit Kats were a slight obsession of Kat's. She originally started to eat them when she was nine because her Mom jokingly told her they were named after her. Ever since then they had always been the candy of choice for her.

Before the fourth hour could start they both decided they'd have enough for the night and Val walked her to the front door. Kat thanked Val with a long hug.

"Look Kat, you have more than a month before you have to make a complete decision. Whatever you choose I'll be by your side. I just hope you don't wait too long, the longer you wait the harder things will be."

17

On the way home Kat pulled over at a scenic rest area to throw away the papers Val had printed up. She appreciated them but didn't want to bring home any evidence for Jasper to find. She got out of the car and walked over to a beat up old green metal trashcan. Of course she shredded them before tossing them in. She wanted to bring home the list of websites but figured she could do a search online instead, there was no way she was going to risk leaving that piece of paper laying around.

Turning around to head back to the car she stopped in her tracks. In front of her was a sight she used to drive a half hour just to see. It didn't even dawn on her that she had pulled over here. She went to the car and shut off the engine before heading to a picnic table that had a view of over seven miles.

The view wasn't at all breath taking; just a regular small hill view of a small town but it was pleasant. Each street, car and house-light glimmered as if it were it's own star. Kat used to come up here any time things got hard in her life. It was sort of her own place. Not many people stopped here since they'd built the highway some twenty years earlier. Her friends used to tell her it was too dangerous to come up here by herself at night, but Kat didn't care; she felt safer here than anywhere else and never ran into any trouble. As a teen, when she was down on herself she used to stare at the miniature houses in the distance and just imagine what wonderful things were going on in each separate house. Of course she imagined they all lived better lives than she. Looking back now she wished to have any one of those adolescent problems rather than the one she had now.

Kat was amazed that after six years of not coming here the sight could still calm her. She laid back on the top of the table to take in the stars. Thin clouds covered most of them but there were still a few for her to marvel at. For the first time all day her mind was off of what was growing in her stomach. She thought of her youth and tried to go through all the different events that brought her up here in the past: fights with boyfriends, bad grades, too many zits, not fitting into a pair of jeans, the list was endless. After going through a few dozen she thought that maybe she made up excuses just to come here.

Almost a full hour went by before she grew tired of the twinkling lights and teen reruns. She headed back to her car in a better mood than she had been in for days. As the engine turned over she realized that she had never come up here with anyone, let alone Jasper. It was always her place, no one else's. But as she pulled out onto the desolate back road she made a promise to herself to bring him up here for a romantic evening; she didn't want it to be just hers anymore.

18

Kat arrived home only an hour and a half before Jasper. She took a quick rinse, got the bed ready then went right to the computer. As the computer screeched and dialed Kat checked the time, forty-one minutes left. She knew that waiting for another day would be smarter but she felt that she had to do research tonight, there were a few things she needed to know.

Doing a quick Yahoo search yielded more than enough sites for her to look at. Not bothering to read the description she quickly double clicked on the first one. Waiting for the page to materialize she caressed her silk. When enough of the page was up to view her heart sank. Before her was a full screen black and white fetus with big red words above it still too blurry to read. This was one thing she really didn't want to see, yet she couldn't take her eyes off of it. It made her think about how something was actually in her stomach. The red word above the picture started to get clearer M... U...R...She quickly hit the back button.

Back at the search results she made sure to read the next tag line. In the next thirty or so minutes she learned more about abortions than she ever thought she would know. Feeling she had acquired a sufficient amount of knowledge on the subject she logged off and headed for the bedroom to think and think and think some more.

Jasper arrived home and they went through their routine, for her a 2 (which she lied and told Jasper a 5) for him a 7. With a quick kiss on the head he said goodnight and rolled over into slumber. It would be several hours when Kat finally made up her mind that she finally fell asleep.

Finally closing her eyes she wasn't happy or sad, just relieved that she'd made up her mind. She promised herself not to go back on it and to be strong. She had some odd dreams that night but nothing that woke her up.

19

Two days later Kat woke up an hour earlier than usual. She moved around the house like a cat burglar, afraid to wake up Jasper. After getting ready for the day and packing an extra bag of snacks, she picked up the phone in the kitchen and dialed work. Kat was mortified calling in sick on only the third day of a new job, but she figured now was the best time since she was still really just organizing the office and going over files. Also the incident the other day gave her a perfect excuse. Being that it was so early she left a message on the office machine saying she felt horrible and was going to a doctor. She was a little leery about them calling the house so she figured that she would call them back again before they could get a chance.

Arriving at Val's she was surprisingly calmer than she'd thought she would be. Val was already outside waiting for her with a sympathetic smile. The two hugged silently for a few seconds before getting into Val's Ford Explorer. The first stop of the day was at Dunkin' Donuts to have a quick breakfast of bagel and microwave egg sandwiches. By quarter of seven they were back on the road to begin their two-hour drive to Boston.

20

"Mifepristone. Or RU-486, it's in pill form. It can take anywhere from 3 days to two weeks to work. What it basically does is give you a miscarriage by deteriorating the cell membrane..." Kat listened to the old man who looked like a construction worker with a white coat on. When he started getting into the technical side of how the medicine worked, she turned her attention to the window-it was painted black to keep protesters wondering what was going on inside. Val noticed the lack of attention by Kat so she listened harder to make sure she didn't miss anything of need.

"So we will need to see you back here to check on the bleeding and make sure everything is alright." Kat was still staring at the black paint. She couldn't help but concentrate on the tiny scratch where light fought to sneak in. It took a nudge from Val to get her to look back at the doctor. She looked at his construction worker eyes. They seemed have been sympathetic at one point but after years of seeing patient after patient they probably gave up.

Finally getting back her attention the burly man went on with his speech that he had probably given more times than a Broadway star has performed Hamlet. He spoke for about another five minutes all of which Kat was numb too. At the completion of his monologue he didn't take a bow instead he left a small pile of papers and a little white box on the counter he was standing in front of. He left without a handshake, wave, good-bye or even a head nod.

Usually you had to take the pill in front of the doctor, but Val had dated his son briefly. He also aborted his own grandson from her, making an odd, silent bond between them. She was young and went to him in confidence. He was stern and made her get the abortion. His son never found out. In front of Kat they acted not to know each other. But in the hallway they exchanged quick greetings and Val asked him to do a favor and let Kat take the pills home. He agreed knowing if he didn't Val had plenty of blackmail power.

"Well that's it, we can leave now." Kat was numb but relieved. It had been four hours since they arrived in the clinic, which felt more like a prison. They checked in, waited, waited some more then finally Kat got an examination following the voluntary psychological exam. Then finally more waiting topped off with the doctor's monologue.

The two walked arm and arm through the waiting room. A few middle aged women, two teens and a girl that looked like she wasn't old enough to spell "sex" sat spread out through the room-each had their own "Val" next to them. Everyone's eyes either looked at the floor or a magazine as if no eye contact meant they weren't there.

Just before reaching the door the security guard stopped them. "Ladies, I'm sorry to stop you but we have a few protesters out there, Greg is going to have to walk you out." Kat was a little shocked, the building wasn't labeled and it was supposed to be a discrete location. A small man in a tan security guard uniform strolled over.

"Ready ladies?" He asked while opening the door. Kat thought he looked more like a doctor than anyone else she'd seen today. As they started out the man gave them some pointers.

"Just don't look at them and ignore everything they say, they won't do anything but yell." They gripped each other a little tighter. Not knowing what to expect they stepped out into the blinding sun. At first they didn't see a thing. It wasn't until halfway to the Explorer did they see the protesters.

Standing on the tree belt two sixty-year-old women walked back and forth wearing sandwich boards. Kat couldn't help but stare at the boards they were wearing, it was the same picture of an aborted fetus she'd seen on the net. The two women watched them get into the vehicle; they were too far away to yell.

"Now don't worry they won't touch the car but they will yell just ignore them, alright? I'll stand here and wait until you're out of sight. You ladies have a nice day now." Kat wished he were her doctor. They pulled out of the spot and headed for the road. Before they could get to the road the women got in position, one on each side of the exit. Kat tried to keep her head down but couldn't help looking.

It felt like slow motion going past the screaming women. Kat would never forget the woman's face. It was wrinkled but not too much, she wore no makeup. Her graying hair was in a bun tied with a tie-dye scrunchie. She couldn't see the color of her eyes but she could tell they were dark and filled with rage. She actually reminded her of her own mother in a way, too tired to wear make-up or do her hair. Just a hard working mother.

"MURDERER! MURDERER! MURDERER!" The screams came out of her mouth with so much emotion that Kat felt like she had just killed the woman's kid. Kat couldn't hear the screams from the other side but that was fine she didn't want to. All she wanted was for the traffic to die down so they could pull out.

"You don't deserve to be a mother, I pray you never have another kid!" Kat had been strong all day until she heard those words.

21

That morning when Jasper woke he was disappointed to find that Kat hadn't woken him again to say goodbye. He suspected something was wrong with her lately. Probably the stress of the new job. That's why today on one of his days off of running he was planning to get her a special gift. He had it all planned out and was very excited about it. With a quick stretch and shower he was out the door.

He dropped off a small package at the Knitting Barn to get stitched. Then went off to work in high spirits. Nothing was going to ruin his day. Being under-staffed and busy had made working at the restaurant stressful lately. But Jasper was determined to not let it get him down today.

Pulling into his parking spot behind Three Worlds Eatery Jasper greeted the two dishwashers who were sweeping around the dumpster. Not only was Jasper the head chef he was also the co-owner and manager. The other owner was a buddy of his, Jack Snider from The Culinary Institute of America where they went to school together. For the past year Jack has been on Kitchen duty at the Thomas Stanoff Minimum Security Prison in Connecticut. Jasper had yet to visit him. The bad publicity of a chef sleeping with a 15-year old busgirl did hurt the place for a bit. But Jasper's cooking kept them coming back regardless.

A few grunts and head nods greeted him as he entered the kitchen. None of his crew usually perked up until after the lunch rush. Like usual he did a quick check to see how everyone's work was coming along. He was satisfied with the chopped parsley, leeks, cracked eggs, soups, sauces, and all around cleanliness. Three years in a row they had won the Shiny Spoon award for the Cleanest Kitchen in Western Massachusetts.

"Darren, I want to see you in my office in five minutes." Darren agreed by raising his eyebrows. The blond haired ex-football player was his main man in the kitchen, and well over-worked. Jasper headed out to the dining room where the greetings were much warmer. He did his check of the settings, salads, bread, the bar, and cleanliness. All passed. It was then off to his office to go over the new food orders.

The office had two desks, only one of which he used now. The walls were plastered with various food logo-ed free gifts from the salesmen. The only normal picture in the place was Kat's. Jasper always kept an 8" by 11" picture of Kat sitting on a dock facing him on his desk. It was his favorite picture of her.

They took it four summers ago on a trip to Lake George New York. It was a horribly planned trip that ended up to be the best time of their lives. Everything went wrong that week, including the weather. It was early May, unseasonably cold and rainy. The two stayed in their rickety old hotel room for the entire week.

They'd both only packed summer wear. After finding out it was in the low fifties they spent most of the time wrapped in the hotel blankets. They only dared to venture to the shore twice since they had to wrap themselves like enchiladas to keep warm. It was a funny sight seeing two grown-ups running around a beach with flower print blankets, luckily for them the place was deserted. Kat had sat on the pier tightly wrapped up with her feet dangling inches above the frigid water. That is when Jasper had taken the picture. She had no clue he even brought the camera down. A smile of pure happiness was on her face as she stared out over the fog-covered lake. Jasper couldn't believe his luck in catching such a true moment forever. They made love nineteen times that week.

A knock startled him out of his stare. Darren entered with a new off-pink sauce stain near his navel.

"What's up chief"?

"I'm going to take the rest of today off, you're in charge. Think you can handle it?"

"Are you all right? Is someone sick?" Darren was honestly nervous for Jasper. In the few years he had known him he had never seen the man take a day off without notice.

"Actually everything is great. I'm going to surprise Kat and celebrate her new job."

"Oh…well that's great. Sure I can handle it."

"Great, I'm going to do some work in here and head out. I'll check with you before I leave. Oh and you pick the specials tonight too." Darren turned around still a little confused but excited. It was his dream to be in charge of the restaurant. His mind started going over a checklist of what to get ready for the night, he was so deep in thought that he left without another word.

22

Jasper finished his paperwork, checked on the kitchen and snuck out the back door so he didn't have to listen to anyone. On his way home he picked up the package from the Knitting Barn and a card from the drug store. Arriving home he tried to remember the last time he was in such a good mood. He had only two more things to do. Call for a dinner reservation at The Federal Hill Club and call Kat to make sure she was coming home right after work.

The reservations were set for 8 to leave plenty of time for pre-dinner lovemaking. Not knowing Kat's new work number off hand he had to go to her office to find it. Along with all the other obsessively organized items she kept an immaculate Rolodex. He flipped through the color system and found the new number under hot pink with exclamation points.

He picked up the phone and sat down in the soft second hand swivel chair. As the line started to ring Jasper noticed a few odd sticky notes on the board. One bright green one said '7 points yes' in purple ink, the next one green ink on pink paper said '5 points no'. Filtering through this he tried to put an explanation to them. Before he could read the third note the phone was answered.

"Guidance office how may I help you?"

"Huh... oh uh sorry, can I speak to Mrs. Cutter please?"

"Mrs. Cutter is out sick today, is there anything I can do for you?" Jasper's heart sank. A million reasons for her being out played through his head. Did she go the hospital? Was she surprising me? Is she cheating on me?

"Did she go home sick?"

"No she called out early this morning, may I ask who's calling?"

"Thanks." Jasper hung up the phone lightly and read the third note. Neon blue ink on a standard yellow sticky note, 4/27 underlined three times. He plucked it off the wall like a dead leaf off a tree.

"What the hell is she doing today?"

23

The first half hour of the ride was silent. They both knew words were useless at the moment. Kat leaned hard against the door as if trying to get away from the pocket book that held the murder weapon. Every few seconds she would glance down and look at it. She thought if this were a movie the bag would be shaking, steam escaping its lips and glowing red on the sides. Even though it just sat there still as can be on the bumpy Boston roads she felt as if it were teasing her.

So far the day had been a hundred times worse than she thought it was going to be. She'd thought that by the time they were on the ride home that it would be all behind her. Jasper's arms were what she was craving more than anything else in the world right now. She wanted to run into his arms and tell him everything, it wasn't too late she could still have the baby. But then she would lose her job, her career, all those years of school for nothing.

A small half giggle half whimper sounded through her nose. Val glanced over at her, wanting to comfort her but chose to keep silent instead. Once again Kat's gaze landed on the once cute but now ominous black DKNY pocket book. And that's when it happened, the bag started to shake violently. Kat jumped and crammed herself against the glass harder than before. The sudden movement startled Val enough to swerve out of her lane but only for a second.

"Jesus Christ! It's only your phone sweetheart."

It took several seconds before Kat could get the image of the black killer bag leaping at her stomach and burrowing through her, out of her mind. Finally snapping out of it she picked up the innocent handbag and pulled out her phone. Across the illuminated blue screen it read, "Call from Hubby!" Kat burst out in tears.

24

Hearing the answering machine Jasper hung up the phone. He gazed around the small room looking for clues. Curiosity had gotten him into trouble his whole life. An attribute he blamed his over-protective mother for. At the age of fifteen he came home to find his mom going through all his drawers. He quickly forgave her, understanding her concern, but when he found out that she did this on a weekly basis he was furious. So in return when he was home alone he would go through his parents' drawers. Ever since then Jasper had to restrain himself from going through any drawer. Not finding anything suspicious he quickly jabbed the on button for the computer.

After a few tense moments the computer was up and running. Without hesitation he clicked on the drop down website history bar. A few dozen or so sites appeared in front of him. This was a new kind of snooping for Jasper. He hated using the computer and only did when he had to research a new recipe.

The first three sites were of no significance to him. The fourth one was Map Quest. "Where did you go honey?" He thought to himself before his eyes hit the fifth site. He could feel his stomach limbering up to tie itself in a knot. www.choices.com was the fifth site, the sixth was www.maclinics.com, and the seventh was www.prochoice.com.

Jaspers stomach tied itself in the biggest hardest knot of its life. "But, it can't be, no way." Shock took over as clues of the past few weeks flooded through his brain. She wasn't acting weird because of the job. She was… no…she was. Wanting not to believe it he clicked on her e-mail account to see if he could find anything else. Waiting for the account to log in he started to nervously rock in the chair and thought to himself "It's Val that's it, yeah she went and got herself knocked up again, damn her! Why does Kat have to support her? She knows how much I'm against it." He started to feel a bit better blaming Val as the pregnant one.

His eyes bounced from email to email. "Here are your directions from Map Quest!" one read. With a double click it opened to reveal driving directions to the Silverstien Clinic in Boston. "Damn it!" The nervousness came back, now he knew where they were going. He had a fifty, fifty chance. Scanning some more he saw one that read "Silverstien Clinic Your Appointment." Jasper made the sign of the cross before opening the email. It was no use.

25

Within five minutes of finding out his wife was getting an abortion Jasper got changed into his running shorts and a t-shirt. He was glad that today was his day off of running because he would have enough energy to burn off some anger and pain before Kat got home. He went back into the office; the screen still had the appointment confirmation up on the screen. Glaring at the computer as if it was the guilty party, Jasper grabbed a thick black marker out of the desk. With one hand he popped the cap off and wrote in big letters across Kat's perfectly kept calendar "WHY".

He threw the marker down and headed for the door. Before he made out of the room he turned back and grabbed the small package he got earlier during the day for Kat. He pulled out the long embroidered silk sachet and wrapped it around his right hand like a boxer getting ready for a fight.

Once it was tight enough he started his jog right there and then, out the door, down the stairs, through the living room and kitchen, right out the back door leaving it wide open.

26

After twenty or so minutes of a slow steady sob, Kat began to settle down. She looked at the evil little handbag again with rage. But this time instead of fearing it she grabbed with both hands as if she didn't it would slip from her grip and run away. Kat brought the bag to face level, ripped it open, and dumped the contents on the floor.

"That's it! I'm pulling over."

"NO! I'm fine, keep driving!"

Val looked at Kat's enraged face and wondered what the hell was going on in her head. But once again she decided to do nothing. That's how she dealt with life any time she got scared: step back and watch.

Kat looked down at the culprit afraid to touch it. In the back of her mind she really felt that just touching the box would abort the baby. Finally after three deep breaths she lowered the window a bit and let the now moist air hit her face. Then with the suddenness of a lion attacking dinner she grabbed the box off the floor along with an innocent tube of lipstick and threw them out the window. Again Val swerved.

"What the hell are you doing?"

"I can't, I can't go through with it."

Val whipped the car to the shoulder and threw it in reverse. After going twenty or so yards she put it in park and jumped out. Kat watched as Val stumbled down the small slope to receive the box. When she returned to the car she threw it in the back seat.

"Look! I'm not going to have you change your mind in hour and have to drive back here and look for the damn things with a flashlight!"

"I'm not changing my mind again."

"Sure you won't, Hun, sure you won't."

Fed up, Val put it in drive and peeled out cutting off an elderly couple. Kat stared out the window with a smile as she thought about Jasper and her playing with their baby in the park.

27

With his legs pumping hard and fast Jasper sucked in the moist air through his clenched teeth. His mind was racing almost as fast as he was down the street. For the first time in his life Jasper hated the image of Kat in his mind. Ever since he first dated Kat he had several imaginary pictures in his head. Pictures that made him happy. The first was Kat on their wedding day. After they got married he replaced the blurred fantasy photo with images of the real thing. The second was an image of Kat washing dishes with a big belly. It was such a simple thought, but it brought such joy to him. The third was of Kat and him lying in bed looking at each other, in between them was a young child sleeping. Jasper's heart rate used to go up at least four beats a minute at the excitement of this. Now his heart rate was reaching 187 beats a minute from his sudden run.

With almost every third stride his track of thought changed. The images in his mind were driving him mad. But worst of all he tried to think of ways to forgive Kat for taking away his only dream in life. He could think of none. He finally broke into a light sweat about a half-mile from the house. As he turned a right onto Adams Street, which was the longest and most desolate stretch of his usual run tears started to fill his eyes. He was thankful that he was running, at least no one would be able to tell they were tears.

A mile into the run sorrow mucus started to fill his nostrils. Having a hard time breathing, he slowed his pace to a walk. Not wanting to be seen by anyone Jasper casually slipped off the road and into the woods across from Pioneer Tool, a small brick factory. Leaning over with a hand on a peeling white birch he tried to blow the snots out. But instead he choked on a sudden wave of hard sobs. It was the hardest he had ever cried. He cried at the loss of a child, the betrayal of a wife, and at an uncertain future. Less than twenty minutes ago his life was perfect. The thought of confronting Kat was making his stomach churn. A few dry heaves helped him cope and gain courage.

After several minutes of stomach cramps, sobbing and heaving, Jasper tried to get a hold of himself. That's when he realized Kat would probably make it home before he'd finish running. He had to get back and leave before she got there. He couldn't handle a confrontation now, not yet.

Jasper bolted from the birch towards the street in a frantic attempt to make it home. As his foot hit the pavement he glanced both ways to see if he could cross, there was only one car at the exit of the factory, but it looked parked, he had time to make it.

Jasper wouldn't make it home, or across the street for that matter.

*Man the sky is so cloudy today, I sure hope it doesn't rain...I want to make love to Kat outside tonight...*Jasper had no concept of how badly he was hurt. He didn't even know a car hit him. All the thoughts of the day's events had drained out of his head along with way too much blood.

"Shit, shit, shit...I don't need this, god damn it...my plane leaves in two hours...FUCK!"

Don McAlister, a forty-two year old bitter salesman stared at the bloody pulp of Jasper's body that laid twenty-five feet in front of his car. A full seven minutes went by on the empty road before Don picked up his cell to call the police.

Jasper started to move his fingernail over the now bloody silk wrapped around his hand. *Why does she love this so much... I wonder if our kids will do it too. I can't wait...* Sirens interrupted his thought. *I wonder what happened... I hope whoever it is, is ok... especially since to... day is such a special day.* A blurry figure appeared above his face. "*Kat... I love you baby*". *Kat started to kiss his neck slowly...* The paramedic felt for pulse, it was weak. *Her hands searched his body gently caressing and touching every part.* They put gauze over gaping wounds to try and stop the blood loss "*Tell me how much you love.*" "*Shhhhhhh*" *Kat replied as she started to wrap her arms around him...* They strapped him to the body board to be placed in the ambulance. "*I don't think I've ever felt you hug me so tightly*" *Jasper smiled as he cherished the warmth of her body around him.* Jasper past away in the ambulance before it ever made it off Adams St.

28

With his very large stomach hanging over his brown pants that were half as old as him Don screamed at the two-way mirror.

"I missed my god damn flight! Look what is wrong with you guys? I gave my statement, now I need to go." Don sat down where his fourth cup of coffee laid half full. He stared at the more milk and sugar than coffee combination while going over the event. He had to keep his story straight or they would know he was not telling the truth. He lied. He lied to cover his ass. Yes it was an accident but it was also his fault. Only the slightest bit of guilt stung his heart. But fear of losing his license, jail, being sued and missing his next meeting won over. Nothing was going to bring that stupid man back he thought. So what's the difference? Why ruin two lives? So what if they think he ran in front of my car on purpose. A nice sympathy card should cover it all.

29

For the first time since finding out she was pregnant, Kat was happy. She actually rubbed her stomach with love and not hatred. It was hard and it took a long time but she decided she was ready for a family. A half a mile from the house traffic came to a crawl as they passed Adams St. A cruiser blocked off the road. Rubber Neckers tried their best to see what sort of excitement was going on. Val was one of the many who slowed down to see nothing.

"I wonder what's going on?" Kat glanced, but she didn't care, she just wanted to get home and go see Jasper at the restaurant to tell him the news.

When they pulled into the street curiosity crossed both their faces when they saw Jasper's car in the driveway. Nervousness set in when the saw the back door to the house wide open. Japer was a worrywart and would never do something like that. Kat jumped out of the vehicle without a word and ran to the house. She bolted through the kitchen not bothering to yell out Jasper's name. Kat checked every downstairs room with nothing more than a quick glance. Then it was the upstairs' turn to be searched. The last room she checked was the office since it was the last place Jasper would be. There on the calendar she saw the word *WHY.* She backed away from it and looked out the window to see if Jasper was outside, that's when she saw the police officer talking to Val.

PART TWO
LIMBO

1

Kat had stood frozen staring out of the window as she watched the officer talk to Val, waiting silently for her reaction. Then after a few strong hand gestures, Val covered her face. The officer tried to comfort her with a hand on the shoulder. Kat was numb, she hadn't been told anything yet but she already knew. When Val started towards the house, Kat dashed for the bedroom. Once inside she locked the door, grabbed her silk sachet and jumped into bed. A moment or two later a soft knock came.

"Sweetie, open the door...I...I need to talk to you."

Kat wrapped herself tightly in the down comforter, and placed a pillow over her head. The pillow smelled of Jasper. She tried to clear her mind of every bad thought. She prayed that if she could just hide long enough everything would be fine...if she didn't hear what happened then in her mind Jasper was fine.

"Kat, please don't do this…this is very important. The police are here Hun."

Val pleaded for more than ten minutes without an answer before the young police officer picked the lock out of fear of suicide. Val walked to the bed and stared down at the cocoon-like figure, she could hear a small whimper from beneath. She sat on the edge and placed a hand on the cocoon.

"Is he going to be alright?" Kat asked in a shallow tone.

"Baby…he…he's…" Val couldn't finish the sentence without crying. Kat violently started screaming "*NO!*" over and over again while thrashing hard in the bed. Val backed up and started crying hysterically.

Thirty minutes later Kat still hadn't come out from under the covers. The paramedics were called in to sedate and bring her to the hospital to be treated for shock. It took two paramedics and one officer to pull the sheets back and inject the cold fluid into her arm. Kat fell into a slumber.

2

When Kat awoke she was in an unfamiliar room but she could instantly tell where she was from the plain colors, beeping noises, and cheap curtains. Her head felt foggy. Scared not knowing why she was there, she immediately called for Jasper. Val was sleeping in a reclining chair in the corner, and by the third "Jasper!" she awoke and rushed to her side. One part of Val wished Kat would never wake up, she dreaded having to tell her the news, again.

"Baby, baby it's me Val. Shhhhh calm down."

She rubbed her hair in a comforting motion. Tears started to form in both their eyes.

"It wasn't a dream…?"

Val couldn't answer the question with words. She shook her head no. Kat shut her eyes and tried to control her breathing.

"He was hit by a car jogging. I'm so sorry."

The two embraced as much as they could. Val sobbed, Kat did not, she refused to believe it.

"No…Nope…not now…"

A man in a cheap suit showed up at the door. He knocked softly. Kat looked at him, not caring who he was. Val turned and quickly stood up.

"I'll be right back honey…this man works for the police department and I need to talk to him, ok? Later on you're going to need to as well." Kat stared blankly at the man's wedding ring.

In the hall the two talked in a half whisper. Kat, feeling she shouldn't be left out of anything to do with her, crept to the door to listen in. She placed her cheek against the cold gray steel of the doorframe to hear better.

"I'm terribly sorry to tell you this but technically I should be filing this as a suicide." the over-the-hill detective said with genuine feeling and straightforward police talk.

"You can't, dear God no. She couldn't take that. She's been here for two days already." Kat's mind swirled. She could barely remember anything but seeing a police officer in her yard and a few moments of foggily asked questions in this room.

"Well with everything you told us, and the note that was left by the victim…"

"Jasper!"

"Yes, I'm sorry, Jasper. Well what Mr. McAlister said was that Jasper bolted out from the woods, right in front of his car as if it was on purpose."

"Jesus…" Kat was amazed at how well she was taking this news. She attributed it to the drugs and the fact that she thought she was still dreaming.

"But there is an insufficient amount of evidence to label it a suicide."

"Thank God."

"But I wanted to tell you so you could decide whether or not to talk Mrs. Cutter about it." Kat had heard enough. She walked back to the bed but to her it was more of a float. When she got back to the bed she looked down and realized that in her haste to get to the door she had pulled out her IV. Noticing this made her so frustrated at her half conscious state that she slammed the IV tower to the ground.

Pressure started to build in her more and more. Kat started to tear at everything in the room but she didn't get far before the detective grabbed her and yelled for the nurses. Within seconds three nurses charged into the room with needles in hand. Kat was off to a long slumber once again.

3

Two weeks later Kat was staying at Val's. The whole event was a complete blur to her. Luckily, Val took care of all the necessary arrangements - everything from identifying the body to picking out the tombstone. It wasn't anything she wanted to do but Kat was in no state to do anything. In fact for most of the two weeks she didn't speak, she was heavily drugged and just stared. Val herself took a leave of absence from her job so she could make sure everything was going to be fine.

Kat's state reminded Val of her volunteer days in the nursing home when she was a teen. She originally volunteered to help the elderly and make them happy. But seeing how so many of them would just sit and stare out a window for hours on end no matter what was said to them was too much for her to handle. She quickly quit.

Kat attended the funeral in a wheelchair with a blank expression on her face. She talked to no one. Val told the large group of mourners that her silence was due to the depression medication. In truth she was on only one anti-depressant. She would have been on more but the doctors were afraid it would harm the baby. They also told Val that this current state was a mental shield to get her through the rough part of mourning, and that sooner rather than later she will start to come out of her state of shock. Tomorrow was to be her first trip to the psychologist to help that process along.

Sitting in the spare bedroom that was void of any of her own personal items, Kat stared at the wall. Her mind was clear. Actually her mind was fine. She was completely sane and no longer in shock. She just didn't feel like talking. She didn't want to have to listen to that quiet low tone that everyone used as they tell you how sorry they were for her. That sickening, forced frown everyone put on to show how upset they were. That's why she hadn't spoken. She knew she would have to soon. Not only that, but she would have to start to face a life without her life, Jasper. She would have to make decisions on things like what to do with the restaurant, the house, their…their…baby.

Kat was actually surprised at how clear she could think about things now without having to break down and cry. Of course at night she didn't sleep, that's when she cried a slow soft stream of steady tears that flowed most of the night. It had only been three or so days since the fog had lifted her mind, and in one sense she wished it were still there.

Val walked into the room with a fake plastered smile. Kat loved that smile even though it was fake, because Val was the only person who didn't pity her. Dozens of friends and family members had visited, but Kat ignored them all. Val told most of them to go away and come back in a few weeks.

"So what ya been up to kid?" Val said in a joking manner. Kat's bloodshot, black ringed eyes which reminded Val of a horror movie victim's eyes in the last reel of a movie, looked up to say hello.

"Not much? Well I got something to give to you Hun. It's not going to be easy for you, but I've had it now for a while and I think it might help you. Well I'm hoping at least." She took her purse off her shoulder and sat down on the end of the bed next to Kat. Kat watched her hands as they trembled, pulling out a small plastic bag. She couldn't imagine what it was that made her so nervous. Val clenched the bag in both hands as she prepared to give a speech.

"Now Sweetie when…oooooh man…when they found…when they took Jasper in the ambulance he had this wrapped around his hand. I'm guessing he was going to give it to you when you got home from work. I talked to the guys at the restaurant and they said he was home because he was going to surprise you and take you out for the night." Kat had heard pieces of the story before and didn't want to hear it again but she nodded since Val was so nervous - it must be important.

"Well I guess…well here." Reluctantly Kat placed down the silk sachet that hadn't left her side in two weeks.

Kat unruffled the bag slowly and reached in even slower. Her fingertips touched the softest silk she had ever felt. At that instant she knew that it was a sachet. She pulled it out to reveal the beauty of it. It was two feet long, powder blue with small glorious butterflies on it amongst some unidentifiable stains. But best of all it was embroidered. In small red threaded letters it read: *My love, you are my everything and you can be anything.* Tears filled her eyes as she wrapped it around her hand.

"I tried to clean it the best I could."

Kat turned to her.

"Thank…you…so much." Val's faced beamed, she didn't respond with any words, just a hug. Hearing her voice after two weeks made every second of emotional stress worth it.

4

It was hard at first but Kat finally began to talk. And talk they did, for three straight hours - neither of them left the bed. They lay holding hands, crying and smiling. They were both relieved that the whole silent part was over. Val could resume work, and Kat could…

They both did their best to keep the conversation light hearted. But most of all they tried to avoid the subject of Kat's pregnancy. When the conversation hit a lull in the third hour, Val used the pause to take a bathroom break. When she returned a few seconds later she found Kat in the same cocoon-like state that she was in when she first heard the news. Her heart sank at the sight. Carefully, Val approached the bed.

"Sugar, what's going on? I thought we were doing good, real good." No answer. She sat down and tried to pull back the cream colored sheet from her face. No luck.

"Baby, you..." At hearing "baby" a small whimper escaped from beneath the velour. Val shut her eyes tight in preparation for the conversation she wasn't ready to have.

"How the hell am I supposed to have a baby alone?" Kat whispered in a shaky voice.

"Come out of there and look at me." The sheets came down just enough to see forehead and eyes.

"You'll be just fine, you've got eight months or so to get ready for it." Both sets of eyes wandered more than they looked at each other. Val caressed Kat's neglect-damaged hair for the thousandth time that week.

"Look, you have me to help you, you'll be a great mother."

"That's not what I'm afraid of, I know I could be a good mother. But I'm afraid that its eyes will look just like Jasper's, that every day for the rest of my life I'll have to look into those eyes and see what I lost. That I'll have to relive the loss every time it asks, 'Where is my Daddy?'. That I'll have to explain that Daddy's...that Daddy..." Val hadn't thought too much about this side of the ball before. She was scared for Kat.

"Honey, I'm sure you'll get used to it. Won't having a piece of Jasper with you be better?" Val choked out with no confidence.

"But how will I ever be able to move on? I'll never be able to. Right now I want nothing more than for it to be a year or two down the road, when I've learned how to cope. When I've started to get on with my...my life was Jasper." The conversation was harder than Val had anticipated. She was trying to be strong for Kat but was having a hard time.

"I don't want to have this baby…what if I blame it for Jasper's death, I know I will, I just know it."

"Don't say such a thing, it was an accident."

"HE KILLED HIMSELF! You don't have to hide it from me anymore…." Val's mouth dropped. She'd never planned on telling her that the detectives thought it might have been suicide. Kat started to have a screaming fit that looked a lot like a seizure. Val was too overwhelmed to do anything.

"I don't want to live! I don't want to live! I don't want this baby, god damn it! It's all my fault."

Val backed away from the bed. The two weeks of everything, having to see Jasper's mangled not yet touched up body, planning funeral arrangements, being the strong one, taking care of Kat and missing work, finally built up in her. She left the room. She couldn't do this anymore.

Val slammed her bedroom door and locked it. With her arms crossed, she paced back and forth in the luxurious room. For the first time since it happened, she was mad. Mad that she couldn't just fix everything, mad because she wanted to do more but couldn't. Or could she? Kat didn't want this baby. She never wanted it. Having this child would mean that she wouldn't be able to follow her career. Then the chances of her ever finding someone else would be even harder-guys didn't want a woman with baggage.

After pacing for five or so minutes Val went to her dresser. Squatting down, she opened the bottom drawer and moved a few junk items aside until she found the box. The box of Mifepristone. She took it out and started to read it. Kat will never willingly take it, even though she doesn't want this child.

For a solid twenty minutes she held the box and thought: *Should I to talk Kat into taking it? She was just out of her first month, but it should still work? But she'll never agree to it, as much as she wanted to get rid of it. Maybe I should give it to her without her knowing it? Would that be murder? But Kat was going to do it herself anyways. Now she has to. She has to take these. She's in no state to have a child, not now, not alone. I mean how would I deal...how would Kat deal with not working and having no life? I have to do this, whether she knows it or not. It's the best thing for her. She'll just think she's had a miscarriage and that will be that.*

5

An hour and a half after leaving Kat's room, Val came back in. In one hand was a tall slender glass of cold water. In the other closed hand were Kat's anti-depressant pills... and the Mifepristone.

"Look sugar, I know I know what you're going through is a trillion times harder than what I'm facing, but you need to understand that I'm having a hard time with this too." Val recited to the now calm Kat who was lying on her side facing the window.

"I'm sorry, I know and I appreciate everything."

Val walked around the bed and sat on the edge.

"Come on, sit up, it's time for your pills."

Kat sat up with the speed of a half-dead snail. Looking at Val she noticed a tiny rim of sweat forming on her forehead. Val handed her the glass of water. She was nervous, not knowing whether or not to tell her that she was giving her some new vitamins or something. Kat put out her hand for the pills. Val's hand shook gently as she placed them in it. Without looking, Kat popped all five pills in her mouth and took a large swallow of water to choke then down. Val anxiously watched Kat's face to see if any signs of suspicion arose. None.

"Good girl, why don't you try to sleep? I'll come in and check on you in the morning." Kat gave a half smile, shut her eyes and slid back down to bed. Val walked out of the room and shut the door. The second it was shut, her entire body began to tremble. She couldn't even walk away from the door. The only thing she was happy about was that she only had to give her one more dose in two days.

6

The next day, while chemically induced changes in her body were about to supply her with her second loss, Kat attended her first therapy session. The doctor who reminded her of Groucho Marx, (mustache and all) was pleasantly surprised by her sudden mental change. After an hour session, the doctor was a hundred and seventy-five dollars richer while Kat on the other hand, felt the same.

Val was waiting for her in the small but elegant reception area.

"So how did it go?" she asked. Kat shrugged her shoulders as the pair headed for the SUV. Once on the road, Kat began to fidget.

"I…I think I'm ready to go home." Val was happy, yet scared. If Kat went home now, she wouldn't be able to give her the second pill and Kat would remain pregnant. Or would she? Even worse, maybe it would just mess the kid up?

"I don't think that's such a good idea, Hun. You just started to talk yesterday…I mean what if…I just think it's too soon." After a few tense moments, Kat agreed.

"All right. But you're going back to work this week and when you do I'm going back to the house. I just need to try and see if I'll be able to live there. I need to know what the hell I'm going to do now." Val was relieved.

The next morning Val went out shopping early to surprise Kat. By the time Kat had woken up Val had a makeshift beauty salon set up in the living room. Kat walked into the room and was shocked at the hairdryers, creams, ointments, rubs, electric massagers, masks, junk food, and videos strewn about the room.

"What is this all about?"

"Honey no offense but you look like something out of a Wes Craven film, today we are going to pig out, get beautiful and watch stupid comedies all day long."

Kat smiled a real smile for the first time in a long while.

The day was a tremendous help to the both of them. Kat finally started to look like part of the human race again and she ate more than she had in the past two weeks combined. But most amazing of all, she finally laughed while watching Tim Robbins's feet on fire in *Nothing To Lose*. Of course the occasional cry occurred but that was to be expected.

All in all the day went great. Finally the two of them felt as if some forward progress had been made. But towards the end of the night Kat noticed that Val had started to get shaky and quiet.

"What's wrong?" Val didn't respond with words and instead just made a face as if she'd bitten a lemon. She shook her head, "No." Right then she left the room. She went to the bathroom to retrieve Kat's daily dose of anti-depressant and the final abortion pill that that she had hidden in her contacts case.

"Do you want to talk?" Val jumped a mile and almost dropped the pills at the sudden appearance of Kat.

"No, no I'm fine sweetie. I'm just getting your medications for ya." She filled the bathroom cup with water and handed it to her. Kat took it without hesitation. Val started to clench the pills in her hand so tightly that if they had been coals they would have turned into diamonds.

I can't do this, why the hell would I kill my best friend's baby? She should decide whether or not to do it. This was stupid of me!

Kat held out her hand for the pills. She was concerned and baffled about Val's condition.

"You know what baby, you don't need these anymore."

"Val I'm scared of what I might be like without them, I need it for now." Val was terrified, not knowing how the hell she was going to get rid of the two evil pills and let her have the rest without making a huge scene and having her ask a million questions. Kat's hand was still outstretched. Val pretended to hand her the pills but instead dropped them all on the floor. The best she could hope for was that the two odd pills would land near her so she could snatch them up discreetly. She was only half lucky.

The five pills spread out on the floor like white cockroaches trying to escape death. Two of the anti-depressants landed on the green bath mat at their feet. The third one rolled and hit the bathtub where it stopped. The two doppelgangers must have had more bounce in them because they spread out the farthest. One shot right behind Kat, the other went to the left of Val and under the toilet.

"I'm so sorry Hun let me get them."

"Don't be silly I'll help." Val dropped to her knees and started to crawl for the one behind Kat, the other one wasn't a threat. Kat instinctively went for the farthest one first. She easily picked up the abortion pill before Val could even make it halfway to it. With a quick blow to clean it she popped it into her mouth and swallowed it dry.

Val stopped moving and stared up at her. She wanted to scream. She wanted to make her throw up, to tell her what she'd done, but she couldn't even speak. Kat hardly noticed that Val was still on the floor, she just kept bending over picking up and popping pills. As she picked up the one next to the tub she asked. "That's the last one right? Four?"

In a low shallow voice Val replied, "Yeah, just four."

She glanced over at the one-imposter pill lying still under the ceramic pot. She could only hope that one pill wouldn't be enough.

7

Three days later Val was going back to work and dropping off Kat at the house for the first time. They pulled into the driveway silently. Kat had a blank expression on her face as she surveyed the yard and house. A million memories and not a single one without Jasper. A young kid down the street that Val had paid to keep up the yard while Kat wasn't there had just cut the grass making the yard smell of early spring.

"Well, this is it Kiddo. Remember, work knows of my situation so if you can't handle it just let me know and I'll come and make sure you're OK." Kat got out and walked around to Val's open window.

"I'll be fine." They kissed each other on the cheek and with a supportive smile, Val backed out of the driveway. As she drove down the street, Val thought to herself: *Two days to two weeks. So the box says. Please God let the next two weeks fly by without incident.*

Kat walked to the door. With slow deep breaths, she slid the key into the lock. She kept her eyes on the floor as she took the first step in. With a final boost of self-confidence she raised her head to look around the living room. Somehow, even though it was the exact way she had left it a little over two weeks ago, the room seemed entirely different. It seemed as if the bright pastel colors of the room had dulled and aged. This was going to be harder than she thought.

As if walking through a field of delicate flowers, Kat stepped through the living room and into the kitchen. There she saw Jasper's cup upside down next to the sink. At the sight of it she had to fight back tears. Jasper had used the oversized red cup long before he'd known Kat. No matter what the occasion was, if he were home he would use it. If it was dirty he would just rinse it out and fill it up. He could never explain why he loved it so much. In actuality she never even knew where he got it. Sitting there by itself it looked so empty and useless, just like she felt.

I've done enough crying for a lifetime. NO MORE, NO MORE. What good does it do me, huh? Nothing. I have to be strong. Kat thought to herself as she closed her eyes tightly. Turning to the kitchen table she saw a note. As she picked it up she instantly knew it was from Val. It read:

Honey, I know today is going to be hard for you. Remember I'm only a phone call away. I put Jasper's ashes upstairs in the linen closet. I know that is a bit odd but I didn't want you to turn a corner and half to face them. This

way when you're ready you know where they are. I love you.
Val

Her heart started racing at the thought of what was left of Jasper, his ashes, were in the house with her now. They were both under the same roof they had shared for four years. She crumpled the note and half-heartedly threw it to the floor.

She walked through the rest of the downstairs doing her best to suppress memories. Finally, after becoming somewhat accustomed to the house, she ventured upstairs. She stood at the top of them and looked down the hallway. The linen closet was straight in front of her at the far end. She wasn't ready. She walked down the hall, never taking her eyes off the closet. For a split-second, her sick subconscious pictured Jasper's mutilated body hanging on the other side of the door. Not having seen Jasper's body until it was made up for viewing at the wake, her mind made the mutilation seem much worse than it was. She had never asked the extent of the damages from the car. She didn't want to have to ever picture it. Yet she did anyway.

Kat side stepped into the office and instantly noticed that her wall calendar was gone. Val had taken it and thrown it in a dumpster a week ago. It was the only evidence of possible suicide. A wave of guilt stronger than she had ever felt before rushed through her body at the sight of the large empty space. She collapsed into the chair.

No way. He would never have done something like that. But what if he did…then this is all my fault. Why else would he sprint out the door and leave it open on the one day he took off from running. Why else would he write "Why" on the board? He definitely found out. I was so careful. Not enough though. But I can't believe he would purposely run in front of a car.

She got angrier and angrier with both herself and the thought of Jasper actually killing himself. She wanted to know the truth. She needed to know the truth. But how could she ever find out?

The two steps across the hall past the closet to the bedroom seemed like an epic journey. She kept her gaze away from the pale white shutters that served as doors. To her, it was as if Medusa's eyes were embedded in them

The bedroom was the hardest room of all. It was where they had made love, where they had their deepest talks, where they had planned their future. Emotional exhaustion was taking over her body. Kat wanted nothing more than to lie down and rest, but she couldn't even bring herself to come within five feet of the bed.

At that moment she realized the house was no longer theirs, but hers. That was something she didn't want. The place had too many memories and smells of Jasper. She saw no possible way of living here alone. It would be like living in a giant photo album, that you were forced to look at but never allowed to add too. Kat started to feel clenching and spasms through out her body. She was amazed at how much her emotions could affect her physical being. A sweat broke out and her knees started to shake so much that she had to back up against the wall and slide down it so she could sit.

Now in a rocking position hugging her knees, the cramps started to beat her stomach so hard that she couldn't concentrate on anything else but them. Then it started to happen. Blood, thick, dark and chunky, started to make its way out of her body.

Terrified, knowing what was happening but not knowing what to do she crawled to the phone, leaving a small dark stain on the white carpet where she had just been sitting. Instinctively, she called Val. Within five seconds of answering the phone Val knew what was happening. Within forty seconds she had her keys in hand and was heading for the door.

8

Val arrived shortly after to find Kat sitting on the toilet. Her head was down on her lap. At first her heart sank, thinking Kat had passed out. But when Kat heard her come in she lifted her head to see her. The makeover from the previous day was certainly gone now. Her face was once again pale and somber. Her eyes looked dry and blood shot as if her tear ducts had run dry.

"I'm losing him." It was the first time either of them had referred to the baby as an actual human being. This took Val off guard and made her hesitate in the doorway. Kat put her head back down.

"How bad is it baby?" Val asked in a low voice as she approached her.

"A lot has come out. I must have flushed fifty times. I couldn't stand knowing what was floating below me."

"Have you called a doctor yet?" Kat shook her head "No". Val was surprised at her demeanor. She had expected to see a sobbing mess but instead she looked like a woman who had gone through much worse in life.

Val slipped out of the bathroom and into the office to call the hospital. Kat had yet to see a doctor about her pregnancy so Val called the Emergency Room to ask what to do. Of course she had been in this situation herself many times, yet she still wanted to call. The woman who answered sounded like a roadside diner waitress with a two pack a day smoking habit. Not only was her voice not welcoming, but her tone and words were much worse. After explaining the situation to the nurse she answered with:

"Look lady we are crazy down here right now. You don't come to the hospital for a miscarriage. There is nothing we can do. Just call your normal doctor and set up an appointment to have a check up." CLICK. With that the woman hung up the phone. And Val made her way back to the bleeding Kat. Walking down the hall Val didn't feel guilt over the miscarriage. In fact she was happy that it was happening. She was always good at doing this, telling herself that what was her fault wasn't. In this case she would never know, and that was probably better.

Kat was sitting up this time when Val appeared again.

"Well sweetie looks like we are going to be staying right here. Do you want me to get you anything?"

Kat shook her head. Val took a seat on the edge of the tub. Kat stared at nothing, a past time that had become her hobby as of late. Val stared at Kat. After several moments of silence, Val spoke.

"All right. I know you don't like being coddled, so tell me what you want. Do you want me to give you a long speech about how common miscarriages are? That well over twenty-five percent of women have them? Do you want me to tell you that no matter how hard this is that it is the best thing for you in the long run?"

Through the short speech Val found herself getting angry and loud. She stopped and closed her eyes.

"I know this is the best thing for me. I never wanted the child in the first place. It's just so ironic and horrifying that I went through so much pain and suffering to just end up having a miscarriage anyway." Kat shook her head as if not to believe it. Stupefied, Val looked at her wondering how the hell she was holding together when she herself felt like she was coming apart at the seams.

Val noticed that Kat's face seemed to change a bit. Color started to come back to it. She looked different. Weathered, stronger, she looked like a woman who'd been through hell and survived, returning stronger from the journey. For the first time that afternoon their eyes met.

"I'm going to make it, Val. I don't know how, but I'm going to make it."

9

The doctor's visit two days later was quick and painless. He expressed his sympathies and told her she would be just fine. Up to that day she still hadn't spent a night in her own home. This time she thought she was ready.

It wasn't hard for her to cross the threshold of the house this time. She felt changed and ready to face the memories that lay within the walls even though the last two times she was here she was met with tragedy.

The living room still looked different and lifeless to her but she chose to sit on the couch anyways. It was completely silent. The only sounds came from her breathing and the subtle whoosh of the silk being run under her nails.

She did her best to stop the flood of memories that tried to barge through her mind. All of course were of Jasper and her in the living room: The time they wrestled and laughed for way too long, the countless times they made love in every inch of the room, the hundreds of cuddles and movies watched, the time Jasper spilled his drink and she yelled at him, to which he only laughed, their first Christmas, their last one.

Before she knew it an hour of her reminiscing with herself went by. Instead of getting upset, she tried to comfort herself by reminding herself that at least she had the memories. Finally, after going through pretty much every attainable memory, she started to think of what she had to do. That's when the reality of her life set in

It was the first time Kat had started to think about doing things, but nothing came to her mind. There wasn't one single thing she needed to do or had to do. Not one. She tried harder and harder to think of something, no job, no husband, no anything. What was she going to do? What was she supposed to do? Everyone had been telling her to rest and take some time to heal. Well, she'd taken two weeks of not even speaking. Now what?

Her life seemed meaningless now. She had no kids to help at school. No husband to make happy or do things with. She got up and started to pace. Millions of people die everyday, what do all the widows do after? A passion! That's it, she needed a passion. Something she could do to take up time until she was ready to go back to work, which was today but the school was making her take a mandatory month (or until a doctor said she was ready) to rest. *Needle point! Writing! Gardening! No...Damn it! I'm not any good at those and don't like them enough to do them for more than ten minutes.* She found herself getting more and more frustrated by the second.

Crazy thoughts about the lack of meaning in her life and her uselessness to the world started to knock around in her brain like bowling balls. That's when she remembered a six-month stint in college when she wanted to drop out to become a professional soccer referee. The thought of it now made her laugh, but it was still something in a time of nothing.

The thought brought her upstairs and into the bedroom closet to dig for her old memory boxes. She was doing pretty well at pretending that being in the bedroom didn't bother her. Back in her sophomore year at college she volunteered to be a soccer ref at the local elementary school games. It only lasted for one season but she had enjoyed it immensely, even if she hadn't thought of it since then. But now in the back of the walk-in closet on her tiptoes, reaching for four blue shoeboxes, it served as a good excuse to occupy herself.

With the four boxes on the ground in front of her, she sat Indian style in the closet. None of the cardboard containers were labeled except with giant Avia logos. A cloud of dust appeared as she removed the first lid. She wasn't sure in which box she would find her old whistle and penalty cards, but she didn't mind. It would be a fun trip down memory lane on the way to finding them. Three of the four boxes were filled with various items, pictures and memories from her past before Jasper. The fourth was from their first year dating.

The first box took her way back to elementary school. She pulled out and played with such items as sea shells, Gumby figurines, coins, love notes (of such immature nature that they talked about holding hands as if it was a night of wild sex) and countless drawings she had made as a kid that her mother put away for her, for moments like these. After a while of sifting, smiling and remembering, she put all the items back in the box and closed the lid. It was now onto box number two.

This box took her back to her teen years. Magnets, pictures of boy bands with big hair, Garbage Pail Kids stickers and a SheRa pin were all on top. She laughed at how she'd had all those items in her locker for four years. Deeper in the box were pictures of high school boyfriends, love notes that talked about and planned out wild nights of sex and drinking (which in reality ended up being nights of puking and thirty seconds of one-sided pleasure). Under the notes was a softball-sized key chain that she had lugged around all of High School. It contained more than twenty-six separate key chains including: a mini koosh ball, a super soaker, a ray gun, stupid slogans like "I'm not a bitch I just act like one" and dozens of others. All that and it used to only have three keys, which at times were very hard to find.

When she hit the bottom of the box she still hadn't found the items she was looking for and she was glad. This was the most fun she'd had in a long time. She hesitated before opening the third box. She knew one was full of painful memories of Jasper and the other was her college years. The only problem was they both looked identical. With a deep breath she chose the box that was next in line. She chose wrong.

The second the lid came off she saw Jaspers big beautiful eyes shining at her. Everything that had been pushed out of her mind for the past few hours rushed right back in. The picture staring back at her was the first one she had ever taken of him. With both hands, she held the lid ready to shove it back on, to seal the pain away for another day, but she hesitated. The desire to plunge in and immerse herself in everything Jasper was strong, but she knew it would be a bad choice. She just wasn't ready. After a long debate with herself she decided to put the lid back on. That was when she saw it, just a tiny corner of it. Amongst the hundreds of pictures, dried petals, old tickets and toys she saw a piece of blue paper with red crayon on it sticking up on the side of the box. She instantly remembered what it was and was disgusted with herself for not thinking of it sooner. She couldn't have been happier that she'd opened the wrong box. Now she had a purpose, something she needed to do, something she must do.

10

As she pulled out the ruffled blue paper the long forgotten memory rushed back. Even though her life had changed drastically in the past two weeks, she knew it was about to change again. The paper was folded four times. She undid each crease to reveal a once diner place mat turned into a crayon drawn contract. She stared down at it and recalled the day she signed it.

It was almost two in the morning when they went to Phil's Diner, the only all-night restaurant in town. They had just finished making love and decided to get some food. Lovemaking was still recently new to them and they had yet to move in together. That's why they were up at such an hour. They could never get around to saying goodbye.

Their faces glowed with love and post climax as Jasper ate chocolate pancakes and Kat nibbled her Belgian waffle with strawberries.

"I feel like an old man in here." Jasper said with a mouthful of food. Kat looked over her shoulder at the group of rowdy drunken teens. Her eyebrows arched at the realization that in fact they were the oldest people there, and yet they weren't even thirty.

"Well you are climbing the hill old man."

"Hey I'm only two years older than you Miss Spring Chicken." They both giggled and ate with their eyes locked on each other.

"What are you going to do when you…you know?"

Jasper asked as he poured more syrup on his already drenched pancakes.

"Boy you must really feel old."

"No, no. I mean I want to be cremated. What about you?" The subject took Kat a little off guard.

"Well I'm not sure, I guess I never really thought of it. I try not to think about death."

"Yeah, but you got to. You never know when you're just going to kick it. My uncle died at 38 and he had nothing planned. My poor father had to do every single thing. It was horrible. I just never want to put anyone through that. I want my plans to be known so at least if something happened I would get what I wanted." Kat jabbed a strawberry with her fork and fed it to Jasper in a halfhearted attempt to change the subject. She hated thinking about things like this.

"Well I guess you're right. So are you telling me what you want done? Does that mean you plan on being with me for some time?" Kat said in a giddy schoolgirl voice. Jasper swallowed, looked her in the eye and replied.

"Yeah. I really do." They leaned in and kissed a soft kiss until one drunk yelled.

"Ohhhhhhhhhhhh yeah baby! Give her more tongue!"

They both cracked up laughing, but didn't acknowledge the kid.

"All right, so I want to tell you my wishes, but you've got to promise not to laugh." Jasper said with all seriousness. Kat cocked her head in a "what the hell are you talking about" manner.

75

"Well… as long as you don't want to have a dress on when you're in the coffin I don't think I will."

"No, nothing like that. Well since I was a kid I've always wanted to drive cross-country. I want so bad to say I've been to all fifty states. But so far it hasn't happened and I don't think it will for a long time. It's too expensive and would take months. Maybe when I retire I'll get a camper and set out. Who knows? But anyway like I said, I want to be cremated. Now here comes the weird part. I want my ashes to be separated into fifty handfuls. Then I want someone to scatter one handful in each state, that way I will have been to all fifty states, making my dream come true. In a weird way it would be as though I was be everywhere all the time. You know? Instead of asking 'Where is Jasper buried?', people can say, 'He's not buried, he's everywhere you go.'" Jasper finished his speech and looked at Kat, waiting for her to laugh. He couldn't believe he had just said that. It sounded like a cheesy moment out of a romance novel, but Kat smiled back a smile that could have melted all the desserts in the diner.

"That's nice. I wish I had a dream like that."

"Really? You don't think I'm stupid?"

Kat reached across and grabbed his hand.

"Not at all. I promise you that if we are still together… which I know we will be, I will do that for you."

Jasper's face got serious. It was at this moment when he first knew he wanted to marry her.

"Promise?"

"I just did. But I'll do even better."

Kat moved her plate aside and turned her blue lacy place mat so it was the long way in front of her. Then she looked at the cup of crayons that was next to the syrups, ketchups and sugars. She chose a red one. Jasper watched with great curiosity as she wrote. Finally she made two big lines across the bottom, put down the crayon and picked up the placemat.

"I, Kathleen Trevington hereby promise to divide Jasper Cutter's ashes into fifty individual piles. Upon doing so I will then scatter one pile in each and every state in America. Fifty in all. This is a legal and binding contract. Signed, Kathleen Trevington. Witnessed by Jasper Cutter. Now my dear, sign right here and we have ourselves a contract." Jasper yanked out a green crayon and signed without hesitation. Kat, as though she were a lawyer, put out her hand for a shake.

"Pleasure doing business with you sir!"

Jasper took the paper folded it in four and placed it in his shirt pocket.

"Ok. Now what can I do for you?" Jasper asked. Kat tapped her finger against her chin thinking.

"Hmmm, well you do realize how much work that would be to go across the whole country? I'll have to think of something good. I'll get back to you on it." The conversation was over and pretty much never brought up again.

As Kat started to refold the paper she felt alive again. Guilt of Jasper's death had been weighing her down. Now she felt that if she did this, things would be right, they would somehow get better. She got up and rushed out of the closet. There was a lot of work to do before she could set out on a cross-country trip.

11

For the next few days Kat did her best to avoid Val and the other family and friends who called or stopped by the house. She also turned the living room into her bedroom, refusing to ever sleep in the bed again. Excitement and nervousness ran through her every second of the day. Today, those feelings were more intense than ever.

She paced in the living room, constantly glancing outside. Twenty-three minutes after they were supposed to arrive, a medium sized moving van backed into the driveway. Kat ran out to greet them. Wearing beat up old jeans and one of Jasper's old Patriots t-shirts, Kat looked like a woman ready to do work. The two bulky, obviously lazy men followed her into the kitchen where ten various sized cardboard boxes sat.

With brief instructions the men started to cart out the boxes with the speed of a sedated sloth. Kat was proud that she was actually doing this. Since reading the contract she'd started going through everything in the house and had packed up only the things she knew she couldn't part with. These were mostly objects of great sentimental value and some irreplaceable knick-knacks.

That was only one of the many things she had done in the past few days. Kat also rented a small storage unit not too far from the house for the boxes. At the mall she also bought herself a new set of luggage.

Jasper's death left Kat with a great deal of money. The life insurance policy check of $500,000 was to be deposited into her account soon. Kat went to the bank and changed all of the accounts over to her name. Along with the house, restaurant, and previous savings she had close to a million dollars. Kat could care less about the money, she had a promise to fulfill. Yes, the money would help but she had lost the only thing that mattered in her life.

Kat also went to several real estate agents until she found one she liked. The house would be up for sale and on the market by the end of the week and the restaurant was to be auctioned off in a few weeks.

Kat didn't dare tell anyone of her plans. She knew that Val and her family would try to stop her and blame it all on stress. They didn't understand because they had never had to live through a situation like this. All they wanted her to do was sit in a house seeped with memories and grief. From the second Kat made her decision, she never thought twice about it. That's what made her know it was right.

The plan for the next three days was to buy a car, (convertible preferable), to hold the estate sale of the items left in the house (which she hired a company to do), and to pack up the few items she was going to bring and then sneak off on her journey.

The only thing she couldn't bring herself to do yet was open the closet that held Jasper's ashes. She knew she had to before the estate sale, but she kept putting it off. She was going to do it though. Tonight…

12

With one hand on each knob of the double closet, Kat stood gathering all the courage she could to open them and face the inevitable. She knew it was only an urn and ashes, nothing that would scare her or look hideous, but the fact that the man she had vowed to spend the rest of her life with was now just a pile of soot in a tin can was horribly depressing.

The doors opened with ease to reveal a normal linen closet filled with towels, cleaning agents and cosmetic supplies. The only item out of place was the small brass urn. It was the first time she had seen it. In fact she'd had no clue what it was going to look like since Val had picked it out. It was plain and looked like any urn she'd seen in a movie. The only difference was a gold chain was wrapped around the neck of it. On the end of the chain was a gold ring. Jasper's wedding ring.

Kat fingered the ring and thought of how much arguing they had gone through to decide on what rings to get. Jasper wanted one of those rings you could spin when you got bored. But Kat wanted a traditional solid gold ring. She'd won.

Her hands gently lifted the urn as though she were carefully picking up a butterfly by its wings. She kept it at arms length while walking down the hallway, down the stairs and into the kitchen. *Who ever thought you could put a human being in a jar,* she thought as she made the short journey. She placed it down on the table and took a seat in front of it.

Staring at it as if Jasper's eyes would appear, Kat didn't move. The house was silent like it had been every night she'd spent here alone.

"I'm going to fulfill my promise." She finally looked away from the urn. Kat couldn't believe she was talking to a jar. But she rationalized it, thinking of people in mourning who pray at a grave or who talk to themselves for comfort. Why couldn't she talk to a jar?

"You're finally going to see the country. Both of us, together." For the first time in the past two days she felt tears. . She did her best to fight them back.

"I've got so much I want to say to you. But not now. We have a long, long trip ahead of us. We're going to be together again. One last trip." Feeling like she was losing her mind, Kat shook her head.

After a few deep breaths she took the necklace off the urn and placed it around her neck. Next, she laid out plastic wrap across the table. Wearing yellow dish gloves, she took the lid off the urn with one quick flick, as if she was scared something would pop out of it. Nothing but a small trail of dust floated out of it.

"All right my love, I'm sorry about this but I'm just doing what you wanted." As gently as possible she poured the ashes out of the urn onto the plastic wrap. A small cloud of ash formed above the pile. Afraid to breathe it in she backed away from it and leaned against the fridge. The thought of breathing in her husband terrified her.

Leaning against the fridge she examined the pile from a distance. The small size of the pile amazed her. Jasper was a little less than two hundred pounds. All that was left of him was a five-pound pile was that was in front of her - she had figured it would have been much more.

Slowly she returned to her seat. It took some effort to force herself to lean in closely and look at the pile. It reminded her of very fine off-gray fish tank rocks. She had expected something more like powdered ashes, than what she saw in front of her.

After getting accustomed to the pile, she finally touched it with her gloved hand. Even though it was a sick thought she couldn't help but wonder what part of Jasper she was touching. She actually felt a little cheated because since

Jasper was an organ donor she knew not all of him was here. The thought of something of Jaspers working in another person's body gave Kat the chills. Val wanted to tell her what organs were used to save which people but Kat had chosen not to listen.

On one of the chairs next to Kat were three boxes of zip lock bags with the zippers. She popped one box open and pulled out a bag. With one of the kitchen spoons she started to scoop the ashes into the bag.

It took the better part of an hour and a half to separate the ashes into fifty-one even bags. With all the bags full, Kat felt great pride in being able to accomplish the task she had so dreaded. Placing the lid back on the urn, she threw it into the trash.

"Now I know you probably think I've gone crazy, but I just think that urn was too...old person-ish. So I got you something that was more suiting."

She left the room and returned with a white box that she placed on the floor. Reaching into it she pulled out a large plastic cookie jar shaped like a cartoon chef.

"Ta da! Isn't it cute? I figured that if you're going to be in the front seat with me the whole time I might as well have a face to look at." She placed the cookie jar next to the fifty-one baggies of Jasper. It wore the traditional white pant and coat with a blue-checkered scarf around the neck. In his left arm was a bowl of batter, in his right hand a spoon. Of course on his head was a big puffy chef's hat. His face didn't look a thing like Jasper's but it was cute with rosy cheeks and a big smile.

Amazingly all the bags just barely fit into the jar. The lid was on a hinge that leaned back. She gently closed the lid.

"There, your new temporary home."

That night Kat slept in the living room with Jasper next to her. It was the first night she had slept for more than five hours in a row. When she woke up in the morning the jar was sitting there smiling. *I must be losing my mind. Why the hell am I doing this? I'm acting like a crazy woman. But then again it's made me happier than I've been in weeks. So what if I talk to the jar? I've seen people talk to graves for hours. I don't care what anyone thinks.*

The doorbell interrupted her thoughts. Glancing at the TV clock she realized she'd overslept and that the estate sales woman must have arrived.

Running to the door, she threw on a pair of jeans and a t-shirt. The woman standing outside reminded Kat of the caseworker in Beetle Juice. She was past old and running into ancient. Wearing a tweed dress and pearls she introduced herself as Mrs. Cummings with an accent that sounded like a bad Mary Poppins impression. Kat took her into the house to discuss the details of the day's events.

After a twenty-minute conversation, Kat assured her that every item in the house could be sold at the company's discretion. Another five minutes later, a crew of five men in suits entered the house with tags and pens to price everything. Overwhelmed by the situation, Kat excused herself from the decrepit Mrs. Cummings by telling her she would be back late in the evening. Grabbing her keys and Jasper, she headed out the door.

13

Two hours later at ten o'clock Val pulled down the street to a shocking sight. Cars were parked along the whole road and people were coming in and out of Kat's house as if it was Grand Central Station. Shocked, confused and angry Val pulled right up onto the front lawn and parked, startling a young couple walking out with a pair of lamps.

She did see the estate sale sign in the yard but knew Kat would never do something like this. Kat had been acting weird the past few days though, but Val had just attributed her behavior to being home for the first time.

Val burst into the house ready to unleash her rage. . Horrified by seeing that every single item in the house had a price tag on it (even some items she'd given to Kat) she looked around for someone to blame. After pushing through several crowded rooms she finally came upon a near death looking woman who was wearing a nametag. It read: "Barbara Cummings".

Mrs. Cummings remained extremely calm at the wave of verbal abuse that streamed out of Val's mouth. The few shoppers that were in the back spare room casually exited with speed. When Val stopped to take a breath, Mrs. Cummings face finally made an expression, she smiled. It was something she was used to. After fifty years in the estate business you get used to irate family members bursting in and asking "how dare they sell so and so's items without telling me?" But to her it didn't matter, as long as she had the sole heir's signature, it wasn't her problem.

"Look deary, I know you're probably upset by this but you really have to take it up with Mrs. Cutter."

"Did you seek her out? Is that it? Do you guys read the obituaries and call people?"

Val felt bad for yelling at a woman who was so close to death. But she felt it was necessary since she really believed Kat would never do this.

"Actually Mrs. Cutter called us. And we don't solicit business." The woman said it with such sugar in her voice that Val wanted to slap her, but of course she didn't. Instead, frustration made her flee the room. She ran down the hall to use the kitchen phone, but just as she got to it a middle-aged, tiny man was taking it off the wall. She grabbed it from him and the two played tug of war.

"Hey lady I got it first!"

"It's not for sale you damn munchkin." The man let go with a disgusted look. Val hooked it back up to the plug and dialed Kat's cell. No answer.

14

Val stayed at the house the whole day waiting for Kat to return. She spent most of it in her SUV (which she finally parked on the street). Piece by piece she watched Kat's house disappear into other people's lives. With each item she saw taken out, she became more and more depressed. Finally around eight at night the decrepit old woman removed the sign. She even smiled and gave Val a wave. Of course this pissed her off even more.

A few minutes after the removal of the sign a large truck with the name *Cummings Estate Auctions* on it backed into the driveway. Several large men loaded items into the truck. In another forty minutes the truck drove off with the rest of the stuff in the house.

The next thirty minutes she spent eating a Taquito from the Seven Eleven down the street. As she finished the last bite of the processed chemical goo, a car she'd never seen pulled into the driveway. It was an emerald green, convertible Sea Breeze. Kat hopped out of it in a giddy mood.

"Well do you like it?" She yelled over to the steps. Val wiped her hands off, trying to calm herself down before she opened her mouth.

"I know you would have gotten a red one but I really liked this one. It's pretty snazzy!"

Again, no response. Kat knew she finally was going to have to face a lengthy speech about her "crazy" behavior. As the door shut she took a look at the cookie jar strapped into the passenger seat. Her chipper mood was fading fast. As she made her way to Val, she did her best to fend off the oncoming speech.

"Look. I don't want a long drawn out speech about how what I did was crazy and how I'm suffering from stress and having a break down. Yada Yada Yada. I'm completely sane and thought everything I'm doing through. Trust me, OK? Let me explain before you go off on me."

Biting her tongue Val nodded her head "Yes". Kat took a seat next to her on the steps. She took her time and explained everything: finding the paper, selling the house and the restaurant, trading in her car for a more fun and reliable one, and finally the whole route she had mapped out in a three-hour meeting with Triple A. Val did not say one word the whole time. When Kat was done she said to Val.

"Well?"

"I think you're crazy. Why didn't you talk to me about this?"

"I just didn't want anyone, not even you trying to talk me out of it."

"Well, you're right I would have tried. But now it's too late."

"Val, don't worry about me, I'll be fine. And I'm going to keep in touch with you. Look, I have enough money to not work for years. Why should I just sit here and do nothing? This trip will let me get right with Jasper. It will clear my head and when I'm done, we'll see what happens. But you know, no matter what, I love you and you'll always be my best friend. I wouldn't have made it through the past few weeks if it wasn't for you."

Val's head was swirling with a million emotions. Even though she needed Kat in her life, she knew she had to let her go. So without saying a word, she hugged her. Kat knew that was her way of approving.

15

After discussing things more openly for another hour, Val warmed up to the whole idea of going cross-country. In fact she was jealous in a way. Finally, they entered the house. It was an odd moment for the both of them. This morning it was still somewhat of a home and now it was merely a shell. They wandered through each room to check for any items left behind. There were none.

The thorough search was done and the two headed back outside. Kat had plans to spend the night at the Bel Aire Motel down the street, but Val pleaded with her to stay her last night at her house. Kat gladly accepted. There was one last thing she had to do before leaving the house for good. Kat told Val she would meet her there and asked to be alone for a bit. Val, a bit nervous, drove off.

Watching the taillights disappear she went back to the convertible and pulled the head back on the little chef. She grabbed one of the baggies, leaving fifty behind. The half moon supplied enough light for her to walk around the back of the house. The yard was a decent size and led into the thick of a rather large forest. It had been one of the selling points of the house. All the others they had looked at had small or no yards for future kids to play in. It wasn't huge, but it was cozy.

Neither Jasper nor Kat had been very good with gardening and being early spring there wasn't much beauty to the yard. Trees, a few bushes, and a red picnic table that came with the house were all that was there (the grill had been one of the first things to sell). She strolled over to the table and sat on the top of it with her feet on the chair part. With both hands she squeezed the bag of ash in her hand as if it was a stress ball. The bright moon brought back memories of the numerous times Jasper and she had snuck out in the backyard to make love, giggling with nervousness, scared that a neighbor might see or hear them.

There was one spot in particular that had been their favorite. Halfway through the back yard to the left side near the shrubs was a rather luscious patch of grass. It was greener, fuller and softer than any other areas. After a long discussion of why that was, they had both agreed that a garden must have been located there some time in the past. They would always bring a blanket since Jasper was such a clean freak, he never wanted to get dirty. The old but soft blanket would be placed over the patch, making it a nature bed of sorts. The normal routine wasn't used out here, instead they would take turns being on bottom so they could each have a fair amount of time staring at the stars. It really was magical for them.

Staring up into the inky dark sky watching the glimmering diamonds, while at the same time being one with the person they loved most and enjoying such sexual pleasure, was to them an ideal evening. They enjoyed it so immensely that they made a pact to never do it more than once a month since they were scared that repeat sessions would make it lose some magic.

Kat walked over to the spot to lie down. It was the first time this season she was out here looking up. It felt soft as ever. After climaxing they would lie on their backs and hold hands. They would stay silent for what seemed like an eternity, just staring at the sky and sometimes each other. Laying there, Kat spread her arms as if to hold Jasper's hand. The thick grass filled the empty space in-between each of her fingers. She longed so much for Jasper that the grass actually felt like his hand.

A smile started to creep across her face as she actually felt like he was with her at that moment. She kept her eyes glued on one particularly dull star, she dared not look away because she knew once she did this, the feeling would be gone. The image of Jasper's face with a post lovemaking smile dimly lit by the blue glow of the moon, filled Kat's mind. It was the closest she had felt to Jasper since his death. The desire to stay in this moment forever was overwhelming.

Unfortunately a bird, or bat, flew in front of the star that was holding her attention. It broke her concentration and brought her back to the real world, where the spot next to her was empty and the fingers between hers were just grass.

Propping herself up on one elbow she grabbed the bag. With her thumb and forefinger she slowly unzipped it. Hesitating, she slowly stood up on the spot where magic used to happen. Without saying a word she closed her eyes and turned the bag upside down. The heavier pieces fell straight down and embedded themselves in the soft ground. The lighter ash fluttered in a gentle breeze across the yard. When she finally opened her eyes, she could see the remaining dust cloud fluttering away. The beauty of it amazed her. The deteriorated cloud sparkled like a handful of glitter thrown into the air. The moon caught each piece just right to make it an unforgettable moment. Kat couldn't have been happier at the first step in the journey.

16

One bag down, forty-nine to go. The extra bag was for her. She didn't know what to do with it, but she did know keeping a small piece of him was important to her.

Kat sat in the car with her hands glued at ten and two. The car was not yet started and was still parked in Val's driveway. Going through a mental checklist she knew she had everything including clothing and toiletry items in the trunk, not much, but enough to get by, plenty of snacks and a small cooler with juice and water to keep her going. On the seat next to her, Jasper's cookie jar was strapped tightly. On the floor in front of him was a stack of maps with bright orange sticky notes hanging out at the edges.

Checking the mirrors for the umpteenth time, Kat decided to take off the necklace with the wedding ring on it. She carefully wrapped it around the rear view mirror so it hung a few inches below.

"Ok…now I'm ready."

Val had been patiently standing next to the car to see her off.

"You know what I was just thinking? As often as you pee you're gonna know every damn bathroom in the country!"

They both laughed, which was good since there was a lot of tension.

"Thank you Val. Thank you so much." After the hundredth hug that morning Kat finally turned over the engine and put it in reverse.

"Well I hope I'll see you soon." Kat responded with a look that made Val's stomach tighten into a nervous knot.

Pulling out of the driveway they both waved and yelled

"I love you."

Kat was finally on the road. It was amazing. In less than five days she had sold pretty much everything she owned and given up what little of a life she had left. All she was now was a woman with a car and promise to keep.

PART THREE
PROMISE

1

Growing up in Massachusetts, ninety percent of Kat's vacations had been in New England. In fact she had only been on a plane twice in her life. The first time was when she was twenty-two to visit her sick aunt in Kentucky, who later died of lung cancer. That trip had only lasted a day and a half, and ninety percent of that time she was in a hospital room saying good-bye to an aunt she hardly knew. The second time was on her honeymoon to Santa Domingo. Jasper and she had always wanted to travel more but having the restaurant made it difficult for them to leave it for too long or to go too far away. So usually they went on three or four day trips to Maine, Vermont, Rhode Island and New Hampshire.

Having been to all the states in New England a dozen times she did her best to speed through this part of the journey so she could start the new and exciting states.

Driving while trying to rub the silk was getting too dangerous and annoying and Kat knew she was going to have to stop it. Cold turkey. It was the only way to go. In fact it really was like an addiction — an addiction that had gotten worse lately. She pulled over to the side of the road and folded the embroidered silk. Quickly she stuffed it in the glove compartment at the bottom. She slammed it shut and instantly wanted it back, but she had to be strong. This trip was about being strong and changing her life.

It took her four days (which with out the silk seemed much longer) to hit all six states in New England. In most cases she only drove a few miles over the borders to the first scenic rest stop to let the ashes soar. Kat found herself rushing through these states and after thinking about it she realized she was just itching to get far away from their hometown as soon as possible.

The only times she slowed down during those first few days were when she let the ashes go. In Maine, which was the third state, she stopped and was finally able to get the courage to keep her eyes on the ashes as she poured them out. It wasn't nearly as bad as she'd thought it was going to be. Actually it seemed to sooth and calm her. It felt like Jasper's soul was being released and set free in each state to roam its beauty and nature.

Finally, after two days of nothing but driving, staring at millions of trees and wondering if she had made the right decision, the satisfaction of watching the ash float away in the wind over the guardrail and down the steep slope into the thick forest, made all the monotonous driving worth while.

The gray cloud floated on the wind with such grace that it seemed alive. Slowly it grew larger and larger covering more and more ground before it slowly started to disappear.

Kat knew Jasper would be happy to see how she was doing this for him.

The enjoyment didn't last long though, because she was still in New England and wanted out. Getting in her car she drove right out of Maine and headed for the remaining three states - excited to get them finished so she could start the real journey

After hitting the upper states, she made her way back through Massachusetts (which made her uncomfortable, but she had no choice). Rhode Island wasn't even a pit stop, she was in and out of it in less than two hours. The break-neck speed was taking a toll on her state of mind. The trip was supposed to be relaxing and freeing and so far it felt like nothing but work. She was starting to feel a little relieved that only Connecticut remained. After that, she would slow down and start to sightsee.

Even though the Mystic Seaport in Connecticut was well out of her way, she made it a point to go there. Jasper and she had spent many weekend trips there. It was a cute old shipping town that was minutes away from a beach and two casinos - making it made for a perfect anytime getaway for them. Jasper had a fond affection for the old shipping boats as well.

Kat had never figured out what he found so interesting about these boats. Yes they were neat, but to her not worth more than one visit. On the other hand, Jasper wanted to tour them every time they were there. Most of the time he won and they would pay the ridiculous fee to walk through five boats that they had been on many times before.

She arrived early in the morning as the seaport opened for the day. Paying what was now not such a ridiculous fee to her, she was the first person of the day to explore these ancient fishing boats from the early eighteen hundreds. The fog was so thick that she couldn't see from one boat to the other. In one respect she was happy because no one would see her pouring ashes on the boats, but on the other hand it ruined the beauty of the harbor that she was looking forward too.

She chose the Charles W. Morgan because it was Jasper's favorite boat. It had the distinct honor of being the last wooden whaling ship in America. Anytime they were on it his face would beam with a smile for hours afterwards, even though he was against killing whales. She asked him once why he loved the boats so much. He said he really didn't know and then went on to tell her about an old plastic copper colored pirate ship he had hanging above his bed as a kid. He used to lay there and look at it, trying to see all the men scurrying about to catch a good wind or stop other pirates from coming on board. After hearing that story she never asked again.

In the belly of the boat, boxes and barrels were set up to simulate what it looked like when in use. Kat pulled out the baggie and reached her arms out behind the coarse ropes that prevented visitors from messing with the artifacts and poured his ashes into a small crack in a barrel.

"Now you can have all the dreams about Pirates and the sea life you want."

It was the sixth time she had to let go a piece of her husband. Kat felt better and better each time. New England was done. Now for the rest of the country.

2

Trying to adjust to life without Kat was rough. Jasper and she were Val's only real family, and she missed them both tremendously. To Val, there was an upside to Jasper's death and that was that she was going to have Kat with her much more - which she did for a while, but now she was gone. And who knew for how long? Was she even going to come back at all?

Val had received four phone calls from Kat the first day, two the second, one the third, and none on the fourth. It worried her that Kat was going to become too independent and forget all about her. But most of all she was scared that Kat was going to do something stupid. She had to refrain from calling her cell all day, every day, and most of the time when she did end up calling it, it was off.

After two days of not hearing from her, sheer panic set in. At work Val was cranky and distant. She dialed Kat's cell phone number so many times she was worried the buttons were going to wear out. Each time, no answer. Then on the third day of not hearing from her Val got a phone call. But it wasn't from Kat. It was from a New York State Police Trooper.

3

Kat took the top down at a rest stop just a few miles from the New York border. She wanted to be ready to take everything in when she crossed it. The only time she had ever been there was on a weekend getaway with Jasper to

Lake George. It was a terribly planned trip and too cold to enjoy anything. Yet it was her favorite vacation by far.

For her entire life, New York City had been only three hours away from her. Yet, she had never gone. It seemed weird to her but then again she had many friends who hadn't gone either. Having the top down was making Kat excited. She worried a bit about stuff flying out of the cab so she did her best to hunker everything down. Back on the highway she was a bit cold but enjoyed the fresh wind blowing through her hair.

Finally the tollbooth was ahead of her. Paying the dollar-fifty, her heart started to race. Three more seconds and she was going to be in New York, only a short ways from the Big Apple. She crossed the state line and was so excited she let out a howl like a drunken frat boy on initiation night.

Tina, her lunch buddy, used to tell her all kinds of wild stories about the city. Of course her wild stories had to be taken with a grain of salt, but Kat was sure there was some truth in them. Tina had once told her about how it was possible to see the city from miles away once you entered the state. Remembering this, Kat got excited to catch her first glimpse of the city. She swerved carelessly as she looked on both sides of the road. A few cars honked at her, she laughed and waved apologetically.

A beat up old red Cougar was in front of her making her first vision of New York come too slowly. On the left of the car was another slow car although this one was in much better condition. So with a quick glance in the side mirror she gunned it into the left lane without a blinker. Then she put the pedal to the metal and rose up to seventy-three miles an hour to get by him.

For a brief instant Kat felt rebellious since she usually drove like an old woman, but then she heard the sirens.

At first she thought that they couldn't be for her. But sure enough they were. Panic surged through her body, putting pains in her chest as she pulled to the small gravel shoulder. With the grace of a drunken sailor, she gathered her license and registration. With a useless attempt to fix her hair she felt not ready at all.

The state trooper, who looked a lot like James Cagney, strutted over. Kat had to hold in a nervous laugh when she realized that their eyes were at the same height with him standing and her sitting. She tried to play pretty and flirt but the officer whose nametag read "Lester" seemed not to notice. Kat wondered if he was gay, or just bitter at all the women who had laughed at him for his height.

While he ran the plates to make sure she wasn't a serial killer, Kat strummed her fingers on the steering wheel. Long after her fingers were sore, he came back.

"Ma'am, did you just buy this car?"

"Yes officer, yesterday."

"And why are you in New York?"

"I'm driving cross country." Kat put on too big of a fake smile that made Lester, who was always suspicious of everyone, even more so suspicious of her.

"And why do you have a cookie jar in the seat next to you?"

Kat was nervous about the answer but what the hell it was the truth.

"That's my husband." Kat responded chipperly before she proceeded to show him the individual baggies. Quickly she realized it hadn't been a good idea to show a cop a mess of wrapped baggies with powdered substance in them, all hidden inside a cookie jar. Ten seconds later the officer had asked her to come to their field station for more questioning and a drug test.

3

The tough-acting officer was nice enough to not cuff Kat as he put her in the back of the black and white. He radioed for a police tow truck to bring her car back to the station for inspection. Kat asked to bring Jasper along with her and he granted the wish but kept the jar up front with him since he still wasn't sure what the substance was.

Lester had seen all kinds of drugs being run through New York but never one like this. Not for a second did he believe her ridiculous story. Come on, a brand new car, nice luggage, and a cookie jar full of a powdery substance? The woman had to be dealing something, and Lester was determined to find out what.

The field station was only a mile away. It was small but useful for incidents relating to the highway, but it had only three desks, a holding cell, and one interrogation room, to which Kat was brought. Looking around the plain gray room, Kat was amazed at how much it actually resembled one of the rooms in a movie with its gray walls, metal chairs, and a two-way mirror. Not once in her life had she been in a police station and in fact, it was only the third time she had been pulled over.

At first she was calm, knowing she hadn't done anything illegal besides passing in the wrong lane but after being alone in the room for thirty minutes she started to break down. The mirror started to freak her out. She suspected that this was what they wanted, to see her break down. There was probably five of them on the other side watching her right now, waiting for the second she was about to crack, so they could bust into the room and act like hard asses. She didn't want that to happen, but she still couldn't handle it even though she was innocent.

This trip was a bad idea. Already nothing had gone right. The first few states were miserable and now, the first day she was happy, she got hauled into a police station. She wondered whether maybe she should just go home but then realized that she didn't have a home any more. That was when the dam broke. Tears came out and the second she started to cry she turned to the door and waited for it to bust open.

And open it did. But it was opened so slowly that she half expected Mr. Kidd to peek his head in. Instead it was Detective Walter Fuller, an older man who looked like he had given up on life and on being in shape about ten years ago. A lazy smile adorned his overly fat face and without saying a word he handed Kat a tissue. She took it and wiped up the already stopped tears.

The man sat down in front of Kat and folded his pork sausage fingers on the table. He just looked at Kat with a static smile, finding it particularly interesting that she rubbed a piece of silk back and forth between her fingers.

"Well... What?" Kat asked, annoyed at the man's silence.

"I'm a terribly good judge of character, I like to observe a person to get a full analysis." His voice was boisterous and affected with fake intellect.

"So then what are you getting from me?"

"Well I think you're a woman who's been through a lot lately. Stressed out, hence your odd habit with the silk, and you're having a crisis. But not guilty of anything."

Kat had never hated a person so much so fast as she did this blob. He spoke as if he knew everything in the world.

Kat had always been able to bite her tongue throughout her life. No matter how bad a situation was she would be the calm one who would not yell and call names. But today was different.

"That's great Sherlock, can I go now since I haven't done anything?" The sentence dripped with so much sarcasm that the man's smile finally faded.

"Well there is no reason for that Mrs. Cutter. I came in here as a friend to you." If the statement had sounded sincere Kat probably would have felt bad, but the man still spoke in that horribly fake tone and it just irked her more.

"Listen, I haven't done anything wrong, now I want you to bring me my husband and I'll be on my way!" Kat was taken back by her actions. As was Detective Fuller. He stood up and headed for the door.

"Well Mrs. Cutter I can see this might take a lot longer than I had anticipated." He reached outside of the door and came back with a handful of papers. They were handed to Kat along with a pen. Kat sighed as she filled out paperwork that hardly pertained to her.

On the other side of the glass Detective Fuller rejoined Lester.

"So what do you think?" Lester asked with his arms folded staring at Kat.

"Well she's not the nicest lady. Probably a mental crack is occurring in her cerebral cortex. But she hasn't done anything wrong." Lester held back from laughing at the load of crap that had just come out of Fuller's mouth.

"Couldn't she be insane though? I mean I got a feeling about her. For crying out loud she has her dead husband in a cookie jar with her."

"Well even so, we can't hold her on it. Only way is if we find something in the car."

For the next few minutes they were silent as they watched Kat fill out the paperwork. They knew she was done when the pen hit the two-way mirror with a soft *tink*.

Reading over her paperwork Fuller decided to give one Valerie Pearson a call to confirm her story. The phone barely rang half a ring when it was picked up.

"Hello?"

"Um yes...May I speak to a Mrs. Pearson please?"

Val first thought that it was a telemarketer, but the odd voice sounded too slow and fake to be one.

"Yes, this is she."

"I'm Detective Fuller from the New York State Police. I'm calling about a Katharine Cutter?" The air was pulled out of Val's chest fast, as if she had been hit in the stomach by a pro boxer. Not hearing from Kat in days she had dreaded this moment. Her own life had been shattered by what had already happened. She couldn't lose Kat too.

"Ma'am are you still there? We have Mrs. Cutter in custody and we need to ask you some questions."

Slowly her lungs started to re-inflate with precious air.

"I'm...here."

Val and Fuller talked for a solid twenty minutes. She told him the whole story and reassured him that she wasn't working for a Cuban drug cartel or that she was turning into a Three Faces of Eve. In return he assured her that she was fine. He also promised to make Kat call her. When he hung up the phone he felt disappointed that he had to let her go. It had been a slow week and he was looking forward to grilling someone with his superb brain - making them squirm with words most people didn't even know.

Only one hope remained to keep her prisoner, and that was the car. Fuller left the building to watch the small team of specialists tear through every inch of the vehicle.

Nothing of suspicion was found. Disappointed again, Fuller and Lester decided to have dinner before releasing her.

After two and a half hours the initial anger passed by Kat. Now she was going crazy with pure boredom. The least they could do was bring her a magazine after almost three hours in a room with no pictures, no windows, nothing, not even something to tap on the table. It was cruel and unusual punishment. Suing came to her mind once or twice but that meant a lot of paperwork and lawyers, so she decided that once she got out of here she'd leave it behind.

The door swung open, startling her almost out of her chair.

"Well. I hope you've had some time to cool off Mrs. Cutter. You see, I know you've been placed in a quandary of such peculiar matter. For that we give you our deepest sympathies." He paused long enough for Kat to arch her eyebrows in anticipation of the next sentence.

"But you see, it was an honest mistake on Officer Lester's behalf. For that we are willing to drop the two tickets you have acquired. But first you must call your friend Valerie, quite a charming woman."

Kat couldn't take another second of this bloated pompous jackass. She put on a fake smile and decided to bite her tongue once again, that way she'd get out of here faster.

She did realize that she had been neglecting Val, but she really hadn't wanted to talk to a soul during her travels through New England. She was going to call today. Unfortunately now she'd have to make it with this jelly man over her shoulder.

The call was quick and filled with hints that she'd call later and explain. Lester then brought Jasper to Kat. He handed the cookie jar to her with a look that said "*I'll get you sooner or later, you evil woman"*. Kat took Jasper back to her car. That's when her rage bubbled up in her like a pit of lava trying to break through the surface. Her luggage was in shambles. It was all closed but she could tell none of it was where it had originally been. The car was also a mess, they must have pulled the dashboard and several other units off to check for drugs. It still looked like a new car but things were off and she could tell.

Kat wanted nothing more than to scream and run back in there to give them hell, but the sun was already setting and she had only gotten two miles into the state. So like a Good Samaritan, she got in the car and drove off into the sunset.

4

The only upside to being detained for so long was that her first sight of the city was spectacular. The sky was purple and pink behind the rows and rows of cutout buildings. It looked like someone had hung up a huge painting. The sight calmed Kat tremendously. As she stared at it this time she made it a point to watch the road.

The original plan to go into the city and be out by dark was of no use now. She contemplated staying outside of the city and going in tomorrow but the new Kat won over this time. The stronger, more daring side that had been slowly emerging said "why not go in now and get a room in the heart of the city".

With the music off, hands at ten and two and eyes wide alert, Kat entered the island. She always heard the stories of how crazy New York drivers were and she was ready for them. Following signs to Times Square, she did her best to not look around in awe of all the lights and buildings. Hitting Forty-fourth Street after only six or seven wrong turns, Kat parked in a garage. Locking up the car, she grabbed her overnight bag, placed Jasper inside it and headed out to find a hotel.

Since money wasn't really an object anymore she walked right by small hotels (even though they would cost a pretty penny just the same) and headed for the Millennium Hotel. The doorman smiled as he let Kat in. The ceiling was massive with black marble everywhere. She felt a bit awkward having only stayed in cheap motels. She was a new person she kept telling herself with a confident strut.

"I know that you're probably booked but I thought I would give it a shot anyway." Kat asked the front desk woman who looked like a model trying to make cash on the side.

"Well you're in luck. It's our slow season and with the amount of rooms in this building, we have a few to spare!" Kat was happy to talk to a pleasant real human being for the first time that day. After a few preference questions she handed her the new bankcard she'd received just a few days ago. It was an account that had all of her money in it, and where the money for the house and restaurant would go once they were sold. Being that she was alone on this trip she decided that having the least amount of paper money on her was best.

"Forty-ninth floor. I got you a room with a view of Times-Square!" Kat was more than pleased with the woman and told her so as she headed for the elevator bay. As the elevator sped up ten floors Kat realized that she had never been in a building over twenty stories high. Finally she felt the excitement she'd expected on this trip.

The room was marvelous: a king size bed with original art work hanging over it, a large TV, oak night stands, two lounge chairs and a coffee table, Kat was thrilled. The best part was that it was a corner room were two large sets of windows. She put her bag down and pulled out Jasper to show him a room he would have loved. She gave the cookie jar a walking tour of the room and then headed to the drawn window curtains. With Jasper under one arm, she walked to the curtain on the side wall and flung it open as she said *Ta Da!* It wasn't that exciting but still a sight she had never experienced. About twenty yards away was another building that kept changing colors from the reflections of the neon signs. Another building was a bit below, keeping her from seeing all the way to the ground.

"Ok, let's try the other one!" Again she flung open the curtain with a *Ta DA!* This time the words were correct. Bright blinking lights of all kinds assaulted her eyes. Speechless, she scanned every inch of the view. Only on TV had she seen Times Square. She was pleasantly surprised to find out she had a perfect view of MTV studios.

After thoroughly absorbing everything, Kat smiled at the cookie jar and placed him on the small coffee table so he still had a view. It was ten o'clock and Kat was pretty beat from the horrible day, so instead of going out to explore she ordered room service - another first in a series of many.

Kat sat on the bed eating Chicken Francaise and watching a *Nick at Night* "I Dream of Jeanie" marathon.

"Fancy New York food my ass! Yours tasted much better Hun! And it cost a fraction of this!" Taking another bite she worried that talking to the cookie jar was bad. It did comfort her but what was going to happen when all the ashes were gone? She put the thought out of her mind. It was a long way off and she didn't want to think about it. That night she slept with the curtains open, letting the multi-colored lights dance on the ceiling.

5

Checkout was at eleven but Kat was already out the door by nine. Back at the car she threw her bag in and placed Jasper in the trunk. She took one baggie with her and went off to explore. Not wanting to be in the city for more than a day or so, she decided that the best way to see a lot was to take an Apple Tour's bus (at least that's what the concierge told her). She picked it up at Fifty-First Street and took a seat on the open top deck. Realizing she hadn't brought a camera, she used her bankcard to purchase a digital camera at one of the dozens of electronic junk stores on the avenue. Sitting on the bus, waiting for more passengers, she quickly scanned the directions, put in the batteries and memory card and took a few test shots. Perfect, she thought. The man had told her in broken English that it could take up to five hundred pictures. A geeky man with curly hair, glasses and a red vest took a seat at the front of the bus. His nasal voice came on the speakers:

"Welcome to the greatest city in the world! You're about to embark on a tour of history, wonderment, and the future." The man sounded like a *Saturday Night Live* character, but Kat found it amusing. For the next three hours she took over thirty pictures and learned more about New York and its history than she had thought she would ever know. The bus made frequent stops and with her all-day pass she could get on and off at leisure. Though the main part of this sight seeing tour was for pleasure, Kat used it as a way to figure out where she wanted to spread Jasper's ashes. It was a tough decision. Originally she'd thought of Central Park because of how nice it was but she realized most of the places she'd spread his ashes would be forest-like, so she decided against it. Her next idea was to walk over the Brooklyn Bridge and let them go there, but then they would just fall to the river and flow out to sea. She then thought of The Statue of Liberty. Quickly she realized how cheesy that would be. She was already on this sappy journey, and spreading the ashes there would be like making it a bad movie. After swallowing that fact she decided to just spread the ashes in the heart of the city, a little here and there on the streets.

When the bus made its way back up to Fourteenth Street and stopped for a pick up, Kat got off. It was less touristy than most of the places the bus had gone. She knew what way North was and decided to walk that way back to the car. It would be a thirty something block walk but it would be a nice experience.

Strolling along Seventh Avenue, Kat slowly snuck her hand into her pocket to open the bag of ashes. Once it was open she palmed it and pulled the bag out. Letting it hang by her side she let ash slowly slip it's zippered mouth out onto the already gritty ground. The thought of millions of people stepping on Jasper upset her, but then she thought of how he would be carried too so many different places that way. Every few blocks she poured out a tiny sprinkle of ash. It was funny how nervous she got – as though she were committing a major crime.

Window-shopping was fun but she didn't need to buy anything since she didn't have a house anymore. She did stop to look at an arrangement of pocketbooks spread out on a blanket.

"Gucci, Gucci, Prada, Prada" Mumbled a large man looking over his shoulder. Kat didn't need a pocket book but a certain backpack caught her eye. It was light brown, fake leather, with a buckle and top that flapped open. It would fit Jasper's cookie jar perfectly so she could carry him around with her. She was worried that that would be going too far, but she bought it anyway.

By the time she reached Thirty-Fourth Street, all of Jasper's ashes had been dispersed, and she was able to do it with no dirty looks. After all, it was New York. In a small cheesy gift shop that was one of thousands, Kat finally gave in and looked around at what was there. Hundreds of items that would be bought by Grandparents for Grandkids, only to be thrown away in a year, covered the shelves. Who would ever want New York nail clippers, toothbrushes or underwear? But they had it. Kat decided before leaving on the trip to not buy souvenirs since by the end of it she would have to get a U-Haul to take them all back. But a small red snakeskin diary with a large "J" on it caught her eye.

She'd never kept a diary for longer than a day or two as a kid but for some reason she felt that documenting everything she was doing was important. Since the journal only had a few hundred pages, she bought two.

6

5/07

Dear Diary.... No that's cheesy. Dear Journal, no that makes me sound like an ancient explorer. Well I don't know who will ever read this besides me. Maybe someday long after I'm gone someone will find this and read it. So in a way I guess I'm writing this for you. A stranger I will never meet. So for sake of myself I will call you DJ so at least I have a name to write down. I'm not sure how much I'll write or if I'll write much at all. But I'll do my best.

Well I have a long story to tell. Right now I'm in a small hotel room somewhere off the New Jersey Turnpike. It's nothing special, just a room. I wanted to go on to Pennsylvania today after spreading Jasper's ashes at a rest stop (I'll tell you more about that later) but it started to pour outside so I'm just going crazy of boredom and loneliness here. I've been traveling for eleven days now. I can't imagine how much more I have to go. It's so long. I've only done eight states so far. Forty-Two more to go. Times like now I'm not sure if I'm going to make it all the way. It hurt me so much when I poured the ashes today because I did it without any feeling. I felt nothing. That scared me. I didn't even take the time to find the best spot I just pulled over on the highway and dumped it. Why did I do that? I'm sorry I did.

Having not written more than a small note in years Kat's hand was sore (She was used to typing, like most people these days). But she enjoyed it. Something about laying on the bed, writing in the book made her feel like a teen. She always expressed her feelings to Val but for some reason putting them down on paper made her feel like she was getting them out for good. Shaking out her wrist, she went right back to writing. She went on and on and told the whole story of what had happened and why she was on the road. Every little detail. It took her several hours and almost half of the first book. But it was out of her head now.

Accomplishing what she wanted to do for the night she put on a light jacket and headed out into the rain to find some food. Running across the parking lot she got pretty wet before getting to Earl's Eat-In. The place looked like a dive, but was fairly clean on the inside even though every item looked as if it were purchased forty years ago. The place was practically empty, there was a single elderly couple sipping tea in a window booth. At the far end, two cooks and three waitresses were playing cards.

Kat plopped herself down on the bar stool and picked up the sticky menu.

"You look like shit!" Kat was startled, not to mention offended (even though it was true) by the loud voice. The little make-up she wore was smeared, she hadn't taken much care of herself lately. All the nightly routines of face scrubs, lotions, plucking, and masks had stopped since the event.

The woman had come from the back kitchen. She was wearing a black apron with at least sixty novelty buttons on it.

"Gee, thanks." Kat replied, acting as if she didn't care.

"Well you do you know. I'm not trying to be mean sister. You look like you're real pretty. You're just a mess right now." The woman's nametag read 'Patty', a name that was destined to become an eternal waitress at a truck stop. Not only was she covered in pins she also had obnoxiously large rings on her fingers with earrings to match. Bracelets covered her forearms almost entirely. Her nails were so long and red that Kat wondered how the hell she could do anything with them.

"Well thank you…Patty."

"You want a coffee or something sister?"

"No, I'll just have a water thanks."

Kat returned her gaze to the menu as Patty poured her water into a hard clear yellow plastic cup. While Kat pondered what to order, Patty stared at her while leaning on the counter just to the left of her. Kat, feeling a little uncomfortable asked,

"So what's good on the menu?"

"I hate when people ask that. You know it's such a dumb question. I mean, I probably like things you don't and vice versa." Kat was amazed at this woman. How did she make tips the ways she acted? Kat put on a fake smile trying to be polite.

"Well then, I'll just have a cheeseburger deluxe with a coke and fries."

"I wouldn't suggest that girl...Hell...I'm just messing with you!" That actually made Kat snicker. Maybe this woman did know what she was doing. Patty strutted over to the table of card players. A few seconds later one of the cooks got up and went to the kitchen.

Kat pulled a map out of her pocket and started to examine it. The route was already marked in a heavy red line but she wanted to re-check it before leaving tomorrow.

"Where ya headed?" The voice again startled her. Patty took a seat next to her.

"Oh... just driving."

"Wow! That was a vague answer." Besides minimal purchases and police badgering, this was the first human contact Kat had had since she'd left on the trip. Finally meeting the woman's eyes, Kat saw that they were a brilliant green and friendlier than she'd expected.

"I'm going cross-country."

"Oh yeah? That's great! Are you with your husband or are you gonna meet him?" The hunger pangs in Kat's stomach turned to a vomiting feeling. Kat looked straight ahead not knowing how to answer. She wasn't used to talking to people who didn't know her husband was dead. This took her off-guard. The lining of her mouth started to go dry as she opened her mouth to speak, but no words came out. Then, something soft and warm was covering her hand. Looking down it was Patty's hand.

"It's OK sister. If you don't want to talk that's fine, but let me tell you I'm one of the best roadside therapists this country has. If he beats you and you're running, you can talk to me about it." The voice was lowered to a soothing tone and the hand was now caressing. Odd as it was it did settle Kat somewhat. Kat started to shake her head "No" in response to the question.

"He passed away huh?...So did Eddie, twelve years ago."

Still holding back her tears Kat broke her stare and slowly turned to the emerald eyes. Finally looking closely at the woman Kat realized she must be sixty even though she looked forty.

"Yeah..." a loud ding cut off their moment.

"That's your food sister. I'll tell you what, it's dead tonight why don't you go sit in a booth and I'll bring your food over and we'll talk, OK?"

"Thanks." Kat was touched by the woman's sympathy and excited for a real conversation.

7

The burger was greasy and tasty, a fatty delight. They made light chitchat at first since Patty wanted to wait for her to finish before they started to really talk. Sopping up the last of the ketchup with the last fry, Patty began to speak with a serious tone.

"Now you already told me it was recent. You know what I was sick of when Eddie first died? Having to tell the story over and over again. It's too hard right away. So I'm not going to ask you anything! I'm just gonna tell you how I dealt with losing my Ed." Kat was relieved to not have to tell the story. Wiping grease and ketchup off of her hands she couldn't help but wonder how often Patty gave this speech.

"I thought my life was over. When I came home to find Ed, my Eddie lying on the kitchen floor I thought, this is it. Now I'll save you the question. He was trying to fix an old plug under the sink and cut the wrong wire. Always messing with stuff my Eddie." She must have told this story many times. But it was OK. Companionship and having someone to relate to for the first time was making the rainy day a bit brighter.

"I was an accountant for a law firm then. Big shot. I made a ton of dough. But none of that mattered once Eddie was gone. He was my life. Afterwards I tried to go back to work, but it was meaningless. About a month had gone by when I first tried to kill myself." Kat felt guilty for thinking the woman was a waitress her whole life. Patty then moved the bracelets on her left arm up high for Kat to see a large diagonal scar.

"Ouch. That's so sad."

"Sister, don't even try to tell me it hasn't crossed your mind." Kat sunk in her chair a bit. Though she hadn't made any attempts it did occupy her thoughts often, before coming here in fact. Though she wouldn't admit it. Not even to herself.

"I was too much of a wuss. Once I saw the blood and felt the pain I had to stop. So the next time, I was ready to take a bunch of pills." The door behind Kat jingled as it

115

opened. Patty gave a dainty wave to a husky man in a suit. One of the card-playing waitresses took care of him.

"But you know what stopped me this time? Do you know why I'm talking to you right now?" Kat shook her head. She didn't know but she was sure she was going to find out.

"Pizza delivery boy." Kat was confused and started to think maybe Patty was just crazy.

"I know what you're thinking… I had a bottle of sleeping pills in one hand and bottle of Scotch in the other. Suddenly the doorbell rang. It was a pizza guy at the wrong house. He saw how much of a mess I was in and looked past me to see what was on the couch. Putting two and two together he wouldn't leave." Kat was now intrigued.

"What did he say to you that changed your mind?"

"He didn't say much. He let himself in and threw away the pills and dumped out the liquor. I tried to stop him but I was weak from crying. He then just sat down with the pizza and gave me a slice. Reluctantly I started to eat and we talked. Not once in the hour he was there did he mention what I was going to do. Nor did he try to talk me out of it. We talked about sports and movies mostly."

The look on Patty's face was of pure joy. Kat could instantly tell she was picturing every second in her head.

"After an hour he left and I no longer wanted to kill myself. Then every Wednesday for a few months he would bring me a pizza and say 'I'll see you next week!' before leaving."

"But I don't understand how that changed your mind about killing yourself?"

A large smile crossed Patty's lips.

"Do you want any dessert sister?" The question was so out of place it took Kat by surprise - she did actually want some ice cream.

"Aren't you going to tell me why?" Kat asked as Patty stood up.

"We have a fantastic pumpkin pie right now."

Kat was in shock of wanting to know. "I could go for a hot fudge Sundae."

"Coming right up!"

Patty disappeared into the kitchen. Kat played the conversation over and over in her head, trying to figure out what could have changed her mind. The conclusion she came to was that she didn't have enough information and would have to get it out of Patty somehow.

When Patty returned she had two humungous Sundaes. She sat back down and dug right in. Kat made small swirls in the whipped cream with the long spoon.

"So are you going to tell me or not?" Patty rested her spoon in the sundae.

"Do you see these pins on my apron?" Kat nodded as she examined the apron that must have had fifteen pounds of cheap metal on it. There had to be over seventy different pins. Everything from movie promotions to smiley faces, state flags, phrases, and animals.

"Well I've gotten these pins from people who thought I liked pins. Actually I never did. I only had this one here." She pointed to a small pin in the shape of a pizza with a slice missing from it.

"People would see it and buy me more thinking I collected them. Now I have four hundred, most at home."

Kat had no clue where she was going with this story and how it related to her question. Patty then removed a pin the size of a quarter. It was a cartoon frog's head with his tongue sticking out.

"I want you to take this pin with you. You don't have to wear it. Just take it with you." Kat took the pin and examined it. On the back were ten tiny numbers written in red ink.

"What are these?"

"Well you asked me how the young boy saved my life. If at any time on your trip you get to the point where you're going to do something stupid like I was, I want you to call that number and ask for me. Then I'll tell you the answer. I'll tell you the sentence that saved my life!" Kat was thoroughly amazed by Patty's odd ways.

"But you must promise me you will do that. No matter how bad you are."

"I do. I promise." The pair then resumed eating their Sundaes.

8

After writing her experience with Patty and her phone number (in case she lost the pin) in her journal, Kat headed for bed. Later that night Kat couldn't sleep because she was wondering what the pizza boy had said to Patty to stop her. Turning the frog pin over and over in her hand she pondered if there was a deeper meaning to the frog than she knew. She had the urge to call the number now and beg her to tell the rest of the story, but she had made another promise as she left to not call unless it was that time.

"You need to figure this out on your own. Trust me. I know you can't figure out why I'm a waitress but someday you will. But let me tell you my worst day here is better than my best day as an accountant and I loved that job."

The image of the angel whose name she couldn't remember from *It's a Wonderful Life* popped in her head. Maybe Patty was sent down as a guardian angel? But the idea quickly left for she had lost the little faith she had as of late.

The next morning Kat poked the frog head pin through the shoulder strap of her new backpack. With ease she placed the cookie jar into it- a perfect cozy fit. This was going to be a much better and more inconspicuous way of carrying around Jasper and she could also take him more places this way. At eight a.m. it was back on the road, this time with a promise to herself to slow down and try to enjoy everything.

5/13/03

Dutch Country was so amusing! I remember watching 'Witness' with Harrison Ford years ago and it's amazing that these people are actually like that! They are so cute with their little horse and buggies. I must say ever since talking to Patty I feel much better about my trip even though I never told her about it or what I'm doing. I was in such a good mood that I went on a full tour of an authentic Amish village. I got to pump water from a well (ok, that wasn't that exciting) and I got a ring made from a nail (again, that wasn't that exciting). But it was something to experience. When the tour group finished and we dispersed to wander around I took the ashes and spread them through the ancient hand-built houses and the farm. Even though this isn't a life Jasper or I would ever like to live I think he would have liked it here.

On the way to the B&B I stopped at an antiques shop. I found the most wonderful brass toothpick holder. The

119

woman said it was made in the 1800's. I bought it and sent it off to Val to sort of apologize for not talking to her as much as I should.

9

It was hideous. Not only had the woman lost her mind she had also lost her sense of style. Val couldn't believe how ugly this...this thing was. It had two little pouches to hold something, with a dead looking rabbit and rooster above it. Digging through the peanuts she finally found the letter from Kat.

Hello from the Road! I miss you so much! Today I'm in Lancaster Pennsylvania staying at the Cameron Estate Inn Bed and Breakfast! It's the most amazing place. It's an old mansion from the...

Val skipped over most of the letter trying to find if Kat had put anything of any actual importance in it. Like how she was, or that she needed Val back in her life. Nothing. Nothing more than fake useless info about her silly trip.

Val really started to feel the sting a week after Kat left. She couldn't function without her. It was silly but Val was the kind of person who needed a constant friend to have, to help and to bug. She'd been crazy lonely without Kat around and had tried to go out with several other girlfriends, but none had the history or the feel of complete comfort she had with Kat - she could say anything no matter how off the wall. Val needed that back. The fact that Kat showed no signs of needing her was the worst part.

More than anything (as horrible as it was) Val wanted Kat to fail, give up and just come home. But deep down she knew Kat was never coming back to this town. She wasn't going to let that happen.

10

The Nifty Nectarine was a lot nicer inside than what the name made it out to be. The fact that it was in Delaware and named after a Nectarine was also confusing. It was a half hour before closing time when Kat arrived. She was seated in a desolate area of the dining room. Then again, most of the place was desolate. She plopped down her backpack next to her on the springy maroon seat. Wearing a lime green windbreaker and jeans, she felt terribly under-dressed for the candle-lit atmosphere but it was late and she didn't care what people thought of her anyway.

Brad was the waiter's name. He was in his early twenties and used flattery to get tips. Kat thought the subtle compliments were cute but phony. She ordered blackened scallops and a French onion soup for an appetizer. Brad told her how wonderful of a choice she'd made.

After the young unattractive man left her table she was quickly bored. This had become a problem of late. Reading was always an option but Kat never had the tolerance to do that. She couldn't just sit there and read unless she had to or if it was a gossip magazine. It was one thing she wished to change and had tried unsuccessfully several times.

To keep herself occupied at times like these, Kat had come up with a new game: People watching. She always loved to look at people but never had the nerve to look longer than a few seconds. Now, she didn't really care much if someone noticed her staring, she would smile and look away. After the first few seconds she would come up with a theory on the person's life and try to guess what their name might be, or their job. On a few rare occasions she'd gotten the courage to ask someone she was watching what their name was, pretending to recognize them. Then she would quickly apologize saying she was mistaken. So far she had yet to be right about someone's name. The closest she came was thinking an elderly man's name was Nate when it was Nick.

When the soup arrived she was in deep thought about a man that was also alone, sitting diagonally across from her. He was slightly older than she and wearing a wrinkled suit. A smile kept crossing his face every now and then as he thought of something. Kat wondered what it was. Two times he caught her looking at him. She smiled.

Definitely computers. Something with computers. That's what this man did. He was overly pale, balding and his nose was more of a beak than a nose. Harold...no, no it had to be something geeky like Larry. Yeah Larry had to be his name. Larry, the computer analyst.

Slurping her soup, she was disappointed that no one else was in her view to guess at. Only Larry. Finishing her soup she noticed Larry was looking at her with a smile. Crap. Eye contact for the third time wasn't a good thing and she'd make the first two, crap.

Shifting slightly in her seat to make sure her line of view would stay far away from Larry, Kat anxiously awaited her food. When it did finally arrive she was forced to look at Brad and thank him. In her peripheral view she could see Larry staring at her. Not good. Being hit on was not what she wanted. And it was all her fault.

On the fifth bite of the semi-rubbery yet flavorful scallops she sensed someone standing next to the table. Sure enough Larry was there with a large smile.

"I couldn't help but notice we caught each other's eye a few times. I'm Kyle." Kyle? Jesus she was off. Kat felt horrible, she did lead the man on. Well not lead on but gave him the signal. How was she supposed to politely get rid of him now?

"Hi Kyle, I'm sorry about that. I didn't mean to flirt. I...I'm only here for tonight, then I'm out of town, sorry." Kyle's smile stayed on his face but his dull eyes seemed to fade to anger.

"Well, one night is all we need." Whoa! She might have brought him over by accident but now he was crossing the line.

"Look, I really didn't mean to lead you on. I'm not looking for anything like that. I'm married." Kyle looked to her hand for proof. His smile seemed to fade only a fraction.

"I'm gonna go sit in the bar for a while. Feel free to stop in. I'll buy you a drink. Or if you want call my cell later." Out of nowhere, startling Kat, he produced a business card. He put it on the table and with one finger slid it across the table to the edge only inches away from her breast. Kat was not amused. She looked up at him with hate in her eyes. Kyle just winked and strolled away as if he was about to get lucky.

Kyle Winterbourne-Magician. Kat was boggled that the man was a performer of any sort. She couldn't picture him outside of a cubicle with Dilbert cartoons on the walls. She picked up the card with just her fingernails as if the sleaze of the man would infect her skin. Without thinking, she tossed it onto the candle wanting to dispose of it. A large orange flash became of the card. It was much brighter and hotter than she thought it would have been. So much so that it scared her enough to toss her water on it putting out both the card and the candle. She felt a bit stupid but at least no one had seen her... Little did she know Kyle was peaking around the corner from the entrance to the bar. He saw it all.

11

Kat paid for her meal and headed for the door. She wasn't particularly excited about going to the hotel tonight. It was just a regular Best Western room. She had been spoiling herself lately so tonight seemed less than thrilling. As she passed the bar she did her best not to look in for fear of making eye contact with the lame magician.

Once outside she breathed a sigh of relief, until she realized she had to walk the length of the bar to get to her car. A dozen or so windows with neon beer signs lined the walk. Eyes locked on the car, she readied her keys. Finally she walked past the main bar entrance leaving her only seven paces away from her car.

A door chime jingled behind her. Dear God no. She quickened her pace. She beeped her alarm button to unlock the door. Footsteps behind her. Fast as she could she opened her car door and jumped in. But when she went to pull it shut it wouldn't budge. Kyle was holding it open. The fake smile on his face was now a grimace.

"You know. You flirted with me first." Kat plunged the key into the ignition and started the car.

"Look I wasn't flirting I was looking at you. I'm sorry if you got that interpretation, now please let go of my door."

"You shouldn't do that to a man. It's not nice. Not nice at all." Kyle slammed the door so quick and hard that for a second Kat thought it was a gunshot. Without hesitation she backed out and started driving.

Kat was shaking so much on the way back to the hotel she almost got lost. Only one other time had a man assaulted her. It was in college and Val and she were walking back to their dorms late at night. Two drunken frat boys started following them, yelling crude remarks about their asses. Kat was nervous but Val wasn't. When they finally came up next to them, one grabbed her and tried to lick her neck. That's when Val whipped out her pepper spray and doused them both. Kat was impressed at how cool Val played it. Even though nothing happened, it still shook her up. But not as much as this had.

Now she had the paranoid feeling of being followed. Every car looked like it was out to get her. She tried to laugh it off but for some reason couldn't. A car was definitely following her, she thought. Maybe she shouldn't pull into the hotel lot.

Not knowing where else to go and afraid of getting lost if she didn't stop, she pulled into the lot. Just her luck no one was out unloading their car. If she could get to the main door she'd be OK. All she had to do was swipe her card to get in. A car pulled in after her. Shit.

It pulled in two spots away from her. Maybe it was just another guest. She kept the engine on and waited to see if the person got out. If it was Kyle she'd peel out backwards and call the police on her cell. Hopefully it wasn't him. Her heart pounded in her chest like a madman sledge hammering his way out of prison.

Her eyes started to dry out from not blinking. She was afraid to miss the person getting out. Through two other car windows she saw the door open. This was a good sign she thought, if he was going to attack he would wait. Right? She couldn't see the head only a shadowy body walking towards the sidewalk and towards her car. Bending her head down to see who it was, she put the car in reverse. It was him.

Kat was ready to gun it back but Kyle never approached the car. He walked right by and to the hotel entrance. He slid a key in and walked through the door. Kat's heart tensed not knowing what to feel. Relief that he was walked by her car or dread that he was staying at the same hotel.

Waiting for a while would be the best idea. Let him get into his room and settle in. She'd just slip by and go to bed. She'd be out in the morning before he ever woke. Ten minutes went by when she finally emerged from her safe-haven like a scared cub leaving the den. The *Mission Impossible* theme song started playing in her head. As she walked to the door she whipped her head in every direction looking for the bad guy.

She made it to the door. Safe. Slid the key in. Still safe. Then it was a wind sprint up two flights to the third floor hallway. Safe. Peering around the corner it looked deserted. Key in hand she made a mad dash past thirty-one doors. At last her door. Hand on handle, no one behind her, slide key in, still safe, inside, shut door, lock it, made it!

She flopped on the bed face first. It was like finishing a marathon but the prize was her life. She felt a bit foolish - he was probably harmless. But better safe than sorry. Her temples were still pounding with adrenaline when she stretched out her arms. On the pillow she felt a small piece of hard paper. Thinking it was a card from the maid she brought it to her face to read: *Kyle Winterbourne Magician.*

Not safe.

12

Frantically she pulled her legs onto the bed, scared he might be under it or in the closet. Most hotel beds nowadays had a board underneath to stop people from losing stuff under it. But she hadn't checked this one. She wanted to call the police but her phone was across the room on the bureau and the hotel phone was by the window on the desk. Besides, they'd probably think she was crazy anyways. Getting to her feet the mattress felt springy and she bounced a bit. A plan started to formulate in her head.

Thank God her bags were still packed. All she needed to do was grab the three of them and get the hell out of Dodge. Get to the car, drive away and get to a new hotel. But what if he was waiting in the room or the hallway? Well…she was going to have to find out. One, Two, OK, OK. Deep breaths were taken to get her nerve up to jump off the bed. Ok. Three, Two, One! Jumping off the right side towards the window she grabbed her overnight sack. Then a quick dash to the bureau to grab her pocket book. One left, Jasper's bag. It was by the door on the chair. Without stopping she grabbed it and nailed the door. With a snap the bottom lock was undone, she pulled on the door but it caught. Shit. Sensing someone behind her she glanced over her shoulder. Nothing. The top latch was still on. Idiot. She closed the door and unhooked it.

Deciding it was better to just burst into the hallway than to peek she rushed out the door. Running, so far no one, the exit was only a few more doors away. Suddenly someone came around the corner in front of her. They slammed into each other so fast she had no clue who it was. She could only assume it was magic Kyle.

On her back, one bag was under her the other two on her sides. It happened so fast she didn't remember hitting the ground. Opening her eyes she saw a hand and foot in front of her face. Panicking she kicked hard. It was followed by a grunt. Whoever it was dropped out of sight next to her. Rolling over she collected her bags and continued down the hall. Finally getting the courage to look over her shoulder she saw an elderly man rolling on the floor in pain. Guilt filled her head but there was no time to stop.

Thirty seconds later she was in the car and backing out. Once on the road her nerves started to settle a bit, constantly she looked in the rearview mirror. No one was behind her. She slowed a bit and that's when she noticed another card under the wiper blade.

It was eleven o' eight when Val's phone rang. Even though she had gone to bed two hours earlier she was not sleeping, not even close. Looking at the caller ID she was thrilled to see Kat's number.

"Baby!"

"Val…Jesus Christ…I'm so scared." Her heart stopped at the sound of distress in Kat's voice. She'd never heard that tone before.

"Honey just calm down…what's wrong?" Kat steadied her voice and explained to Val the whole situation. Val knew that being on her own like this was a bad idea.

"Why don't you just fly home?" Val waited a while for a response.

"I don't have a home anymore." That's not what she wanted to hear.

"You always have a place with me and you know that. In fact I'm better off with you. I've been so damn lost lately."

"Val I have to do this. I have nothing else to live for right now." That statement made Val panic, thinking Kat didn't value her life anymore.

"Well what should I do about this whole thing?"

Val took a deep breath. She just wanted to scream, "Come home you fucking moron!" But couldn't. She knew how sensitive she was.

"Well technically he didn't try to do anything, he just creeped you out. So the cops can't help you. Especially since you're not in one place more than a day. I suggest at the next town you stop and get yourself some pepper spray. You remember how I like that stuff!"

They both laughed.

"Besides you'll probably never see this guy again."

"I guess you're right."

The two talked for three hours that night until Kat was in Maryland and checked into a Sheraton hotel. Val was still awake at three in the morning. That's when she made a decision to take some personal days off work and surprise Kat on the road. During their conversation she had hinted at it but Kat seemed completely uninterested at the idea of company on her trip.

The hard part was going to be tracking her down. Kat rarely answered her cell and almost never gave exact locations of where she was. All she knew right now was that she was in Maryland. But probably before days end tomorrow she'd be in one of three places, West Virginia, Virginia or Washington D.C. That would make it hard, too hard to find her?

Val's best idea was to fly to D.C., get a rental car and call Kat hoping she would tell her where she was. After the incident tonight she hoped Kat would be more likely to answer her phone. Val only hoped she could leave by tomorrow evening. She was anxious to see Kat.

13

After going to bed so late, Kat slept until eleven thirty the next day, which was rare for her. The previous night's events were still on her mind and now in her journal. Now that they were behind her she looked at it as something she was almost happy to have happened. She knew it was sick to think of it that way but no harm was done and it would make a great story to tell. If she had someone to tell it to.

Kat decided to relax a bit while in Maryland. After getting up she went to the front desk to tell them she'd be staying another night. This would be a first for the trip, so far she hadn't stayed anywhere more than one night. It will be nice not to have to pack today.

She ate breakfast at a near-by IHOP trying her best not to look at anyone or try to guess what they did. But she still couldn't help it. After feeling bloated and full from her five-stack of blueberry pancakes, Kat made a promise to herself to eat better or else by the time she got to Oklahoma she'd weigh three-hundred pounds!

The first planned stop for the day was the Lillypons Water Garden in Frederick County. A brochure of it in the lobby caught her eye. It would be a great place to disperse the ashes. Arriving, she was blown away by the amount of lily pads. Far as the eye could see were giant, green lush pads. She strolled along for quite some time before pulling out the packet of ash in her pocket.

For some odd reason Kat had a hard time opening the bag. She couldn't tell if it was stuck or if she just didn't want to. The last few were so rushed and emotionless. This time she felt the grieving come back. She had done well at pushing it out of her mind and occupying it with thoughts of the mission she was on. Hell, she'd been talking to the cookie jar so much she felt like Jasper was actually there.

After a few glances around the park she was confident no one was close enough to see her. She knelt down at the edge of the path next to some over grown pads. Touching the thick plastic-like leaf she thought about how amazing nature was. She suddenly remembered learning that ashes fertilize plants and wondered whether Jasper's ashes would help these lily pads? She wondered if she came back in three years and looked at this exact spot if this one plant would have grown more than the others, having used Jaspers remains to feed its own life and growth? It was an odd thought but it actually made her happy. To think that a little piece of him would grow inside of other things. It was almost as if he would still exist in some sort of odd way.

The thoughts cheered her up and gave her the courage to open the baggie. She chose one particularly small lily pad. It was much smaller and weaker than the rest and it didn't even have one of the beautiful white flowers on it. Carefully she dispersed all of the ashes around the pad. The gray flakes darkened and changed color as they hit the water and floated down. After a few inches she couldn't see them anymore. Then on top of the pad she poured out the remainder of the ash. It sat in the middle of the green like some odd urn made by a hippy.

Nodding her head in approval she stood up. Taking another look around to make sure no one was watching, Kat suddenly felt totally alone. No one was in sight. Just acres and acres of lily pads. After a few deep breaths she started the long walk back to her car. Alone.

14

Three suitcases and two backpacks. Shit, that's definitely not going to work. Looking at the clock she only had two hours left before her flight. Some of these bags had to go. But she needed everything. Or so she told herself. Val couldn't believe she was doing this. She had done some crazy things in her life but this was definitely the biggest.

Last night after getting off the phone with Kat she got out of bed and hit the computer to book an afternoon flight. Even though the last minute flight cost an extra two hundred dollars, she was ecstatic. The plane was to arrive in Washington D.C. at four-thirty three. From there she was to pick up her rental car. That was as far as the plan went. From there she could only hope Kat would answer her phone and divulge where she was.

Nervous and excited, she slept maybe a half of what was left of that night. First thing in the morning she called the school and gave a sob story about how her aunt had died and she needed to take care of the arrangements. She told them it would be at least a week. More likely than not the time would come from her personal days, but she didn't care.

Frantically she unzipped the bags to figure out what to leave behind. She threw clothing all over the place. The main problem was that she had no clue how long she was going to be away. She vowed to herself to not leave until she had Kat with her coming home. But what if she wouldn't go? That was a thought she didn't want to face just yet. The thought of quitting her job and traveling across country with Kat was exciting but what would she do afterwards? What about money? She had enough for a little while and she could always sell the house. Wait. Why the hell was she thinking such thoughts? She was going to find Kat and talk some sense into her.

It took almost an hour of tossing clothing up in the air before she got it down to two suitcases and one backpack. In the middle of getting it all ready she needed to swallow a half of a bottle of Pepto Bismol. Her stomach ached with nerves. With only an hour before the flight she left her house praying to not miss it.

15

After leaving the gardens Kat decided to take in a movie. She was just driving by and suddenly she pulled in. It was going to be a treat. The last movie she'd seen in the theater was over three years ago. Jasper and she just never had time. A rental was always much easier.

It took five minutes of hemming and hawing before deciding on the new Mel Gibson movie. With a large popcorn and Cherry Coke she sat right in the middle of the empty theater. Only one young couple sat in the very back. They looked like they were skipping school and probably weren't going to watch more than a minute of the film anyway.

Even though just this morning she had vowed to eat better she lied to herself and decided that the buttery salty popcorn was low in fat. Well she had to, you couldn't go to a movie without popcorn. The opening credits disappeared and Mel came out shooting a gun. After a few explosions he went back to his apartment to shower.

Kat had always had a thing for Mel. She'd always said he was the best looking man in Hollywood. He stripped off his shirt and for the first time in a while Kat felt the tingling sensation of lust. Immediately her face got flushed, the old feelings she once loved rushed through her body. She felt awkward even though the place was empty.

Masturbation was never a major thing with Kat. But she did do her share of it when she was single. Maybe once a week sometimes three. During her marriage she still did it once or twice a month if Jasper wasn't around and she was in the mood or if he asked to watch her. But it wasn't until now when she saw the water falling from the showerhead over Mel's half naked body that she finally had the urge to please herself.

Obviously the feeling would pass in a minute once she saw a dead body on the screen, but she started to worry about when she was finally going to do it. How would it feel? Would it make her cry? Or would it be OK? Of course she was going to think of Jasper and that was the problem. Maybe she should think of someone else? No way. Then guilt would wreck havoc on her brain.

She was able to concentrate on the rest of the movie but the second it ended and Mel flashed his twenty-million-dollar smile, the feeling came back again. She rushed out of the theater and jumped in the car. The desire was bad. She wanted pleasure more than anything at that moment. The hotel was only ten minutes away. Kat didn't have one clean thought on the whole drive back.

Finally in her room she locked the door and shut the shades. She paced back and forth, nervously contemplating whether or not to go through with it. Her heart was racing and her clitoris started to swell with anticipation. She had to do it. Without wasting time she took off her shirt, pants, and bra before hopping under the covers.

Her chest rose and fell quickly as her breath started to increase. A tingle of pleasure burst through her body as she started to caress her stomach. Images of Jasper loving her sweetly raced through her mind. Then her pelvis twitched as her fingers finally touched her panties. Slowly her fingers started to rub. Pleasure instantly burst through her body. How did she go so long without doing this? One minute into it her whole body started to move with ecstasy then, the phone rang. She tried to ignore it but it broke her concentration. Frustrated she searched her pocket book for the cell and answered it.

16

"What!?" Val was totally thrown off by Kat's tone.

"Uh…Hey honey." She could hear Kat breathing deeply on the other side of the phone. She had to play it safe. If she told her she was in D.C. Kat would never say where she was staying. Val had to get about it in a round about way.

"What are you doing baby?"

"I'm…I was taking a shower." Val was confused and didn't really believe the answer. Why the hell would she answer if she was in the shower? Oh well, she had to step carefully.

"So are you feeling better today sweetie?"

After a deep sigh Kat answered. "I'm fine."

"Oh did you make it to D.C. already?"

"No. No look I got to go could I call you back tomorrow?"

"Wait Uh... I was wondering if you... I had something to send you and I needed to know where you are?" Val knew she sounded stupid and desperate but what was she to do? She was in the middle of Regan airport with nowhere to go.

"Val. Please I need to get back in the shower I'm freezing. I have no clue where I'm going to be day to day you'll just have to save it for me, OK? I'll talk to you tomorrow." Beep. The phone was hung up. Val was in a total state of panic.

After the bad start to this last minute trip Val went and got her rental car, a mid-sized Taurus. She was used to better but she wanted to conserve money just in case. With a cheesy tourist map she navigated her way from the airport to The George Hotel. She hadn't planned on staying there or anywhere for that matter, but Val spotted it while driving around and remembered seeing it on the Travel Channel. She was lucky they had a room.

It was definitely an interesting room. Very modern with bright colors, sharp edges and elegance. It even had a large psychedelic painting of the one-dollar bill above the bed. Val flopped onto the large bed and fingered her cell phone. She was nervous. If Kat didn't answer again today then the whole day would be a waste. For all she knew Kat could already be on her way to Virginia.

Reciting a prayer in her head, Val pushed the send button. It took a few tense seconds for the phone to connect. Then her machine picked up. No ring. Kat had shut her phone off. Leaving a message would be pointless. She was just going to have to keep trying back. In the meantime she might as well walk around and see the sights.

Even with the interruption it was still worth it. Kat couldn't believe she'd waited this long to do it. The best part was she didn't feel guilty afterwards. She knew Jasper would want her to please herself. As long as she thought of him and that she sure did.

Her face was hot and her nipples still hard as she closed her eyes and spread out her arms to relax. Her whole body felt free and loose.

"Nine and a half." She said out loud from habit. She laughed at herself. A slight sweat covered her lower back. She rolled on her side to wipe it off. For the first time in a while her mind was blank as she drifted off to sleep.

An hour and forty-three minutes later she woke up. Her face had returned to its normal color and her nipples were once again soft. She got up and retrieved a pair of sweatpants and nightshirt from her bag. Putting them on she turned her cell back on. Usually she would leave it off but after last night she felt more comfortable to have it accessible.

It was only four-fifteen and she had nothing to do. The trip was going to be a lot more boring than she had anticipated. She could go out to eat but she didn't feel like getting dressed up. Maybe she'd go to a drive through and get some burgers. So much for eating healthy.

The phone rang, making Kat jump. It never rang unless it was Val. Her relatives and few other friends had given up calling since she never returned their calls. Knowing who it had to be she picked up and hesitated, she wanted to shut the ringer off and not answer it but she felt bad being rude earlier. Using a fake chipper voice she said hello to Val.

"Wow! That is a different mood than what I heard earlier." Kat laughed in response.

"So what's up?" Having plotted for some time Val was ready.

"Well I was just watching *The Travel Channel* and they did a piece on D.C. I was wondering if you were there yet? Because if you haven't gotten a hotel yet you have to go to this one I saw."

"Ok. Well I'm still in Maryland I was going to leave tomorrow morning for it. Let me grab a pen and I'll write the name down." Kat snatched the hotel stationary off the desk and readied the pen.

"Go ahead."

"Well it's called the Hotel George. It's right near the capital building. Uh…Fifteen East Street. I wrote it down because it looked so amazing! You're going to love it!"

"Well that was nice of you." Kat thought it was a bit odd for her to give advice like that. It must be one hell of a place for Val to call like that. Or maybe she just missed her that much.

The two chatted about a few other things before letting the other go. Kat was excited to go to D.C. tomorrow - there she could do a lot of site seeing for once.

Val's heart pounded with excitement. She couldn't believe it had worked! All she had to do now was wait in the lobby for her. Or she could just ask what room she was in later and pop in to surprise her. Granted, she was petrified how it would go, but she hoped for the best and planned for the worst.

17

At eleven a.m. Val took her post in the lobby. It was a small but modern lobby. She hid on the balcony above the reception desk. Sitting in a large leather couch Val played with a cue ball from the pool table next to her. She knew it might be hours before Kat showed up but she didn't want to miss her. Her eyes roamed the red carpet, grand piano and fresh flower bouquets below.

The first twenty minutes went by as if it was an hour. This was ridiculous. She could easily just come down and check with the front desk every now and then. No. What if she checked in and then went out for hours? Still she would be able to catch her that night. Ah hell, she'd wait another hour then go to her room and order some room service for lunch.

The two well-groomed young women at the front desk kept looking up at her wondering what she was doing. Finally after another forty-five minutes, one of the two made their way up the stairs to her.

"Ma'am is everything OK?"

"Oh yes. I'm just waiting for a friend."

"Would you like me to point her in your direction when she gets here?"

"Oh no, no, no. It's a big surprise! She has no clue I'm here. After she checks in I want to get her room number and surprise her then." The young business like woman was pretty baffled why anyone would wait up there for so long to just get a room number. It took her a few seconds to respond.

"Well…if you want to wait in your room I can call you when she checks in." At this point Val was also in a state of confusion. Not wanting to miss Kat come in but also feeling like an idiot for sitting in the lobby for so long, she agreed to the woman's suggestion. Val gave her the information she needed and headed off to her room. At least here she would have a TV to keep her mind occupied for a while.

Not wanting to take Kat too off guard she decided that once she got the phone call, she'd wait an hour before going to the room. In the third hour of waiting she felt like she was going to explode. As she was about to take a shower to calm her nerves, the phone rang.

Kat left Maryland early that morning. The trip wasn't long but she was in no rush, so she drove slowly with the top down. It was a bit chilly but she was enjoying it. Occasionally she stopped for a pee break and a snack. Around one-thirty she arrived in D.C but it took her a while to find the hotel since it wasn't on her itinerary. After asking few locals she finally found it.

Approaching the outside of the hotel Kat wasn't that impressed. It looked small but nice, nothing grand. The lobby on the other hand was much different. It was elegantly modern and she loved it. She had to remember to get a postcard for Val. The room was even better than the downstairs. She took out her camera to take pictures of it. The big picture of the dollar bill above her bed cracked her up. In the closet she even found an umbrella and robe, something she'd never seen before in a hotel.

Enjoying the room so much and knowing there was much to see here, she made a mental note to stay longer than just tonight. Anxious to get out and see the town, she put down her bags and headed out the door.

Val got the call that Kat had checked into room 437. It was three floors below her own. Her blood started to pump through her system like a freight train. Nerves were tightening like knots. Waiting any longer would drive her insane. Val left her room to deliver the surprise.

Standing in the elevator she tried to control her breathing like she was in *Lamaz*e class. She rubbed her eyes to get the lack of sleep out of them. As she circled her eyes with hard knuckles, the door rang as it opened on a lower floor. Still rubbing she heard someone get in.

The elevator door opened and Kat strolled in. The only other person in there was rubbing her eyes fiercely. She didn't pay much attention to her and stood slightly in front. That's when she heard a loud gasp. Concerned, Kat turned her head to see if the woman was OK.

Val stood with her mouth wide-open, face pale and eyes blood shot. Though she was on the way to meet Kat, she was not expecting this at all. The pair locked eyes in a sort of shocked stare-off. The elevator bell rang for the lobby floor.

Kat had no idea what was going on or how to react. She was thrilled to see a familiar face she could hug but at the same time she felt a bit of betrayal. She better wait to hear the story before she got all pissy with her.

"So…The Hotel George huh? Saw it on *The Travel Channel*?" Color started to fill Val's face in the form of blushing.

"Well I did. I didn't lie. I just didn't tell you I was here." A smile crossed Kat's face making the billion pounds of pressure on Val's chest start to fade. The two embraced and the elevator doors shut and headed back up the shaft. The hug lasted six floors until the doors opened back up for an elderly rich couple with three poodles. The man had a crooked smile from seeing the two hug. The woman turned her nose up. Both Kat and Val laughed.

18

Sitting in front of the Capitol Building the two munched on hot dogs and Cheetos. With a mouthful of food Kat started to speak.

"You know if I wasn't so lonely I would be pissed you're here. But I must say it's good to see you."

Val's heart bounced with joy. It was the few words she needed to hear to make the whole trip worth it.

"Well thank you sugar. I just couldn't go without my Kat fix. I was worried about what happened the other day. Thought you might like some cheering up." Kat bobbed her head to agree.

"So how long are you staying? A few days?" Kat questioned. Val instantly took a big bite of her hot dog to delay having to answer. Chewing on the mustard covered meat she tried to summon the nerve to have a talk with her about coming home. Kat quickly saw that she was trying to not answer the question.

"Look. Don't even try to give me the come home speech. I told you Val, I don't have a home anymore. It just reminds me too much of Jasper to stay there. Plus I made a promise and I'm going to fulfill it."

This day was just one emotional roller coaster for Val. Way too many ups and downs. Not ready to make a rebuttal she just nodded. She would have to work something better out in her head to win this one.

After a long silence Kat tossed a Cheeto to a nearby squirrel. The cute little guy picked it up and munched it down to her surprise.

"Who knew squirrels liked Cheetos?" Val followed suit and tossed a few orange sticks to another squirrel. Before they knew it six of them started to come closer. The two laughed at how quick they scooped them up. Kat kept trying to get them closer and closer, which they did. Then she was able to feed one by hand. Val freaked out.

"Jesus Kat, those things have diseases! Be careful."

Kat laughed and turned to Val to jokingly toss a Cheeto at her feet, but stopped when she saw was a big fluffy squirrel perched on the bench inches away from Val's head. Kat could not hold in her laughter.

"What? WHAT?" Val turned her head towards the small creature. In an instant her last bite of hot dog was up in the air. Val started screaming and running. She didn't stop her sprint until she was almost fifty yards away. Breathing hard she brushed her body as if they were all over her. Kat hadn't laughed that hard in a long, long time. She was happy Val had come down, regardless of the reason.

Strolling around the Capitol Building looking at the massive structure Kat told her all about the trip so far. How it wasn't nearly what she'd thought it was going to be. How the first part was miserable. But most of all she talked about Patty. Besides today, it was the only human contact she'd had.

Val tried to put in her two cents about coming back home, often.

"Why don't you move in with me?" Kat ignored it and kept talking. She even told her why she was so snippy yesterday on the phone.

"I'm sure you could get your job back again or at another school." Kat went on as if Val hadn't spoken a word. She told her how excited she was to see the rest of the country. It would be much more exciting than so far. At least she hoped.

The rest of the day they went sightseeing to all the major tourist traps. Then that night they went back to the hotel and watched movies in Val's room. Around nine-thirty a bellboy brought them bottled water and green apples on a silver platter. The two had no clue why, but he said it was a nightly compliment of the hotel. They laughed and ate Kit Kat's instead of the fruit.

Around one they decided to hit the hay. They both stayed in Val's room that night, not wanting to leave each other.

"When you going back home?" Kat asked with her eyes closed.

"Not sure. I want to go with you. Be crazy and travel cross country." Kat thought about how wonderful it would be to have company the whole time. But on the same side it would be sort of annoying. This was supposed to be a solo trip.

Drifting off to sleep, Val thought about how much fun it would be to go wild and actually do it. But she couldn't, she had a life back home. Though it wasn't much. So why not?

Kat heard a low squealing come from Val's side of the bed. It was the familiar sound of early sleep coming from her. For the next hour Kat thought about what to do if Val actually wanted to come along. Finally making a decision, she was able to go to sleep. She needed rest, tomorrow they had planned on seeing the last few monuments that they'd missed today.

19

Waking up before Val, Kat went downstairs to her room to shower and change. She didn't sleep well knowing Jasper wasn't in the same room as her. When she got back she told him and her journal all about Val's surprise visit. She was in a very chipper mood. Thinking about all the beautiful sights she'd seen yesterday and looking forward to the new ones today, Kat felt a bit sad that she hadn't planned on D.C. when she separated the ashes. She had made fifty-one baggies but the extra one was for herself. The thought of dividing one up to have some to release here crossed her mind, but she decided against it.

Val knocked on her door shortly after she was ready. With confidence Val strutted in.

"I've decided I want to go with you!" Kat gave her a crooked smile.

"But you won't." Val's mouth opened to protest but Kat cut her off.

"Look I won't let you for a plethora of reasons. One: you have a great job and house."

"Which you did too might I add."

Kat shot her a dirty look and ignored the comment.

"Two: I want to do this alone. And Three: I've come up with a plan." Val's eye's squinted with interest.

"I have more money than I'll ever use. Especially if I ever get a job again. What I want to offer is to fly you out to wherever I am every two weeks for a weekend. It'll be great. I'll get to do my thing alone and you'll get to see places you never have." Val tried to hold back the excitement in her face. This was perfect. As much as she wanted to, she knew quitting her job never would happen. And since talking her into coming home was next to impossible, this was the next best thing.

"Wellll… I'll have to think about it."

Kat picked up a pillow and threw it at her. On impact Val squealed. She ran to Kat and jumped on her bringing her to the bed. They play wrestled to celebrate the agreement.

Kat and Val were in the highest of spirits the rest of the day as they toured the Lincoln and Vietnam Memorials. They had to hold back their giddiness out of respect on more than one occasion.

Later that day Val made plans to catch a flight back the next morning. Dinner reservations were set at the Jefferson Pub on Independence Avenue near the Botanical Gardens. Kat made them on the suggestion of the concierge at the hotel. He said they had a decent dinner and free shows almost every night.

Reservations were set for eight. After another shower and change of clothing the two decided to walk over to the restaurant. The inside was reminiscent of a cheesy Atlantic City dinner theater. They were seated three tables away from the stage. The waitress, a young girl who looked like she'd lived fifty years already, told them the show was three different acts: a band, a comedian, and something else she couldn't remember.

Kat ate steak while Val had a gourmet salad. When the plates were cleared and the desserts brought out the show began. The Asian owner warmed up the crowed with a few witty one-liners before introducing a young comedian named Sparky Murphy. He had a few good jokes but overall was pretty lame. Kat and Val gave each other an *oh brother* look several times.

By the time they were done with their chocolate cakes that were too dry, the band began to play. They were a Pearl Jam cover band and not that bad. The two of them sang along and shook their hair more than once. Already having had two glasses of wine each, Val ordered them kamikaze shots. Kat was having too much fun to say no. They downed them with a yelp and ordered beers to follow.

The band finished after six songs. The girls wanted more. The host came back on and zinged a few. Kat didn't care if it was the alcohol, but he seemed much funnier now. Clinking their glasses in a toast to each other they didn't hear what the next act was. The light dimmed and eerie music began to play. The curtains opened slower than usual and fog bellowed out of them accompanied by a strobe light.

As the fog cleared, a big beam of light appeared at the center of the stage, illuminating a small glass box. It then started to fill with green smoke. The music became more dramatic. Suddenly the box burst open and a man appeared dressed, in an all black tuxedo. It was hard to see his face through the fog. The inebriated audience clapped heartily. Everyone except Kat.

The man jumped down and bowed. He was pale, balding and had a beak-like nose.

20

Breathing was impossible. Kat tried to suck in air but she couldn't, her body was not allowing it. A deep booming voice announced the man.

"Ladies and Gentlemen, Master Magician Kyle Winterbourne!" Val clapped and whistled until a stiff hand grabbed at her sleeve. She turned to see Kat white as snow with her mouth tightly squeezed shut. She's gonna get sick Val thought. Without hesitating she helped Kat up and rushed her into the bathroom. Kat still couldn't breathe well.

In the bathroom Val kicked open a stall and tried to push Kat to her knees.

"NO!"

"Huh? What's wrong Hun?" Kat turned to her with terror in her eyes.

"That's him."

"What? What are you talking about?" Kat had never felt this scared before. Her mind was a bit foggy and she wondered if it was the alcohol raising her fear.

"The man I told you…who attacked me."

"Where was he?" Kat looked at her not knowing why she didn't understand.

"The magician!" Val finally got it.

"Are you sure?" She nodded. Val wasn't sure what to do. He most likely hadn't seen Kat in the audience. But then again when performers are backstage they usually have peepholes to check out the audience.

"What should we do? Do you want to just leave?"

Kat was feeling a little better as air started to slowly fill her lungs again. This time she wasn't alone so she didn't have to worry nearly as much. Maybe they should face him.

After a few moments Kat calmed down and they began to talk rationally. More likely than not the guy wouldn't remember her. He probably ran into women like her every night. Why not go out and finish watching the show? If he came up to her afterwards, Val was by her side and she always carried her pepper spray.

Back at their seats they both ordered coffee to clear their minds. On stage, the magician was spinning around a box to show that it had no escape. Kat was a bit nervous but feeling confident that nothing would happen to her. The trick finished and a woman came out in one piece to hear the audience applaud. Then the house lights came up.

"Thank you ladies…and gentlemen."

Kat had the strange feeling that he looked at her when he said "ladies". But that was probably just her paranoia.

"For my next trick I need a volunteer from the audience." Both their hearts started to pound hard. A spot light started to roam the audience, it passed over them a few times. Then, just as they both feared, it stopped on their table. Everything went quiet in Kat's ears. The light blinded her. She felt totally helpless and vulnerable. *Run! Run! Run!* But her body wouldn't move. She tried to look to Val but the light was so bright she could only see an outline and wisps of hair.

A hand was on hers, the light started to fade, the crowd started to clap. Once her vision started to focus, her stomach churned, seeing Kyle Winterbourne's face inches away from her own. Kyle had to use both hands to help her out of the chair. Kat was in a daze, wanting to run. He wouldn't do anything to her in front of an audience? Would he?

Val was in the same predicament. Should she grab Kat and run out, embarrassing themselves? Or politely try to decline having her go on stage? What's the worst that could happen? Val stood up.

"Uh. I don't think she's in too good of shape to go up there. Too many drinks you know?" Kyle shot her a look that sent ice water through her veins. Val instantly sat down and dug her hand in her purse. Once her fingers were wrapped around the spray she felt a bit better. But she knew she wasn't going to blast a guy doing a show. She'd be arrested.

"Don't worry ma'am I'm sure she'll be just fine."

Kat reluctantly followed his lead up onto the stage. His fingers felt warm and slimy around her cold hand. Once on the stage he let go of her. Again the lights were blinding, giving the whole event an eerie surreal feeling.

"Now what's your name?" Kat never did tell him her name. Maybe she should lie and give a fake name so he wouldn't know who she really was. Then again he'd found her hotel room so he must know.

"Sandy." Kyle looked at the audience.

"Now do you people think she looks like a Sandy?"

Shit. He knew. If he knew her name than he'd done a lot of snooping. Maybe even knew she was in D.C. Maybe even paid the concierge to tell them to come here tonight. No. That was crazy.

Hearing the crowd that she could only see shadows of, Kat's mouth started to become dry. The situation was becoming too much to handle.

"Now what is your real name dear? I have a feeling it starts with a K?"

Cursing herself for letting him take Kat on stage, Val sat watching horrified. What could she do now? Nothing short of running on stage and pulling her off. But that would be crazy. Only if something bad was going to happen.

"Katharine"

Kat finally admitted. No use in a lying anymore. Kyle made a quick joke about how she must be using a fake name to hide from an affair.

"So...may I call you Kat?" She didn't respond. Kyle walked behind her and placed his hands on her shoulders. Carefully, but comically he shook her.

"Loosen up sweetie!" The practically invisible audience laughed. The heat from his slimy hands radiated through her blouse onto her shoulders. It was more than she could take. With a hard jerk she wrenched away from him. Then for the first time in her life she punched someone.

The impact wasn't that bad, Kyle saw it coming and was able to move his head enough to lessen the blow. It took him a second to gain his composure while she ran off stage and out of the building. Rubbing and moving his jaw as though he was in an old boxing movie, Kyle played it up to the crowd.

"Wow. That was the worst case of stage freight I've ever seen! Either that or I must have reminded her of an old boyfriend! Well then, let's get a new volunteer! One that won't bite!" Kyle was much angrier than he showed. But it was OK, he knew he would see Kat again soon, real soon.

21

Val chased Kat into the parking lot, expecting to see her sobbing on the curb or running down the street frantically. But she wasn't. Kat was laughing so hard she was hunched over with her hands on her knees. Val was so taken aback at the sight that she stopped ten feet from her. Val was nervous that Kat was having a break down.

Kat couldn't stop laughing. The sight of Val's face standing there made her laugh even more. She'd never punched anyone nor wanted too. But she had to admit it felt great to crack that grease ball a good one. All the fear of him was gone. She stood up for herself, once and for all. Kyle wanted to make a fool of her. Well she showed him.

"What are you looking at? Was that not great or what?" Kat said in between breaths. Val was still not sure what was going on inside of that head, but she felt it was safe to approach.

"I feel great! If I knew punching someone felt like that I would have done it years ago!" Hearing that, Val knew Kat was fine. Better in fact.

"You did get him good! Embarrassed the hell out of him!" Val gave her a high five. It was awkward and their hands only connected slightly, but it was an effort of toughness. The two wrapped arms around each other and headed down the street. They wobbled as if still drunk.

After two blocks, the adrenaline high wore off and more serious talk started. "Do you think it was a coincidence that he was doing the show that we were at? Man. What the hell are the chances of that? There has to be more to it some how."

"I don't know, that is a tough one. I mean why would someone go through a whole bunch of work to get you on stage? Actually, it has to be a coincidence, how would he know we would ask the concierge where to go? He couldn't have. And he can't be following you, acts like that are booked months in advance." Kat thought about what Val had said. It was true. More likely than not he just happened to see her in the audience. He was probably just as shocked as she was. "You know he wouldn't be so creepy if I didn't find his card in my room. I mean he would have just been a sleazy guy. But the card…I mean that's borderline stalking."

Val believed her story but when it came to the card she really thought maybe Kat forgot it was in her pocket and it fell out onto the bed. It made a lot more sense than the guy knowing what room she was in and breaking in just to leave a lousy card. It was like robbing a house and calling the cops to let them know you did it. But Val didn't have the heart to say it to Kat, she would get too upset.

It took them a long time to get back to the hotel. They enjoyed the crisp, cool, city air and the smell of bums on every street asking for change or yelling sexual comments at them. One in particular asked if they wanted to taste a southern fudge-cicle and whipped out his shriveled crusty penis. They found it funny rather than scary. The streets were brightly lit, people were out, so there was no real threat.

Once inside the hotel they decided to stay together in Val's room again for the night since she was leaving in the morning. Kat didn't bother to stop at her room. The next morning after Val had left she would wish she had.

22

Val left early and Kat saw her off in the lobby. It was a happy good-bye since they knew it wasn't for long. They were both very excited about the new plan they had. Last night's events were totally out of her mind, until in the elevator she put her hand in her pocket to find a small metal tube. For a second she had no clue what it was. Pulling it out she laughed. It was Val's pepper spray. It had a note taped down on all four sides covering most of the label. It read: *Magician Be Gone! Works on all types of men! Just felt a bit safer with you having this. Love Val.*

Kat was tickled by the gift. On the walk back to her room she read the instructions on how to use the can. Once in the room she put it down along with her purse on the desk. She made a mental note to clear the side pouch so it had nothing but the can in it.

The room was spotless. But then again she'd been here for two days and hadn't spent more than a half hour in the room. She wanted to take a shower before checking out and heading back on the road. She undressed and turned on the

TV. She loved the fact that the bathroom had speakers for the television in it. Kat found it amusing to pee and hear *The Simpsons* playing loud and clear in the same room. She clicked around for a bit until deciding to leave it on an old episode of *The Cosby's.*

Clicking on the bathroom light she heard Bill Cosby talking about how he wanted to eat his sub in peace and quiet. She turned on the water in the shower and turned around to grab the bath mat. But some bright color caught her attention. Kat turned to the mirror. Stuck right in the middle was a pink sticky note. *What the hell?* Kat thought. With the steadiness of a cat on the hunt she approached it.

Strike two. Was written in beautiful calligraphy. Nothing else. Just those two words. Kyle. It had to be. Who else would leave such a note? This time instead of fear, rage ran through her blood. Kat stomped out of the bathroom naked, she knew no one was in the room. He couldn't be hiding under the bed and the closet door was open. She threw on a pair of jeans, a t-shirt and marched downstairs.

Five minutes later she was back in the room with the hotel manager and head of security. She was proud of how she'd handled the situation downstairs. Instead of being meek and apologetic, she demanded to see the manager, chewed him out and made him follow her up here. Now standing in the bathroom the three tilted their heads examining the note.

"I want to know who the hell let someone in my room! If I was here last night I could have been raped or murdered! That would be some great press now wouldn't it? Finding a body in your hotel? What do you have to say for yourself?"

The first response to her angry question seemed to be laughter, but it was just the TV that was still on. The head of security didn't seem to be bothered by the comments or the laughing.

"Ma'am I understand you are upset. But please let's handle this rationally." Kat felt she was being rational but maybe her voice was a little louder than she thought. The manager left the cramped room. A few seconds later the laughter went silent and he returned.

"Now you said you know who did this? Let's talk about that. Also we need to figure out if you want the police involved." Hell yeah! She wanted his ass arrested. But wait. She'd physically assaulted him. All he'd done was break in and leave a note, which she knew but couldn't prove. Damn it. She was screwed.

After she calmed down, the three had a long chat in her room. They came upon several conclusions. One: Kat and Val would be reimbursed for their two nights and they would receive a complimentary suite the next time either of them was in town. Two: there was nothing she could do about the situation. They offered to bring in the police so she could get a restraining order, but that would mean staying in town for weeks until they got a court date. And besides what the hell would a restraining order do? Finally three: she was about to learn a lot more about the magician.

Kat learned that Buck, the head of security, was a former FBI agent who made a lot of money protecting the hotel since a lot of political figures stayed there. He had a lot of connections all over the country and agreed to do some digging on Kyle. Kat agreed to stay for a few extra hours until he found out about Mr. Winterbourne's past.

Buck placed a security guard outside of Kat's room. A bit unnecessary, but she didn't argue. Figuring it would take awhile, she took a long hot bath. Afterwards she started to watch a movie on Comedy Central. She had no clue what movie it was, but Gary Shandling's penis kept vibrating. The phone rang, startling her a bit. It was Buck asking if it was OK for him to come back up. She said yes.

Kat dressed while awaiting the arrival of the tough-looking bearded old man. Once he was back in the room he asked her to sit down. Kat sat on the bed and he pulled up a chair. He had a manila folder in his hand.

"Well, I wish I had better news to tell you."

Kat's heart sank a bit. If she was involved with some psychopath she didn't know what she was going to do.

"There is no record for a Kyle Winterbourne but then again that's because he didn't exist until three years ago. His real name is Leo Freeman." Well she wasn't that far off then! She thought he looked like a Larry and he was a Leo!

"He changed it to his stage name after a few incidents. It seems he was becoming a big magician and it got to his head. Thought he could get any girl he wanted. Forced himself a bit too much." Kat felt like she was shrinking as she listened to Buck. She was so confident after punching him. Now she was getting nervous that he was going to want revenge.

"He was accused of raping five separate women but got off on every single count. The bastard had a top-notch manager who thought Kyle was going to be the next David Copperfield, supposedly he had a TV special in the works with *ABC*. He only had one trial. The other girls dropped their suits and settled out of court. I'm guessing the agent put up some big dough. But after the trial, *ABC* dropped him saying they didn't want to be associated with any bad press. After that, his career went South and now he tours around doing tiny little bars and clubs. He hasn't had any suits since, but someone like that doesn't change. He's probably just more careful now. Careful and bitter." Kat was having a hard time breathing. Buck noticed and grabbed a bottle of water from the mini fridge. She took it and drank half of it in three large gulps.

"I know that this is a lot to drop on you. Especially since there is nothing we can do about him. But I also found something that might be of use."

Buck pulled out several sheets of paper stapled together.

"I've got his entire tour schedule for the next six months. Seems like he's the kind of guy to never miss a gig, so I don't think he will be following you. What I suggest is you just make sure you're not in the same state as he is." That piece of info made Kat feel much better. She looked at the paper. Her schedule would have to change a bit but that was fine. Her safety was most important.

"How the hell did you get all this so fast?" Buck gave her a cocked grin.

"I told you, I got connections." Kat was amazed and thankful for what Buck had done. She thanked him over and over again.

Buck walked Kat to her car and made sure she had his number just in case she needed some help. She gave him a light hug and he blushed as if it was the first time a girl had ever touched him. She left the parking garage not knowing if she should be happy or scared. She didn't expect to see Kyle again. But now for the rest of the trip she knew looking over her shoulder would become the norm.

23

5/18

Dear DJ,

Well I just arrived in Williamsburg Virginia. The next stop on Psychotic Magic Man's tour is Ohio so hopefully that will put enough distance so I can relax a bit. Originally I was supposed to go to West Virginia first but figured this would be a better idea to go off track and sort of flee.

So far this state looks pretty much like every other one I've seen. But then again I'm still in a foul mood so that could be it. I plan on touring Historic Williamsburg later today and maybe even go to Busch Gardens tomorrow before I leave for North Carolina.

But what can I say right now? The dream trip has been an on again and off again nightmare so far. It's hard but hopefully the whole stalker thing is behind me. And now with something to look forward to every few weeks with Val coming down, it should start to get better soon. I hope. If not I don't know what to do. I want the trip to be over so bad but at the same time I'm petrified for it to end. When it's over what the hell do I do then? I mean do I start over? A whole new life? I don't know if I can do that. I don't know if I want to do that.

One day at a time I guess. Maybe the trip will get better. Maybe it'll never end.

Kat closed her journal and took a deep breath. The room was just like any other on the way. Nothing exciting. It was about an hour before sunset and Kat wanted to take some time with Jasper's ashes and spread them tonight. She felt like she had neglected him the past few days. It was strange how she felt guilt over not talking to a cookie jar. It was odd but for now it was all she had.

After a quick talk to a sweet old woman at the front desk, Kat headed out to an old battleground called James Town. It wasn't a long drive. Actually it was kind of nice driving down a long windy wooded road. She drove along the ocean for about a half a mile before heading up a steep hill. Once on top she saw vast fields that seemed to go for miles. Following tourism street signs she found a small, three-car parking spot next to an old cannon. No one else was there.

With a big stretch Kat put on the backpack with the cookie jar in it. She glanced at a few historical info signs but she didn't care to know that much. It would just be forgotten in a little while anyway. All she needed to know was this place was a battleground.

Jasper would have loved this. The old cannons behind grass mounds where men fought for their lives. Finding one particular base comforting, she decided to spread the ashes there. It was about thirty feet around with mounds of earth fifteen feet high. Small holes were cut out for the cannons and supported by ancient wood. Only one narrow path led from the circle, but it lead to nowhere. On the outside, sharpened logs where stuck in the earth making scaling the walls practically impossible.

Taking off the pack she sat in the middle of the grass. Only three canons remained sticking out of the windows. The other four windows were empty, letting her see patches of blue. It was eerie to think that hundreds of years ago men risked their lives in this very spot. She wondered how many died here.

Pulling out a baggie of ashes she wondered if anyone's remains where still here. Probably. Well, this would be the first place Jasper would have company. Opening the bag she hesitated before dumping it on the grass. Instead she poured it onto her hand for the first time. She actually had yet to touch the ash. She'd been afraid to.

Some were sharp, all were rough as they hit her palm. Moving the life fragments in her hand caused a subtle amount of dust to arise. Kat brought the pile close to her face to examine it.

How? How the hell could this be my husband?

Not one thing in the pile of white and gray chips resembled a human. It boggled her mind. For the fist time she felt a bit stupid talking to the ash. It was really just a pile of nothing.

I can't keep doing this to myself! I need to get in a better mood and enjoy this trip. Kat stood up, losing a few pieces in the process. She looked to the sky just as a huge fluffy cloud moved its way in front of the sun. Her hand closed around the ash. It felt like a dozen small insects were biting her hand. She squeezed it tighter and tighter out of anger.

Kat was never religious. Jasper believed but never practiced. Looking at the sky she started to shake her fist.

"Why! WHY! Why would you do this? Huh? Give me a child then take away my husband and the child? What kind of God are you?" She felt like a lunatic yelling at the sky, but it was the first time she'd brought religion into this whole thing. At the wake, dozens of people came through and prayed at Jasper's coffin then came to her and said blessings. She'd ignored them all. Ignored everyone. Religion would have stayed totally out of the picture too if she were having a decent time on the trip. But everything was so horrible that she needed someone to blame for having to endure such pain. So who better?

Holding her fist to the sky she stopped yelling. What good is this going to do? If praying did anything then with all the prayers said at the funeral she should be having the time of her life. Trying to calm down she brought her fist to her face. Holding it to her cheek she tried to fight back a river of tears. Amazingly it had been a few days since she'd wept.

Her hand started to ache from ash piercing her skin. With trembling lips she gave her hand a kiss. Instead of just letting them go, this time with all her might she threw the handful in the air.

A few minutes later she took a walk to the bluff on the other side of the field. The sun was just about to set. It was a spectacular view. An old bench was placed a few yards from the edge of the cliff providing a perfect place to watch the sun disappear. She placed Jasper next to her to watch.

Having gotten some rage out she started to relax. Her palm was red and spotted with indents from the ash. She didn't mind - the violet and red streaks of light put her mind at ease. The picturesque view eased her so much that she made a promise to herself to have a good time. No matter what.

PART FOUR
REST

1

Almost a month and nine states after sitting on that small bench in Virginia, Kat found herself in Arkansas. She was exhausted. The constant driving and always being on the go had her running ragged. A break was needed.

The crazy magician's schedule had Kat's entire route screwed up. She was way off course, but so far she hadn't run into him again. That made it worth the while. Kat was going to have to go the entire way back East to West Virginia and then loop back through the upper states to finish what she missed.

Over the past month almost nothing eventful had happened. Nine separate times she had spread the ashes in various places and settings. It was becoming more of a routine than anything symbolic or meaningful. She was having a much better time though. Staying in a place for no more than three days was just driving her crazy. Val visited her in New Orleans and the two had a blast. Kat got plastered and didn't remember half the night, but she knew she didn't do anything like Val, who flashed about a hundred horny guys to get three-cent beads.

In Florida she wanted to go farther in for the tourist stuff, but she was starting to find amusement parks depressing. They were just places she really didn't want to go to alone. Waiting in line and going on a ride alone was pretty miserable. She decided the trip down to Florida's tip would take too much time and wasn't worth it.

The Carolinas were boring. Alabama was all right. The Mississippi River wasn't nearly as exciting as she'd hoped it to be. Georgia was beautiful in parts (she took a few extra pictures there in case she ever wanted to go back and get a big old southern house).

Twenty states down...thirty...thirty to go. So far those twenty felt like she'd been to ninety. It was now mid-June and Kat had been on the road for almost two months. It was time for a break. She didn't pick Arkansas for any reason at all, it just happened to be where her body ran out of gas. Kat had been driving up Route Seven when she saw a sign that read: *Next Right Jasper.*

She knew it was just a town, but out of curiosity and instinct she took the right. Driving around she took in the sites. It was exactly like she'd pictured the middle of the country to look like. Mountains, rivers, openness, fresh air, small streets with local stores. Just like in the movies. Her heart started to fill with joy. This was the place for her to rest and take a few weeks vacation from her duty.

The first hotel she found was a small, family run place called Ned's Nature Inn. It only had fifteen rooms and looked like Ned and his wife were the only employees. She checked in and had a nice chat with Ned. She told him that she wanted to maybe stay in town for a few weeks and he was nice enough to give her the names of few places she could get an efficiency room or a bed and breakfast, if she wanted to spend money.

Ned waddled as he walked Kat to her room. Number eight. It was old and the smell reminded her of the cedar balls her aunt used to use in the storage closet. It wasn't too pleasant of a smell, but Ned didn't seem to notice. Tugging on his suspenders the old man showed her around the room and how to use the thermostat before leaving.

Alone in the room Kat felt a bit uncomfortable. It was decorated like it was still the late sixties. Everything looked fragile and aged and it made her afraid to touch anything. It must have been a nice place in its day but now it was like a movie flashback. She quickly checked the bed to see if it was sleepable. It was clean but the sheets had a tacky brown flower print on them.

One night was the limit for her here. If the old man weren't so nice she would have tried to find a newer place in a second, something with a name brand. But for now, getting out and driving around the town would have to do.

A warm tingly feeling started in her throat and spread throughout her body. She instantly new it was excitement of not having to pack and drive again tomorrow. Besides, this felt like a place she could be happy in. For a while at least. Kat couldn't really place why, but she did tried to tell herself that it had nothing to do with the town's name. If anything it would be an annoying constant reminder.

The streets reminded her of sappy nostalgic movies, where the sun would spread a blanket of gold across everything, and everyone would smile and say hello to you whether they knew you or not. Having the top down and it only being sixty-six degrees did get her some odd looks from locals - they must have thought she was an odd tourist.

After an hour of touring around the streets, Kat was happy with her decision to stay in the town until she felt well rested. At least a few weeks, maybe more. The first task would be to find a suitable place to stay. After a few drive-bys of the places the old man recommended to her she wasn't satisfied. It needed to be a place totally different from anywhere she'd stayed lately - a place that wouldn't bring out memories of the past and instead would bring out a new Kat. And then she found it: the Bucking Bull Ranch was just what she was looking for.

Stopping for lunch at a small diner, she stumbled upon a brochure rack near the bathrooms. For a long five minutes Kat poured over each one to find out what was around the area. Most didn't really appeal to her but she put a few in her pocketbook. Finally, she pulled out one with a gorgeous picture of a Ranch on a mountainside. In big letters painted to look like wood it read: *The Bucking Bull Ranch! Play Like a Cowboy, Live Like A King at Arkansas Best All Inclusive Resort*! She couldn't help but laugh at how stupid the slogan was, but the place did look amazing - offering horseback riding, luxury suits with room service, and mountain climbing among other things.

The waitress told her it was only four miles from the diner so Kat didn't hesitate to head out on the road for it. The drive was steep and winding. The sign at the bottom said *Mount Vincent.* Occasionally on the way up there would be a break in the trees showing off some magnificent scenery, but Kat was too scared to look away from the road long enough to enjoy it.

After about two miles (which took fifteen-minutes) it started to level out, letting Kat breathe a little better. When she was almost to the top, the road split. A small wooden sign pointed towards the direction of the Ranch. The next half a mile was dense woods but at least the road was flat.

Up ahead Kat could see a giant wooden archway. It had to be the ranch. Flashes of a dozen different camp movies flipped through Kat's head. She'd never really seen an arch like this. Excitement flushed her face, giving a pinkish tint to it. The first building she came upon was the office and in the distance she could see a few dozen log cabins around a man-made lake. The view was too good to be real.

Getting out of the car, Kat took a deep breath in. It was the freshest air to ever enter her lungs. She was so excited that a small knot started to form in her stomach at the thought of them being entirely booked. It was a good possibility. It was almost time for schools to get out and families would be on vacation soon. She sucked in another chest full of air to calm herself.

The lobby was just as she'd expected it to be - lots of wood and dead animals. She wasn't too thrilled about all the dead animals, but it was to be expected in a place like this. Hell, if it didn't have the head of at least one deer on the wall, she would be nervous. The front desk looked like it was carved right out of a tree that used to stand in that very spot. Kat rang the bell.

A Mrs. Partridge look-a-like strolled out from the back with a pleasant smile on her face and a limp in her walk.

"Welcome to the Bucking Bull Ranch! My name is Margaret. My husband Buck and I are the owners. Now how may I help you my dear?" Kat felt genuinely welcomed by her. Returning the smile, Kat answered her,

"Well I was hoping you still had a cabin available."

"Yes, in deedy do we do! For how long would it be?"

"That's the thing I'm not sure about, I'm actually thinking a few weeks." Margaret was taken aback, but the smile never left her face.

"Well, can't say many people pop in and ask for a few weeks at a time. You a writer my dear?" She started to pull out the reservation log as Kat searched her brain, trying to figure out how to answer.

"Uh…yes I'm actually traveling cross country and writing a novel." Well hopefully now she wouldn't need to explain anything about why she was alone.

"Oh, that is so wonderful my dear! We had a writer stay a few years back…the whole winter, hardly left the place! Have you written anything I would know? Buck and I read an awful lot up here!" Oh shit.

"This is my…first novel." Judging the next question Kat answered to her surprise,

"It's about an orphaned boy who hitchhikes cross country… in the seventies." Boy did she pull that out of her ass, but Margaret's eyes showed signs of excitement.

"Sounds very interesting! Now let me look here. Hmmm… Well… we do have openings for the next two weeks. The only problem is it wouldn't be the same cabin, you would have to move once… Maybe twice."

"That would be absolutely fine!" The woman looked pleased that Kat was happy.

"Let me get you some paperwork and…would you like to see one of the cabins before you go off and pay for it?"

Kat was amazed that the woman cared more about her happiness than getting money.

Margaret came out from behind the counter to give Kat a tour of the place. She was surprised to find out she had a fake leg. Kat had noticed the slight limp but never expected she was missing a leg. It actually looked pretty real but there was no question it wasn't. The two walked around the entire place, which took almost a half hour.

The two-dozen cabins were spread out over a large flat patch of land in the middle of the mountain. When she looked up, she saw a cloud-kissed mountaintop and when she looked down and she saw endless valleys and fields of crops that looked like a patchwork blanket. The lake was small but perfect for a swim or fishing since it was stocked with bass.

The log cabins were modest but cute as could be. They had one bedroom (some had two) each with a king size bed, kitchen, bath and living room. Kat was surprised to find they all had central air and satellite TV. Margaret explained that people loved to think they are roughing it but take them away from AC and TV for five minutes too long and all hell broke loose.

Next they strolled by the dining facilities. They served three hot meals a day. It was a large semi-open air mess hall style eatery with plenty of room for dancing. The horse stables were across the field from it.

"Well, what do you think? Still want to stay here?"

"I think you might have talked me into a third week!"

Margaret laughed and the two filled out the paperwork. It was much more expensive than Kat had thought it would be. She almost didn't want to pay so much, but the new rebellious side took over and yelled that she could afford it. Kat paid in full, which also made her a bit nervous. What if she got sick of it and left half way through her stay? She would lose a few thousand dollars! No, No. It was fine. She refused to let herself worry about it.

Not wanting to stay in the crappy little hotel, Kat drove down and grabbed the few bags she'd left in the room. She messed up the bed to make it look like she'd slept in it before sneaking to her car and taking off for the night. She was going to have to go back and return the key in the morning but this was going to be worth it.

2

It was late when she got back to cabin three, which was to be her cabin for the first week, maybe longer if Margaret could talk the other guests into a different cabin. She explored her new temporary home with excitement. It was warm and felt like home. She was quite thankful no dead animals were on display.

Roaming around the four rooms she explored each nook and cranny. Nothing was out of the ordinary, just usual hotel stuff in good condition. The one thing she couldn't figure out was why the kitchen had every necessary tool and serving piece to make a Thanksgiving dinner. It boggled her mind especially since all meals were included.

Satisfied that she'd looked in every corner of her new home, Kat went out to her car and for the first time and brought in all her luggage. The next hour was spent unpacking and settling in. This was going to be nice - a much needed break.

The next morning, Kat woke up extra early to get back to the hotel and return the key before the old man realized she hadn't spent the night. It went successfully and when he asked how her night went she told him the truth. It was wonderful! Heading back to the ranch she spotted a grocery store. Having not bought or cooked food in a long time, she decided to pull in and get some items.

While shopping, she realized why there was a kitchen - for people like her. Kat didn't buy much, but enough to not let her use the express line.

Back in the cabin, Kat put the food away and grabbed the events schedule off the fridge. Most of the stuff on it wasn't too interesting to her: games for families, arts and crafts, swimming lessons. But there were a few things she didn't want to miss like hiking and horseback riding.

The only time she had ever gone horseback riding was when she was nine and it wasn't a cherished memory. Her aunt Tillie had taken her for her birthday and she remembered how excited she'd been to ride Black Beauty. Of course when she got there the horse was brown with white spots and sickly looking, but nonetheless she was excited. Walking to the horse, her aunt held her hand and tried to guide her around the mounds of crap but Aunt Tillie was unsuccessful. Trying to step over a rather large pile herself, Aunt Tillie wasn't paying much attention to Kat. She pulled her behind and right into it the large steaming pile of horse manure. Kat fell on top of it and covered the front of her new pink dress that her Grandma had bought her. She was horribly upset, but it got worse. When Aunt Tillie tried to pull her up, she started to gag from the stench of the crap and instead of brushing it off, Aunt Tillie grabbed the bottom of Kat's dress and whipped it off right over her head. Kat was mortified. Pulling it over her head caused the crap to smear on her face and she stood there in her flower print undies with crap smeared on her face in front of everyone. Even though it was only a few people, Kat remembered it as thousands and to top it all off she never got to ride the horse.

She hoped today's experience would be much better. The lessons were at twelve or three. Since it was only eleven and Kat had nothing else to do, she called the front desk and reserved a slot in the twelve o'clock class.

3

It was an overcast and slightly windy day but the view from the Ranch was still amazing and the air was still fresh. Using the lodge's picture map to find her way to the stables, Kat felt a little nervous. But then again what did she have to be nervous about? Certainly she could step over a pile of crap now!

Inside a large fenced-in area more than a dozen perfectly groomed horses roamed around. Only a few people stood by the entrance. As Kat approached she could tell that it was a family of three and a newlywed couple, since they were all lovey dovey. An awkward feeling of not belonging started to bubble in Kat's head.

Everyone greeted her with a smile but she was sure that behind those smiles they were all wondering why she was alone. She didn't even want to think of all the different reasons that might be flowing through their heads.

"Is this the group for horseback riding?" Kat asked, trying to break the tension that was only felt by her.

"YES! YES it is! I'm going to ride the most beautiful horse!" A blond six-year-old wearing a Britney Spears t-shirt blurted out. The rest of the group smiled with a *isn't she cute* expression. Kat bent down to the child's level.

"Awesome! Have you ridden a horse before?"

"Nope! But my Mommy used to have a horse when she was my age. I want to get one but we live in an apartment and a horse wouldn't fit." This was the first interaction with a young kid since she'd miscarried and Kat had to hold back tears at the thought of her own child. Luckily a loud voice broke up her thoughts.

"Whoooooo hooooo!"

Kat's head whipped up to see a cowboy. The man wore dusty old jeans, boots, thick belt, plaid shirt cut off at the tops of the arm and of course the cowboy hat. Her first reaction was that he was wearing the get up just for show to make the guests feel like they are on an actual ranch. With his brim down low she couldn't see his face.

"Well dip me in butter and call me Sally! We got ourselves a small group today! You sure all are lucky!"

The cowboy said approaching the group. Kat could finally see his face. It was covered in stubble. He reminded her of Mel Gibson - definitely a Mad Max Mel when he was still really young.

Kat felt a small flutter in her heart. She tried to tell herself it was just nerves of riding a horse.

"Well they call me Billy, what are ya'll called?"

He spoke clearly but with a mid west accent that seemed a bit played up. They all introduced themselves, Jean and Al Campbell with their daughter Megan from New Jersey. And Mr. and Mrs. Nick Dicarlo from Seattle. The young bride didn't give her name because she was too excited to be able to say Mrs. Nick! Kat liked that they were so in love. She missed that feeling.

When Kat introduced herself, Billy looked her up and down and said.

"Are you ready to ride, Mrs. Kitty?" She couldn't recall anyone calling her Kitty except for a college boyfriend who just wanted to say it when they were in bed. He thought it sounded naughty. The extra attention made her blush a bit, seeing her cheeks getting flushed Billy winked at her.

"All right all you city slickers let's get going."

For the next hour Billy taught the group the dos and don'ts of riding. One by one he had each person sit on Gary, his most trusted horse and walked them around the stable to make sure they had the hang of it. Once he was satisfied he let everyone pick what horse they wanted to ride. Kat choose one of the three black ones. Finally she was going to get to ride her Black Beauty.

Billy rode Gary and led the way up the trail. The Campbell's followed first then Kat. The newlyweds went last so they could try and lean over for sneak kisses. Kat was a bit nervous having such a large beast between her legs. She did get the hand of it pretty fast but then again so did everyone else. Megan leaned off her horse she was riding with her dad and waved at Kat. Looked like she had a new friend.

About twenty minutes into it Kat's ass and thighs started to ache from the pounding. She wondered how the hell Billy took this every day. He must have a calloused tush. She pictured his butt naked. It had no calluses on it. The thought shocked her. She hadn't thought of another man in a sexual way (besides celebrities) in ages. Quickly she sunk her hand into her pocket to hold the baggie of Jasper.

The trail became narrow, allowing for only one horse to pass at a time. They formed a single line to pass through the thick brush. Up ahead it seemed to be brighter, Kat thought there must be a clearing up there. If there was the view must be ridiculous since the whole ride they had been going higher and higher. Sure enough it was a large picnic area. Billy hopped off his horse and tied it to a large wood fence. One by one he tied off each horse and helped the passengers off. Kat tried not to make eye contact with him as he gently held her hand and put the other on her back to steady her.

"Ya'll doin' real good. I'll make cowboys out of you yet!"

"Hey…Cowgirls too!" A squeaky voice chirped out of Megan.

"Of course, cowgirls too! We'll have a thirty-minute rest here before heading back on the south trail to the ranch. That's the outhouse over there and don't wander too far." Everyone started to go their own ways, almost every one of them rubbing their behind.

The view wasn't as nice as from her cabin since it was higher and she could only really see other mountains. It was still beautiful though. Kat walked by a few picnic tables to a small footpath that no one had seemed to notice. About forty yards down the path there was a tiny clearing to the left. Kat peeked through it to see a ledge about ten feet down. It looked like a perfect place to sit. Carefully holding onto branches, she made her way down to it. Just as she suspected, the perfect place to sit. It had a great view and the rock was smooth enough to lean back comfortably. She dangled her feet off it and daydreamed about how nice it would be to have someone here with her. Val should be coming soon, maybe next week, she'd love it here.

Kat took out the pouch with Jasper in it. She wasn't planning on spreading his ashes today. It was meant to be more of a good luck charm than anything, but it seemed so nice here, so private. Leaning forward she looked down. It made her head spin a bit - sixty, maybe seventy feet sloping down and nothing but jagged rock the whole way. She made a mental note to be careful getting up. Man that would hurt falling down there…it would hurt a lot. So would getting hit by a car.

Jasper must have been in such pain. She looked at the dusty fragments in the bag with sympathy. The thought had crossed her mind and she'd even asked Val about it but Val had said it was so quick he must have felt nothing. The thought of the actual impact hadn't really stuck in her mind until now, as she was looking down at what could easily be her death. It would be so easy to just slip off the hard seat and fall. So easy. Yes it would hurt, but the pain would be over in a matter of a few seconds. Why not? So far nothing had gone as well as she'd wanted it to. And what the hell was she going to do when she finished? Everyone would think it was just an accident and then Jasper and she would be reunited. Even though she didn't believe in Heaven and Hell, she wanted to believe that when she died she'd be back with Jasper.

Kat scooted a few inches closer to the edge. A rock the size of a golf ball fell off from where she was sitting. It seemed like an eternity before it hit the wall several times and rolled to a stop a painful distance down. Her heart started to thump. *What have I got to lose?* She placed her hand on her heaving chest over the windbreaker to feel the pounding of her heart. On the palm of her hand she felt cold metal. Moving her hand she looked at her jacket. A frog stuck its tongue out at her. Kat had completely forgotten she had put it on her jacket last week in Louisiana. Her thoughts wandered from slipping off the edge to wondering what the hell the pizza boy had said to Patty. Damn! She was good! The first time she was close to actually killing herself and her mind went right to Patty. She was amazing. *If Patty could make it so can I.* Kat scooted back until her shoulders touched moist rock. The bag unzipped with ease. She reached out as far as possible to make sure the ash would spread down the mountain. Slowly the ash slipped out and got caught in the wind. When the pieces fell twenty or so feet she lost eye contact with them.

"Not yet my love. Not yet." There was a crunching noise behind her.

"What's that pretty lady?" Billy was making his way down the hill to the ledge. Kat gave the bag a quick shake and thrust it into her pocket.

"What was that you were dumping?" Panicked, she felt as if she had been caught breaking some sort of law.

"Oh…uh just some crumbs of a sandwich." Billy had seen all the ash fall out. He was curious as to what she was doing but saw the panic in Kitty's face and didn't want to push the issue. He took a seat right next to her.

"You know you found my favorite spot?"

Kat made eye contact with him and smiled. His eyes had a smoky gray look to them. They were eyes with the power to intimidate or melt a heart at will. She bet he knew how to use them. Feeling like his gaze was transfixing her, she turned her attention across to the mountains.

"I eat lunch here all the time. Or when I'm feeling blue I might sit here for hours. I'm surprised you found it. Most people just walk right by it, never knowing it was here." Billy waited for a response, but Kat's mind was swirling too much to answer. A few seconds ago she was going to kill herself and now she was talking to a cowboy who looked like Mel Gibson.

"It's not the best view we've got up here but for some reason, I feel safe here. It's like my own private place in the world."

Finally Kat mustered up some words. "I'm sorry, I didn't mean to intrude on your area."

"No, no, no! I didn't mean it like that. Sometimes you got to share things in life. But it can still feel like it's yours."

Kat felt relieved, for a second she thought he was upset that she was here.

"Actually I'm glad you found it. Shows me you're special."

Oh Crap! He's hitting on me. Just as her heartbeat returned to regular it picked up speed again. What could she do? How could she get out of this?

"So ya married huh?" Billy gestured to the ring. Her emotional bungee jump went down at the relief that he wasn't hitting on her. But it quickly sprung back up at the thought of having to explain.

"Well...sort of." She didn't want to talk about this. Not now, not to a cowboy tour guide.

"Don't want to talk about it huh? That's fine. I hate when people try to pry things out of me too."

The bungee ride was finally over, coming to a gentle swing, but something was odd. Billy seemed not to have his accent anymore. She looked at him with and inquisitively raised her eyebrow. Before she could say anything he spoke.

"I know, the accent. If I tell you a secret do you promise not to tell the others?"

"I promise."

"Well, I'm not from Arkansas. I'm originally from New York City. Born and raised in Brooklyn. I was just sick of the hustle and bustle of the Big Apple. So I moved out here when I was twenty. Learned to ride, had a few jobs as a farm hand. Then I met Margaret and Buck at a horse show and they offered me a job. It's been five years now and I love it." Kat let her jaw drop a bit to show him shock and surprise. It was interesting though and she totally understood someone wanting to live here and have a simple life.

"That's fantastic." It was Billy's turn for blushing. Embarrassed, he looked at his watch.

"Whoa…we better get back." He helped her up the step slate and onto the path. Before walking back he stopped her.

"Look, I never told a guest my story, so please don't tell anyone…and oh…Buck doesn't know, Margaret does though. So just if you could…keep it to yourself." Kat crossed her heart and hoped to die. If only he knew she really did hope to die. On the walk back Kat couldn't help but wonder why he'd told her his secret. She was after all a total stranger. Why would he pick her and no one else? Was he just using it as a line or did he really see something in her that made him want to open up? It occupied her mind the whole way back.

4

6/13

DJ, it's been a while since I've written but my emotions have been getting the best of me. The trip has been hard. Nothing as I expected. But I'm finally taking some much-needed rest. I'm staying at a wonderful Ranch in Arkansas. I'm only worried that I'll run out of activities rather soon. I'm considering getting a job to take up some time while I try to let my emotions heal and I set out again.

I also considered actually killing myself for the first time. That fact terrified me that I'd actually hit such a low. I think it was more of the setting and moment though. Patty's pin saved me. I want to call and thank her but she was very strict about making sure I only call if I'm about to. Hopefully that call will never have to be made.

The major thing that started as a small seed in my brain and now is a full-grown tree is the question whether or not Jasper killed himself. It's been on my mind constantly. I've done my best for the past few months to try and not think of it. But it's getting to the point where I can't help it. But how the hell will I ever find out? When I overheard the police say they thought it was suicide, it crushed me. If that's what they believe, and they deal with that kind of thing all the time, then maybe they are right.

I just don't know what to do. I could track down the man who hit him but...I just don't know if I could look at him without...trying to hurt him. I know it's awful and it was an accident (or was it?) but I can't help but feel hatred. I don't care if he is the nicest man in the world. He took my Jasper away. I could write him a letter asking him what happened, but then he would have time to mould his answer and make him look like he was the good guy. I just don't know what to do. But I do know I need to find out.

5

Kat was starving and ready for dinner. She was a bit worried about having to eat alone, but the hunger won out and she left her cabin and headed to the nightly feast. Since it was still early June, the ranch wasn't totally booked - leaving plenty of open seats in the eatery.

Tonight was buffet style. She grabbed a plate and piled it high with roast beef, potatoes and mixed vegetables. She grabbed a separate plate for her salad. The two plates were almost too much to carry. Kat balanced them like a high wire act on the way to a seat. Glancing around she saw a few completely empty tables but she figured she would really stick out. On her second look around she saw a tiny hand enthusiastically waving at her. When she saw Al Campbell wave her over she decided it was safe to go and sit with them. Hell, it would be nice to have conversation at dinner for once.

She sat down next to Megan who surprised her with a hug.

"Well I guess you like her, huh Meggy?" Her mother said with surprise.

"She really doesn't like that many people, you should feel lucky!" Al said jokingly. Kat smiled and asked how the rest of their day went. They had light chitchat for a few minutes before the dreaded question came.

"So…Kat you on vacation?" Getting used to being in this situation Kat's stomach only did two summersaults instead of the usual ten.

"I'm a writer. I'm traveling cross-country to do research on a book. I'm actually taking a break right now. I'm going to stay here for a few weeks before heading on."

Hell, it had worked with Margaret at the front desk. She might as well keep it up for the remainder of the stay here. They looked satisfied with the answer and asked all kinds of questions on the book. Kat almost laughed at how good of a liar she had become. She had an answer for everything, but she could tell that one question was killing them. It must be knocking around in their heads like a wrecking ball gone crazy. Just trying to get out. The question she knew they wouldn't ask out of politeness: "Where's your husband?"

"Mmmm mm um mm mmmm! Doesn't this food look good enough to eat?" From the sound of the thick fake accent Kat immediately knew the New Yorker was standing behind her.

"Well howdy folks! Mind if I sit here Mrs. Kitty?

He plopped down a bit too close to Kat. His sleeveless arm touched hers. Billy plucked off his hat and hooked it on his knee before digging into his food. Beans first. He moaned with pleasure as if the food was the best he'd ever had, making Megan giggle and the rest smile. After a hard swallow he began to talk.

"So did you folks have a good time on the trails?"

They all agreed and nodded. Megan rambled on and on about how wonderful it was and that she couldn't wait to tell all her friends. Kat watched the discussion between the two. Billy seemed to know just how to talk to her. Kat was impressed.

"So you should all be ready for a sore bum tomorrow!"

Again they all smiled more out of politeness than actual amusement.

Dinner was over and dessert was finished. Pretty much everyone felt like they'd pop if poked in the stomach. The Campbells excused themselves saying it was Megan's bedtime. She protested but finally agreed to go with the promise of watching TV if she brushed her teeth real good. With a quick hug for Kat and one for Billy, they left, leaving Kat alone with Billy.

She wasn't scared to be left alone with him.

It was just that she didn't want to have to reject him if he came on to her. She was never very good at saying no to people. She could recall a dozen or so slime balls that had stuck their tongues down her throat. Most of them had made her gag, but she'd allowed it because she never knew how to say no. But when it came to anything farther than that she would make up an elaborate excuse to get out of it. Now that she thought of it, maybe she'd always been a good liar.

"Well… just you and me, Kitty." She nodded and sipped her coffee. Billy spoke again in his normal voice.

"So do I make you uncomfortable? During dinner you were a chatterbox. Now you don't have anything to say."

Kat felt very rude. She wasn't used to people saying how they felt, so it took her by surprise that he'd come right out with that. Turning towards him to talk she got caught in his smoky gaze.

"I'm sorry. It's just. I'm not… good at… Rejecting people. I don't want to hurt you." A smile started on his face and grew until he couldn't keep the laugh in any longer. Kat sat silent, not knowing why he was laughing.

"Mrs. Kitty you have a ring on your finger. I'm not some scumbag who is going to try and pick you up. I'm just a nice guy who has an amazing sense when someone needs a shoulder."

Again the red hue spread across her cheeks like wild fire. She was so embarrassed.

"I'm…" She tried to talk but just started to laugh instead. With that out of the way Kat was ready to open up to him. It would be great to talk to someone besides Val. She didn't want to spill the whole story and have to tell it over again, but she had a sense that he would pick it up rather easily.

6

Billy took her for a walk on a nature trail just on the edge of the ranch. The night was perfect. The clouds from earlier in the day had moved on, leaving the sky to look like a deep dark purple blanket with hundreds of sequins studded all over it. Looking up, Kat had a hard time keeping her mind off of making love to Jasper under the stars.

Billy sure did talk a lot but then again she was pretty quiet so he had to. She learned a lot about the man and actually found him very interesting. Kat did engage him by asking questions but she had yet to reveal anything about herself. It was wonderful to be the listener for a change. After an hour or so the silence between subjects seemed to get longer and longer. Kat realized she should finally start to talk some.

"I'm thinking about trying to get a job for the few weeks I'm here."

"What for? Need some money?"

"No, no. Not at all, I'm pretty set for money. Just something to do. It's been a while since I was settled down in a place. I just figured I'm gonna get too bored if I don't do something." Billy showed expressions of deep thinking on his stubble-ridden face.

"Well that's a toughie. You said you were only gonna be here a few weeks. Don't know many people willing to hire somebody for just a short while." Kat had thought of that. She knew it would be the one obstacle during this stay here.

"Yeah I know…" Billy's grey eyes widened with excitement.

"Well wait a hot damn minute! Do you like children, I mean you seem like you do?"

"Yeah, I love them I actually used to be a…guidance counselor." In a past life she thought. Somehow in his excitement Billy slipped back into his fake accent.

"Well I'll be. You said you don't care about money… you could volunteer at Camp Chipwood!" Billy looked so

184

thrilled he'd thought of it. He smiled and walked proudly for a moment.

"Well… do you want to tell me about it?"

Kat asked. Billy shook his head with a laugh.

"Gosh, I forgot you don't live around here for a second. Camp Chipwood is for poor, underprivileged and troubled kids. I think it's for ages nine through fifteen or something like that. I teach horse riding there every now and then. They are really sweet kids. Means the world to them to get to do things they normally wouldn't."

Right up my alley Kat thought.

"That would be fantastic! Thank you Billy."

"You're sure welcome Mrs. Kitty! I'll get you their number when we get back."

The rest of the walk was filled with more idle chitchat. Kat did do a lot of talking this time. She told him about her childhood, college and her job at the schools. She even mentioned Val a few times. But not once did she speak of Jasper. It was obvious that she was leaving some major holes in her life story, but amazingly Billy didn't push for answers. Not once did he ask her about her husband. Somehow he could tell she didn't want to talk about it. Kat was amazed he had such restraint. There was no way she would have.

Back at the main lodge Billy wrote down the number of the camp and wished her goodnight. It was a bit awkward. A hug seemed appropriate but given the situation, neither one attempted. They both smiled and nodded at each other as they walked in separate directions to their cabins.

The whole walk back to her cabin Kat had a huge grin on her face. She couldn't figure out if it was from the conversation or the fact that she might be able to work at a camp with kids. But she didn't care, it felt good to smile again.

Once back in the cabin her smile faded at the sight of the cookie jar. Suddenly she felt guilty for spending time with a man she found attractive - even if it was innocent. Kat avoided eye contact with the jar, worried Jasper might be able to tell she was up to something. *This is ridiculous, it's just ash. And if Jasper could actually hear me then he would have seen the whole night and known it was harmless.* She went to bed that night with a mix of guilt and excitement running through her head.

7

Val was happier now that she got to visit Kat every so often. It wasn't her ideal plan but it was much better than nothing. And besides getting to travel to places she would have never gone to otherwise was wonderful. She still wished Kat would call her more though. On average she called every other day. Sometimes three days without a call would go by. That always annoyed her.

So many nights she'd be home doing nothing. She would pop on a movie and sit with the phone in her lap just waiting and hoping Kat would call. It had gotten to the point recently that Val had started to question why she needed Kat so much. Her psychologist suggested it was a motherly instinct she was trying to fulfill and with the absence of a significant other to give her love to, she put it on the only person she did love. But what did quacks know?

Tonight was no different than the last few. Val sat on the sofa eating a pint of LoMein out of the carton, watching

Cruel Intentions. Starting to feel a bit full, she glanced down at her stomach. It bulged ever so slightly over her pajama pants. Since Kat left she'd gained nine pounds. Just another reason to get mad about her leaving.

Just as Sarah Michelle Gellar was about to kiss Selma Blair, the phone rang. It startled her a bit but she crammed a pile of noodles in her mouth anyways. With her mouth overly stuffed she answered.

"…el…oh…"

"What the hell you eating now? It's nine-thirty!"

"Chin…ease…" Val swallowed and took a sip of her diet Coke.

"So…where in the world is Katharine Cutter today?"

"Drum roll please!"

Val made a cheesy drum sound with her tongue.

"Arkansas!"

"Oh…baby I'm sorry. Stuck in Hicksville?"

"Nooooo…it's actually amazing here. I'm staying at the Bucking Bull Ranch! It's so beautiful, I even rode a horse yesterday!"

"Miss Poopy face got past her fear of horseshit? Congratulations!" Ever since Val had heard the horse crap story she loved to tease Kat about it.

"Yup! But guess what? I'm goanna stay here for a few weeks, maybe a month. I need to relax. The constant go has been draining me."

Val felt her heart get put into a vice. Someone started to crank the handle to tighten it. A full month in one state? She shot out of her seat and ran to her computer room. On the wall was a map of the country, a yellow pin was in each state Kat had gone to so far. She tried to count it quick enough so Kat wouldn't question her silence. Twenty. Only twenty states she'd gone to and it had been over a month

If Kat stayed there a month then she still had thirty more to go, this trip would never end!

"Why are you going to go and do that?"

Kat was a bit offended at her tone, it was like being scolded by her mother.

"Val calm down. I just need to rest for a bit. Look I already got a job for a month, I start tomorrow."

"WHAT? WHAT? Why did you go and do that? You don't need money."

"All right Val, if you don't relax I'm going to hang up." Val bit her lip to try and calm herself. She knew she was over-reacting but she wanted Kat back in her life on a daily basis. Damn it! She should have tried to make sure Kat had the baby. That would have made her stay. Why didn't she think of that?

"I'm sorry...I just worry about you."

"Gee thanks Ma...now let me explain everything to you without you getting mad, OK?" Val agreed and listened to her stories. After hearing it all she understood why she needed a break. She wasn't happy with it but she understood.

Her job sounded wonderful. Val knew it would do wonders for Kat to be working with kids again. Kat told her she was going to work five days a week as a volunteer counselor helping with everything from arts and crafts to teaching kids how to deal with bullies. She seemed thrilled to be doing it.

The name Billy came up often in her conversation. It seemed odd to Val. She told her the whole story but she just seemed to talk just a bit too nicely about him. And just a bit too much to be just a friend. Val knew Kat enough to know she wasn't doing something, more than likely, deep down there was some sort of spark.

Val didn't want her to be falling in love. It was too soon. And again if she did she would lose her. She'd just have to hope everything stayed the way it was until she went out there next weekend. They made the plans for her to come out on a Friday and go back Sunday night.

They were going to have an amazing time if the place was half as nice as Kat explained it. Hanging up the phone Val sprinted to the computer with the giddiness of a teenage girl with an IM date. She booked her flight and looked up the Ranch online. And wouldn't you know it, Billy Orbison, the resident Horse wrangler's picture was on it. Val's heart sank. He was gorgeous and looked like a young Mel. *Kat's in trouble*, she thought.

8

It felt like going to High School for the first time freshman year. Would they like her? Would she fit in? All morning long through her orientation, Kat worried. She arrived two hours early in order to get shown around and meet the other counselors. She felt funny wearing khaki shorts and a red t-shirt with the Camp Chipwood logo on it and for the second time this week *Meatballs* and a dozen other eighties camp movies raced through her head. She made an extra careful effort to keep the *Slasher* ones out. Jason Voorhees always scared the crap out of her.

All the other counselors, most of whom were younger than she, treated her nicer than she could have imagined. Probably because she had a degree in this field and more experience than all of them together. They went through all the rules and guidelines. The woman explaining them obviously felt out of place doing it. She kept saying, "Well you know what to do so if you want to do it a different way that's OK ".

Kat was flattered that they thought so highly of her but it did get a bit annoying. At ten o'clock, several large yellow buses pulled down the dirt road. Kat's heart rate quickened. With a muffled hydraulic burst the doors opened, letting out a flood of kids. The young ones ran and hugged particular counselors, the older ones strutted out - too cool to be excited.

The lead counselor, an older man wearing a blue shirt blew on a whistle three times. Kat was only briefly introduced to him. At the sound of the toots all the kids lined up in four separate lines according to age groups. Kat guessed there were ten or so in each line. The counselors then broke into three groups, one group per line. Kat was the odd number. She'd requested to be with the youngest kids. One of the counselors waved her over to the last line.

The kids started looking at her with curiosity. Some of them turned to whisper questions about the new counselor. Most of them looked about nine or ten and giddy to be there. The one male counselor in her group raised his arm and they all stopped fidgeting. The other two counselors scooted down the line and Kat wasn't sure where she should go. The front was fine she guessed.

The lead counselor turned and started to march towards a dirt path. The other groups did the same but in different directions. Kat followed next to the leader. She felt even more of an outsider. In only a minute or two they reached an athletic field with a few sets of bleachers. The kids climbed up on them and started to chat. The grown-ups stood in front. Nick, who had been leading the group pulled out his clipboard and started roll call. Everyone was present except one young girl who'd already called in sick.

"Guys, guys quiet down! We want to introduce our newest counselor, Kat!" She did love the idea of the having the kids call her by her first name. Being called Mrs. and Ma'am all the time made her feel ancient. In unison with a few stragglers all the children blurted out,

"Hi Kat!" It made her beam with joy.

The day went wonderfully. Without a doubt it had to be the best day she'd had since Jasper died. All her problems and thoughts of life not being worth it melted away as she watched the children. First they made popsicle stick cabins. Then it was on to kickball (Kat was the pitcher). But what Kat enjoyed the most was free time, when the kids were allowed to play games or do whatever they wanted.

That was when she really got to talk to the kids one on one. One little boy in particular almost made her cry. His name was Jonnie. He was small for nine and had bright blonde hair that was shaved short. Kat saw him on the swings by himself. After braiding one girl's hair she sat down next to him and started to swing.

Kat was very cautious, using all textbook techniques, as she tried to get the child to talk. He was very quiet at first but when she mentioned Sponge Bob Square Pants he looked her in the face with excitement. After a while Kat found out why he was so blue. It made some of her guilt slip away.

Johnny's father died when he was too young to remember. She didn't get how, but that didn't matter. Obviously he'd learned how to live without him but today a group of older kids had teased him on the bus about how he had no Dad.

Kat didn't find out most of the comments until later that day when she asked the bus monitor. They were horrible things, things that Johnny was too young to understand. Like, "Has your mommy taught you how to change a tampon?" Kat was furious at the older kids and made it a point to schedule a meeting with them and another counselor.

They talked throughout the remainder of free time. Kat learned a lot about him and for the first time she saw how hard it could be on a child to not have a father. Though she knew millions of kids were raised without one parent and came out just fine, she still felt better about having a miscarriage even if it had been half induced. Kat wasn't stupid. She knew what Val was up to in the bathroom that night which felt like years ago. She'd had no clue she'd taken the first dose of the abortion pill until it was too late and when Val was out she rummaged through her things because she knew something was wrong. That's when she found the pills, the ones that were still left. At first, she didn't know what to feel. Most people would have flipped out at Val and never talked to her again. But at that time Kat didn't want the baby no matter how much she wished she did. Crazy as it was Kat actually felt that Val was being brave. She saw Kat's state and knew it wasn't the time for her to have a child.

Kat still liked to think a miscarriage would have happened regardless, because of the amount of stress and medication she had been under. But there were no regrets. Regrets are handcuffs on your freedom...or that was what Kat had come up with after all that had happened. It was hard, but she was doing her best to not regret anything that had happened and just move on.

When the bell clanged to let the kids know free time was over, Johnny stood up and asked Kat if she was gonna be at the camp for a while. When she said yes, a smile crossed his face and he ran off. Kat was excited to have a child to look forward to seeing each day especially since it looked like he needed a buddy.

On and off during the day Kat's mind wandered to Billy. She wanted to tell him how much fun she was having here and she wanted to thank him for it specially. During the drive home she thought of nothing but him. It bothered her tremendously that it wasn't Jasper on her mind. She felt guilty but justified it by saying he was the first person she was a friend with on this whole trip and that it wasn't sexual.

She pulled into her designated spot at the ranch. Getting out, Kat could see Billy in the distance working on a fence. Walking over she found her pace getting quicker and quicker. Concentration was needed to slow it down. About thirty yards away she saw he was shirtless and sweaty. Her pulse rose.

Finally noticing her approaching, Billy tipped his cowboy hat. She smiled at him. He was covered in sweat and streaks of dirt. Large gloves covered his hands. His body was attractive. Not too skinny. No fat, and a decent amount of muscles. Kat thought he should be in a *Cowboy a Month* calendar.

With his forearm Billy wiped away the sweat on his brow. "Well Mrs. Kitty. How was your first day?" He rested his chin on a wooden post that he was about to drop in a deep hole at his feet.

"Incredible...I can't thank you enough!"

"Sure you can. You can be my date for the Friday night dance! Purely platonic of course!" Kat was flattered but thoughts of Jasper shot into her mind like lighting bolts. The last time she danced was at Jasper's good friend's wedding. And it was with Jasper. Come to think of it, she hadn't danced with another man in…hell who knows. "Well…Uh. I don't know."

"Nonsense you just said it yourself. You owe me."

Kat did feel a debt of gratitude towards him.

"Fine. But I don't dance well so you only get like two songs or so." Billy answered with a smile and plunged the pole into the ground.

Friday was two days away, and Val would be there then too.

9

That night Kat felt particularly lonely. Not wanting to go to the nightly dinner (partly to avoid Billy) she opted to make English muffin pizzas. She turned the radio on to a light rock station while constructing the small pies. Sauce, cheese, pepperoni and mushrooms on six halves. It would probably be way too much but she could always use it for a snack later. After popping them in the oven she laid on the couch with a glass of wine from a bottle she never expected to open.

She played over the day's events in her mind's eye. Maybe her stay here would be even longer than she thought. She was loving it and having the camp to go to was giving her a reason to wake up in the morning. The remote was in her hand but she hesitated to turn the TV on. No need to really, she was being entertained by her mind and the smooth voice of Billy Joel singing a ballad she couldn't remember the name of. She opted to close her eyes and daydream a bit longer.

Minutes or it might have even been seconds later Kat was sound asleep. She dreamt of being in bed with Jasper just laying there talking. She couldn't make out the words but she could tell they were laughing. Wait a minute. It wasn't Jasper. Well it was him but he had Billy's face and body. Even though he was under the blanket she could see his upper body was still sweaty and streaked with dirt crystals. She wondered where his hat was.

The dream was silent. She couldn't hear the rustle of the sheets as he scooted a little closer. Oddly she wasn't scared that he was going to touch her. But then why should she be? It was only Jasper…yet Billy. As he leaned in for a kiss, a foul ashen scent fill her nostrils. It was harsh and it stung her lungs. The smell stopped the kiss short. His lips moved to say something. It must have been about the smell.

Kat felt herself yelling "No" in her head as she smiled and reached under the blankets toward his crotch. He shut his eyes in anticipation. She could feel something hot in her hand but not a penis. His eyes squeezed tighter when she started to pull it out from under the sheets. He looked like he was enjoying it even though whatever it was, wasn't attached to his body.

She didn't know if her hand could keep a hold on it much longer it was getting hotter and hotter. At first she thought it might be a pile of hot mashed potatoes then she saw what it actually was. It was a pile of ash. Not any ash. She knew it was Jaspers. And it was hot and smoking as if just cremated. Kat saw herself scream silently and let it go. As she did his face contorted and mouth dropped open as if having an orgasm. Kat watched his face until finally a noise pierced her skull. The sound was so loud it felt like foot long needles being shot through her head at a hundred miles an hour. Jasper continued his silent orgasm, not noticing the sound.

With a loud slam Kat's eyes popped open. She expected to see the oak wood ceiling but she couldn't. All she could see was a cloud. Her nose burned. Smoke. Another slam. It sounded like wood splintering. The oven! Shit!

Kat sprung up coughing. She whipped her head around trying to shake the sleep off. Another crash, followed quickly by a scream.

"KITTY!"

"Billy?"

She could see the gray billowing smoke funnel out what she figured must be the door. Billy was only a shadow. It came closer. Kat was actually frightened by his figure approaching. It looked more like a monster in a movie than human. But once he was a few feet away she could start to see the features of his handsome face. The monster movie then turned into a heroic one.

With no effort at all he scooped Kat up in his arms and ran outside. She could have run herself but he didn't know that. And beside she wouldn't have this amazing memory of being rescued by a cowboy!

Once outside he set her down on the soft grass. It was a bit moist and she could feel the seat of her pants getting wet. She coughed a bit but not badly, being on the couch she had been lower than most of the smoke. Billy still had his arm around her back propping her up. He quickly scanned her body for injuries. None. Then with more panic and concern than Kat had ever seen in someone's face, his watering, smoky gray eyes met hers.

"You alright Mrs. Kitty?" She tried to bite back a smile. The whole event was just too surreal. It seemed fake. These things only happen in movies. Hell it feels like a movie. Why not give it a memorable movie line she thought.

"I am now cowboy!" He laughed but it quickly faded as he turned to the cabin.

"I've got to see if I can stop it. The fire department is twenty minutes away." Before Kat could protest he had already disappeared into the smoke filled door.

Kat got to her feet but her legs felt like they wouldn't hold her. The fear and panic of the actual moment had finally set in. Only a few minutes ago she was having a bizarre dream but now she was realizing what was happening. Her heart dropped out. For a minute she thought it had actually stopped. A crowed was gathering. She could sense people staring at her in curiosity but she refused to take her eyes off of the doorway.

"Come back...come back..."

Kat was muttering with out realizing. She could hear Margaret in the background frantically yelling at Buck, who she had yet to meet, to get the hose. Everything seemed to move slower and slower as she waited for her...hero.

Then in the doorway a cowboy appeared. Kat half expected music to swell up. But it didn't. He strutted out calmly but shaken. Margaret ran and started to touch him all over to look for wounds. He grabbed her wrists to calm her.

"Everything is fine!" Billy screamed to the now big crowd. Sighs of relief were heard scattered throughout the gawkers.

"There was no big fire. Just food burning in the oven."

Kat's heart swelled with relief for both the cabin and Billy. But the instant her mind was satisfied that everything was OK, it filled with embarrassment.

10

Sipping water, Billy and Kat waited with Margaret and Buck (who she was finally introduced to under such horrible circumstances) for the fire department to give them the all clear.

"This is the most embarrassing thing I've ever…I feel like such an idiot." Kat moaned with her head down. Billy put an arm around her and rubbed her back. It felt warm and comforting in the chilly air. She didn't mind having it there at all.

"Don't be so hard on yourself dear. It could happen to anyone." *Jesus this woman is calm at anything. I practically burnt her ranch down and she's comforting me?* Kat thought as she avoided eye contact from everyone.

A large fireman dressed in yellow gear took clunky, heavy steps towards them. Kat could see the others packing up their gear.

"Well folks no problem. Just a little smoke damage. Nothing a little elbow grease and paint can't fix. You'll probably have to air the place out for a while or you can call restorators." Margaret and Buck (who was even bigger than the fireman in full gear) walked away to talk some more leaving Billy and Kat alone. Watching them walk to the cabin Kat suddenly realized she was leaning her head on Billy's shoulder. And his hand! It was on her hip. Oh my God! It was an amazingly comforting and safe feeling but at the same time she felt like leaping away with a scream. Under the circumstances she decided it was OK, so instead of staying or leaping she slowly eased back. He seemed a bit hesitant to let go but that could have been in her mind.

Billy's heart was pounding. He'd wanted to hold her from the second he'd laid eyes on her. When he got close enough to see she had a ring on, his heart broke, but in his many talks with her he could tell something was up. Maybe she left him. Billy ran a million possibilities through his head just trying to somehow make her available to him. It was terrifying for Billy to meet her. Love was never a specialty with him. Girlfriends had come and gone as did love, but he never felt the way he did about Kitty with any other girl (except maybe one). And he truly thought he was in love before. But he was wrong. Maybe it was just an infatuation with Kitty but he didn't care. All he knew was that he'd never felt so emotionally high on life before. Every second since he had seen Kat she had been on his mind. He knew she was only here for a few weeks. That gave him time though. Time to express how he felt, but first to really impress her. The fact that he happened to be walking by just when the smoke was coming out was a miracle (well not really he'd been walking by ten or more times a night hoping he'd run in to her). But he did feel like a hero. Even if her life was never in any real danger, it must have scored some points with her. Hell, he was holding her now right. But then she had started to pull away. He'd hesitated in easing up his grip because he didn't want the moment to end. It was too perfect. Too special. But in a matter of seconds it was over. Now she sat beside him. He wanted so badly to just feel the warmth of her skin through her sweatshirt and to inhale the light flowery smell of her hair (which of course now smelled like smoke). She scooted over casually. Just a few inches away, but to Billy they seemed like a mile.

There was a long silence between them. Billy's heart hammered with too much excitement to let him talk. Kat was embarrassed and felt awkward. They both felt that if the silence went any longer they would scream. Kat's mouth slowly opened to speak, afraid of what might come out. But Billy spoke first, saving her.

"You know I see a lot of shooting stars up here at night. Better than anywhere else in the state."

She turned to him. His head was tilted straight back. Billy wasn't lying, he had seen tons up here. He wished more than ever to see one now. Kat studied his face for a bit before turning to look up. There were more stars than she'd ever seen. She never knew so many were up there. *It would be so amazing to make love under this sky. God...Jasper would have loved this.* The thought of Jasper on top of her with this view was enough to send a plump tear down her cheek. She tried to change her thought.

The only other time she'd seen anywhere close to this many stars was at the rest stop she loved so much. Thinking of that now, she realized the last time she was there she'd made a promise to herself to bring Jasper there. Another tear streaked out onto the cheek facing Billy. Kat was in too deep of thought to wipe the tear off or to realize Billy was staring at her.

Billy was trying to take a mental picture of every detail on Kitty's face when he saw the tear escape from the corner of her eye. He didn't even bother to wonder what was going on in her mind. He just hoped someday she would open up to him. Reaching out with fear of repercussion, he let the droplet settle on his index finger. Kat jumped a bit when she felt something touch her face. She looked at Billy with wet eyes, even more embarrassed than before. His face looked so serious she didn't bother to say anything. On his finger was her tear. He leaned in closer to her, keeping the finger steady. With the intensity of a diamond cutter Billy examined it. Kat was curious as to why. It stayed on the tip in perfect droplet form. The slightest movement would puncture its seal and let the salty liquid spill over his nail onto the ground.

"The Tinowa tribe that used to inhabit this area used to think tears were droplets of your soul. They believed if another person consumed your tears they would know your pain and fears. They would carry leather bags around their necks at all times. When they cried they would let the tears fall in the bags to keep them safe from others. When they would go into the bags later to retrieve the tears they were always gone. They believed the God Pinula would consume them. She was the God of Pain and Grieving. By having her consume your tears the pain was supposed to go away..." He sighed deeply before finishing.

"Too bad it it's not that easy." Ever so gently he blew the tear off his finger. It burst into a thousand miniature tears and dissolved before hitting the grass.

The speech took Kat's breath away. It was just what she needed to hear. This man confounded her. He never pushed or asked questions why. Kat loved that about him. She loved a lot more than just that though. Above the two of them, without them knowing, a shooting star burned silently in the night.

11

The entire cabin reeked of charbroiled English muffin pizzas. Kat actually laughed out loud when she saw the tiny hockey puck like remains in the trash. The cookie sheet was also beyond salvage. Luckily her bedroom door was shut, keeping most of the smoke out. It still had a faint smell but at least her clothing was safe in the closet and bureau.

Kat had apologized to Margaret and Buck over and over again, offering to pay for the clean up, but they wouldn't hear of it. They said that's why they had insurance in the first place! Jasper's cookie jar was on the nightstand. She flipped the lid open and shut while trying to recall the details of her dream. Bits and pieces were there but not enough to put it all together. She felt like she should explain how Billy put his arm around her. But she didn't. She didn't say a word to Jasper that night. But she did do a lot of writing in her journal.

Exiting her bedroom the next morning a wave of wet stale ash aroma hit her like a brick wall. She had to hold her nose the rest of the way to the bathroom. Shortly after her morning routine, a knock came upon her door. It was an older man from the Smoke Restoration Clinic. She was impressed at their speed in getting there, it was only eight. Margaret must have called them darn early. She let the man in and several other workers followed with odd machines that looked like space-aged vacuums. Kat let them get to work as she headed to camp.

Camp was great once again. She wasn't as chipper as the day before but that had to do with the previous night's events. But Johnny was there and excited to see her. He made her day once again. This time Johnny was much more talkative. They talked about all kinds of things, baseball, Sponge Bob (of course), toys and Spider-Man. He even mentioned how the guys on the bus didn't bother him today. The talk with them must have done the trick. Being that it was getting warm Kat thought it was weird that Jonnie wore a long sleeve t-shirt with his Ninja Turtle shorts. Immediately abuse came to her mind. He did seem to have a troubled past. So to check for injuries without it being obvious she kept patting him on the back and arms to see if he'd flinch. He did. So she decided to make a comment on it.

"I really like your skater shirt!" It was white and had a picture of a skateboarding teenager on it.

"Yeah? Thanks Kat!"

"But aren't you hot with the long sleeves?"

His face changed a bit and Kat had a hard time telling if it was confusion or fear.

"N...no...mommy likes me wearing them." Johnny abruptly got up and started to run. He got a few yards away and turned back to Kat.

"Come on! Let's play in the sand box!" Kat was relieved he wasn't upset but she feared she was right about him getting abused. But nothing was on his legs or face. She had time to work on him and find out.

Driving back to the cabin, Kat realized she was getting a farmer's tan from being in the sun all day. She thought about going tanning so she wouldn't have lines for the dance but it would be too late anyway. The dance was tomorrow. Dang it. She was going to look funny in a dress with half white arms. A dress. What was she going to wear? She hadn't packed anything exciting.

Back at the cabin she parked the car, feeling like a schoolgirl going to the prom for the first time. Swinging open the door she had totally forgotten the cleaning crew was there early. Seeing the furniture arranged differently than when she left made the memory of space aged vacuums snap back into her mind. She closed the door and looked around for signs of smoke damage. None. Next test, take a deep breath through the nose. Air flowed through her nose at the speed of coke through an addict who just one won the lottery. It had an orange yet pine smell. It was certainly better than what had accosted her in the morning. But pine and orange? Not a good combination she thought. But who was she to complain? It was probably costing Margaret a few grand. She'd definitely have to do something for them.

Kat stripped off her clothes and left them in a pile on the brown shag carpet in the hall. Turning on the water she noticed the toilet seat was up. At first it was amusing to her. Typical guys. But then she saw the dried yellow flecks of urine on the lip of the toilet and a much bigger still wet puddle on the tile floor next to it. Trying not to gag she balled up a wad of toilet paper and rubbed the spots with her breath held. Being somewhat still fresh the piss wiped up with ease. Kat tossed the paper into the toilet as if it was on fire and flushed it in a hurry. Jasper would leave the seat up but at least he would wipe up if he missed.

Touching piss turned her chipper mood sullen, as she lathered herself in the shower it came back slowly. Rubbing her pink loofa over her body, thoughts of Jasper sneaking into the shower crept up on her and took over all other thoughts. Every once in a while Jasper would whip back their yellow shower curtain scaring and exciting the hell out of her. It would always catch her off guard for a split second, but then once she realized it was Jasper she knew he was going to take her. He would always be naked and already hard.

Jasper would hop in, slide the curtain shut, grab Kat from behind and pull her back against his stomach. She would feel his penis push to the side straining to go back to its normal position. That's when he would start to kiss her neck with big sloppy kisses since she was already wet. One hand would cup her slippery breasts and the other would find its way to the small strip of hair between her legs.

His fingers would explore until she needed to be kissed on the mouth. Kat would spin around and they would kiss hard. Feeling each other's bodies all wet, sliding together would make their breath start to quicken. Jasper would always sneak a hand away to turn up the hot water. She never knew why and never asked, but he seemed to like it.

Not even realizing it Kat was now on her back in the tub touching herself lightly. It was only the second time since Delaware. The ring of water beat down on her stomach and splashed in her face. She kept her eyes shut tight and only opened them once to guide her foot on the hot water to turn it up.

Being almost a foot shorter than Jasper, Kat would step up onto the ledge of the tub. One foot in the corner the other on the lip. It was dangerous but pretty much the only somewhat comfortable way for Jasper to take her. It would always be quick, but filled with lust.

Kat finished out of breath and close to burning from the scolding water. But it was worth it. Kat had actually wanted to touch herself for a few days now but she was terrified that Billy would come into mind during it. She was relieved he did not. But that was probably because it was spur of the moment.

Toweling off Kat couldn't believe the red ring on her stomach. It looked as if someone took a giant cookie cutter and tried their hardest to make a Kat cookie. She wanted to go show Jasper what her lust for him had done. Finally dry, she put her hair up in the towel and walked naked into the bedroom.

The door was still shut. Kat threw it open, put her hand on her hips and made a mock angry face.

"Now look what you did!"

She said to the nightstand where Jasper should have been. It was empty.

12

Her hands dropped to her side. From where she stood she could survey the whole room. Trying not to panic she told herself that the cleaners must have just moved it. Her head slowly went from extreme right to extreme left. No cookie jar in sight. Again she looked back and forth. Still no sign of it.

The circle on her belly started to itch but she didn't bother to satisfy its request. She stood completely still except for her head which kept going back and forth. Kat knew it couldn't be anywhere that wasn't viewable from this spot, unless it was put in the closet or under the bed. But that made no sense. Why the hell would someone do that? But then again no one would steal a nineteen-dollar cookie jar filled with baggies of ash.

Fueled by the need to find Jasper Kat finally started to enter the room. She crept almost as if not to wake a sleeping baby. On the other side of the bed, nothing. She knelt down and pulled up the hand knit bedspread, nothing but a golf ball and blue sock.

Kat turned her attention to the dresser. She knew there was no way it would fit in any of the drawers but she checked anyway. Not there either. One last place. The closet. With her hand on the knob she had a flashback of the first time she was opening the closet to find Jasper's ashes. But this time they weren't in there.

Having exhausted all the possibilities of the room, Kat started to feel the panic crawl up her back. It felt like a dozen ants on stilts made of needles crawling their way from her buttocks to the tip of her skull. It made her shiver with fear. Fear that her Jasper was gone. Fear that her only reason to live, was no more.

Her legs were weak, unstable at best as she stepped over the clothing in the hallway. The parade of ants turned into a dozen drops of sweat that trickled its way down her back. She didn't bother checking the bathroom, she was just in there. From the entrance to the kitchen she scanned it and the living room. Nothing.

The slow refrained pace she was taking to try and keep herself calm finally snapped. She rushed so fast to the cabinets that the towel fell off her head. She hardly noticed. She looked like a mad woman, completely naked, opening and slamming cabinet doors one after another. Every inch of the kitchen was searched, refrigerator and trashcan included. Nothing.

The living room offered much less to search. Practically nothing actually, only the closet offered a big enough hiding space. Figuring it was the last possible place for her cookie jar to be Kat placed her hand on the knob and closed her eyes. She swung it open. Tears started to work their way out of her tightly shut lids.

"Please…please…please…" Kat whimpered. She didn't want to open her eyes. It wasn't going to be in there. Why would it be? She cracked them open a bit. Through her blurred vision she thought she saw it. All she could make out through the salty flood in her eyes was a white spot with a stripe of blue. The little chef cookie jar was white and he had a blue hanky on his neck. With the back of her hands, she wiped the tears away. It took a second for her eyes to focus. There was an old vacuum, metal coat hangers and a blue and white hatbox on the top shelf. No chef cookie jar. Her fear started to melt into rage. *Who the fuck has a hat box anymore? Especially in a rental place!* Kat leapt up and plucked the box off the shelf. She threw it harder than she'd ever thrown anything in her life. With an empty *thunk* the box slammed into the television. The lid popped off and shot back, the box fell straight down spilling its contents of nine mothballs onto the carpet. Kat looked at the lid and noticed a few dozen tiny slits cut into it. She wondered why she didn't smell it until she took a deep breath, her lungs were filled with orange pine once again. She felt stupid for throwing it but only for a second, her mind quickly went back to the horror at hand.

It was amazing how she could feel like the queen of the world and then in an instant feel like a bug being squished under someone's boot. She headed for the bedroom but didn't make it. She collapsed on her knees in the hallway. Picking up her camp shirt she strangled it as if trying to kill a snake. She kept picturing the cleaners stealing the jar, thinking it was drugs. Slipping it out in a bag so their boss wouldn't see. She saw them at a rest stop opening it up with wide eyes ready to get high, then realizing it was nothing. They probably threw it out the window. Her Jasper was probably broken into a hundred pieces being run over by cars, the baggies being torn open spilling her husband's ashes. She felt Jasper was lost to her forever. In slow motion she kept seeing the chef thrown out a window and shattering. What the hell was she going to do? If he was really gone for good what was there to do? Her one fear had been to finish her journey because then her reason to stay alive was over. What if it was cut short? What if Arkansas was as far as this trip was going to go?

The ledge! The private area she'd found while horse back riding came into her mind. *End it.* She thought. *Without Jasper I have nothing. No reason to push on. What am I going to do, stay here? No I can't. I can't go home. I just... The ledge seemed so easy the other day. It would be now too. An accident. That would be the cause of death. Just like Jasper. An accident.* Kat fell onto her side almost hyperventilating.

This was it. The end of the road. All because of some damn hick cleaners with sticky fingers. The vision of the cookie jar falling kept playing in her head but now it was accompanied by her falling, but she never saw herself hit the bottom.

Pain, fear, anger and grief pumped through her veins so hard and fast, she thought she was having a heart attack. Every part of her body hurt. She was making herself sick and she knew it. She started to cough and hack on nothing. This moment was worse. Far worse than when she realized Jasper was dead. She couldn't believe it, but it was. It was like losing him a second time but this time her life was being taken too. The frog pin flashed in her mind's eye. It paused the pain for an instant but not long enough. *Patty saved my life once but this is different. Much different. I don't care what the fuck that pizza boy said, it's not going to take this pain away, nothing will.* Her face was practically purple from so much coughing and crying. A gob of tear-induced phlegm was splattered on her face.

Death was her choice. She wanted it now. This instant. She used to read about people who killed themselves in the paper and think about how stupid they were. Why the hell would you ever do something like that? She thought they were idiots and had no pity for people that weak. But then again she had never experienced this pain. She now felt guilty forever thinking that. Death *was* an option in life.

After what seemed like hours she crawled to her room and dressed. What does one wear to die? Khaki shorts and a Plymouth t-shirt would do. Kat held her head up high, pretending to be confident about her decision as she marched out of the cabin. Outside the fresh air hit her face and dried the streaks of tears that had slowed but remained constant. How does one not cry at a moment like this?

Her body was shaking all over. It was a good two-mile walk up the hill. Twenty yards past her car, she stopped and wondered if she should take the road up. She worried her legs would give out half way there. *Do people about to kill themselves think about this crap? Do they worry about being too tired before dying?* A short story she'd read by Stephen King came into her mind. The name of it eluded her but it was about a salesman who was about to shoot himself. He kept worrying about what to do with his notebook filled with bathroom quotes. So maybe people did think about silly stuff before offing themselves.

The car. That would be much easier. Also, if someone found her car up the hill abandoned then they would find her body quicker. Billy would probably be the one to find it. She felt bad about that. Writing him a note to apologize crossed her mind, but she wanted it to look like an accident. No note.

Kat turned and started to walk towards the car. When she was a few yards away, a bright light hit her in the eyes. It hurt her pupils enough for her to bring her hand up to block it. What the hell was it? It seemed to come from the car. She took a few steps closer. It still glared at her. Jasper's wedding ring, hanging from the rearview window gleaming. Once she realized what it was the thought of death started to fade. Even though the ring was hurting her eyes she stared at it. Kat never believed in supernatural stuff but the sun wasn't out at the moment. The light seemed to be reflected from nowhere. After a few seconds the glare faded and the ring returned to its dull gold color. It hung completely still.

"No! Jasper didn't kill himself. And neither will I. I refuse to believe that he ran in front of that car. That man hit him. It was his fault! I know it. I know it."

Kat said out loud not realizing it.

This journey wasn't going to end. And for that she needed her husband. Damn it, she was going to get him back. What was the stupid name? Fire Restoration something. Margaret will have it. How was she going to explain that someone stole her cookie jar that just happened to have her husband's ashes in it? Well so much for the writer story. Getting it back was more important than what people thought of her.

She found herself running across the parking lot towards the office. Out of breath, she threw back the flimsy screen door. It slammed against the outside wall and popped off its hinge. It hung crooked, refusing to come back. The lobby was empty, thank God. Kat ran up to the desk and slapped the tin bell five times hard. Its small round button made several impact dents in the palm of her hand. She rubbed her palm, trying to calm down. The football player sized Buck stumbled out from the back looking like a giant woken from his slumber.

It wasn't whom Kat wanted to see. She swallowed the stream of angry words that wanted to burst out. Buck's blood-thirsty eyes settled down when he saw whom it was. He was starting to think this woman was crazy. He met her last night for the first time and she was bawling having almost burnt down the resort. Now here she was, slamming on the bell and again with tears in her eyes. Buck wondered what she looked like with make-up and a dress on. Probably would have been his type back in his stud days.

"Now settle down Mrs. Cutter." The giant said with a slow calm drawl. Kat hadn't noticed how thick his accent was, much thicker than anyone else she'd met here. Made her think he was raised in the woods. Kat wanted so badly to talk to Margaret she didn't know how to approach Buck with this.

"Is…Margaret here?" She squeaked out under her once again watering eyes. Kat wondered for the first time how many tears must have fallen from her face the past few months. It had to be a few dozen milk jugs worth.

"Margaret went to town to shop Mrs. Cutter. Are you all right? …Uh…Er…I think I might know what this is about."

Kat didn't want to hear that she was out, but it wouldn't stop her from finding Jasper's ashes. Wait a minute. What was the last thing he said? Kat was now confused along with upset.

"What…did you say?"

Buck's face started to look just as awkward as hers. The tiny spot of his cheek visible from under his beard started to turn a deep red.

"I was hoping Ma, err…Margaret would have been back before you came to the office. I'm not good with emotional things." Kat's tears stopped. She was too confused to cry. Could he know what was wrong? Maybe they thought the ash was drugs too. Did the restoration guys turn it in thinking it was an illegal substance? Or is big burly Buck thinking of something totally different?

"What do you know?" Kat asked with caution, yet not sure why. Buck started to back away from the counter. Kat thought he was about to break into a run for the woods. He looked so nervous she thought he might run right on up the mountain and live the rest of his days a hermit. Without a word he backed into the same doorway he emerged out of. Kat was perplexed. What to do now? Just leave? Go in after him? From the back room she could hear Buck talking. Whether it was to her or not she didn't know. She could only make out a few words.

"…I could…it's still wet…" Buck came back out holding what Kat thought she would never see again. It felt like a boulder just rolled of her whole body. Seeing it was enough, she just wanted to drop to the ground and collapse from emotional exhaustion.

"Thank you, thank you…" Buck placed the cookie jar on the counter as if it were a bubble he'd just blown and didn't want to pop. She now understood the mumbling that came from the back. It had two giant wet glistening cracks one on the right side under its arm and the other went from its feet to the chin. Buck looked at Kat and saw how pleased she was. It must have been very important to her. It made him crack a little smile. He knew he could fix it. Margaret thought otherwise.

"Margaret went out to get you a new one in case I couldn't fix it. It doesn't look too bad? I'm sure it will hold."

"It's perfect Buck…thank you." Then it hit her. What about the ashes? Were they still in it? He hadn't said anything. Carefully she plucked back the head to peer in. Buck's face contorted fearful that his glue job will slide apart being still wet. It was empty. Her heart sank again. She didn't want to show disrespect to Buck, he obviously worked hard to fix this. He must have the ashes in the back.

Buck saw her face twitch at the hollow chef's stomach.

"Oh! OH! Don't worry they're all in the back. I put them in a grocery bag for now. I had to glue it on both sides." Kat wanted to jump on the counter and hug the big man. She'd never hugged anyone that big before. It must be like hugging a much less hairy (well not that much less) grizzly bear.

Buck was polite and asked her if she wanted any coffee while she sat in the lobby waiting for it to dry. She said she was OK. He sat across from her on the love seat, making the two-person seat look like a small chair for one. The silence was a bit awkward but they both seemed content not to talk. Kat waited for questions about the baggies of ashes in a cookie jar but they didn't come. She was starting to think the men in Arkansas were extremely polite, or just overly shy. Buck did speak a few sentences but it was only to tell her what had happened. Apparently the cleaners knocked it off the end table. Buck protested that such a hard plastic could be broken by such a small fall, but what's the use in arguing with people these days? But they had been nice enough to bring it to the office to say they broke it. After the explanation Buck went quiet. His face looked as if he was searching his brain for a conversation starter.

After three or so minutes of silence, Buck went to the counter to check on the glue. That was when Margaret walked through the broken door. She looked at it curiously. Kat had forgotten all about it and was feeling horrible. Margaret's hands were filled with several large bags and the second she saw Kat her mouth formed an "OH". It reminded Kat of a silent movie actor showing shock, but she knew it was real and not fake.

Margaret was nervous that Kat was going to be upset with her. At the same time she was nervous that Buck had to talk to her alone. He'd never been good with talking to people he didn't know. She placed the bags down by her feet and went to Kat with her arms out. Kat thought it was odd but she stood up and accepted the hug. It felt good. Damn good.

It was such a motherly hug. Kat hadn't had one of those since her Mom had died twelve years ago. It was a sudden death and came at a bad time. But then again was there ever a good time for death? Kat was away on her senior trip to Cape Cod and by the time she got the call her mother had been dead for over a day. No one in her family wanted to call her. She was furious with everyone for taking so long and it caused many fights that lasted some time.

Pepper. Pepper was what killed her. She was allergic to it. Not black crushed pepper, she loved that and could eat mounds. She was allergic to fresh green and red peppers. One night out at a restaurant she made it clear, as always, to the waiter to make sure there were no peppers in her meal. She ordered lasagna, the chef said he didn't use peppers in the sauce. He lied, he'd used a half a dozen. Charges were pressed against him for some time but dropped after a year as it was too hard on the family to keep it up. She finished the whole plate and three hours later she was in the bathroom for the rest of the night. Actually she never made it out of it. Doctors never thought she would die from the allergy but the throwing up along with her throat swelling made her drown in her own vomit. Before Kat's father knew it she was unconscious.

The death was hard and it delayed her entry into college a year. The only good thing that came out of it was meeting Val. If she were in her original class she would have never met her.

But being in Margaret's arms right now was like hugging her Mom that she missed so much. Her arms actually started to squeeze a bit hard but Margaret didn't mind. Buck looked at the smile on her face and the two lovers' eyes met. They could never have kids. Buck didn't mind too much. He was content with his life, but Margaret did mind. Billy had been the closest thing to a child they had. That's why they loved the ranch so much. They got to see kids and play with them all the time. Buck might not have been good with people but children were a different story. Kids from two to fifteen seemed to take a shining to him, as he to them. Buck could always make them laugh, he would play for hours no matter how tired he got. Sometimes Margaret thought it was just a way to not have to sit with the adults and have real conversations.

Kat finally let go. She was surprised to not be crying, instead she was smiling from ear to ear. *Jesus! I almost killed myself today. I would have, too.* Kat thought as Margaret went back for her bags. She placed them on the coffee table.

"Now I see Buck has fixed your cookie jar up just right, but I got a few new ones for you to choose from just in case."

"Oh, no, no. You guys have already been to kind to me. The jar will be fine, don't worry about it."

"Nonsense! I bought three. Take a look at them first. If you like one, it's yours. If not, don't worry about it. Some of the cabins could use a cookie jar."

Kat smiled. She didn't know what do. The chef jar had meaning to it and she wanted to keep it. The glue job was good enough, but at the same time she didn't want to upset Margaret. The woman must have gone to ten stores to find a new one.

"Now I couldn't find a chef but I did find a Cowboy!"

She pulled it out and showed her. It was one of those obnoxious ones that said something when you pulled back its head. The side of the box had word bubbles next to the picture, they said *Eat um up cowboy! Get your paws of my jerky! Draw...a cookie that is...yeeehaawww!* Kat figured that Margaret had no clue it spoke. The second one wasn't much better. It was a policeman with similar (if not worse) stupid sayings. The third one made Kat laugh. It was the Pillsbury Dough Boy. It had a button in the stomach that giggled each time she pushed it.

"Well, what do you think my dear?" She looked the three over for a second trying, to act like she was thinking.

"Thank you so much, but I'm gonna keep mine, sentimental value." Margaret had a smile on her face but Kat could tell she was hurt. She felt bad, it was like hurting her own mother. But she figured it was probably much better than hurting Buck.

Over tea (which she only accepted to not hurt Margaret again) Kat explained in a vague but telling way, her story. Margaret was almost in tears. Buck just had a scowl on his face through the whole story. It wasn't a mean scowl it was a sad scowl. She hugged Kat again when it was over. This one lasted much longer. Kat liked it so much she thought about coming down here for a hug instead of a cup of coffee in the morning. When tea was done the jar was dry. The three of them placed each baggie in it together. It felt like a family. Kat liked that. It was a feeling she'd been missing.

13

Later that day, Margaret took Kat to get a new dress for the dance on Friday. After several stores they decided on a simple sundress. It was yellow with flowers on it. Kat had never worn anything like that before but she liked it. The dance wasn't that formal so the dress would be perfect. After picking it out they went to the salon (the only one in town owned by a chain smoking old woman with a beehive hairdo). She got a wash and trim to get rid of some dead ends. If it was a nicer place she would have spent a few hours and got the works, but the smoke and attitude of the owner annoyed her.

Back at the ranch Kat gave Margaret another deep hug and thanked her over and over again for everything. The two said goodnight and went their separate ways. Entering the cabin Kat was washed with shame. The place was a mess from her afternoon panic attack. Drawers were open, clothing in the hallway, the hatbox was dented along with mothballs spread out on the floor. Sighing, she went about tidying up.

While on her knees picking up mothballs with a Kleenex, her cell phone rang. Knowing whom it had to be she took her time answering it.

"Yes, my dear?"

"Hey honey! You excited?" Kat paused wondering what she was talking about.

"You forgot I was coming up didn't you!" Yes she had. The thought of Val being there tomorrow made her horrible day get a little better.

"No! Of course not! I'm excited!" Then she realized that the dance was also tomorrow.

"What time does your flight get in?"

"Six thirty three!" Well that would give her enough time to pick her up get back here and go to the dance. Val was just going to have to come. Not like she ever had a problem meeting new people. Actually she'll probably love the idea.

"Ok…bring a nice dress for tomorrow." Val questioned why and Kat told her it was a big surprise plan to take her to the cowboy formal. Val seemed thrilled. She then started to go on about meaningless little things at work, but Kat wasn't in the mood to talk much so she politely listened for a few minutes before cutting her off.

"Val, why don't you save your stories for this weekend? We'll have all the time in the world to talk about them." Val was upset but tried not to show it. She would talk to Kat for two hours a day if she could, but she knew she had to be gentle on the subject. And besides she was going to be there in another day.

Kat hung up and finished replacing the balls and shoved the hatbox back in place. It was nine o'clock and she was exhausted but she knew sleep would be impossible. The McDonalds that Margaret had made her eat was bubbling in her stomach. But that wasn't what was going to keep her up. Playing through the day's events in her head was. A walk was in order.

She went to the door and peaked out before exiting. Billy was walking by. She craved talking to him. To go sit under the stars and tell him how horrible of a day she had. He would probably offer his shoulder, but Kat was too embarrassed to do that right now. He was close to Buck and Margaret, and they would most likely tell him her story. She didn't mind, but she would prefer to tell it to him herself.

Kat let the old brittle curtain slip back in place. No walk tonight.

Billy walked by for what felt like the hundredth time that night. It was the first time he'd seen her in the window. She peaked out for only a second. He wanted to wave but thought that it might look creepy, like he was waiting out there, which he was but in a harmless concerned way, not a cut you up and feed you to the mountain lions way.

Over dinner Buck had told him the whole story about Kat. His heart ached for her. He wanted to hug her and tell her it would be OK. He wanted to make it OL. The dance was tomorrow and he couldn't wait. He wanted to see her tonight, but knocking on her door and asking to take a walk would be too straightforward. Or would it? At least a dozen times he decided to do it but chickened out at the last minute.

Disappointed that she wasn't going to get fresh air, Kat headed for the bedroom. Jasper was back standing guard next to her bed. The cracks weren't noticeable unless she was close to it. She didn't mind, as long as she still had him with her. She stared at the plastic smiling face. It never moved, never changed - just always a big old grin and two painted on dimples. She stared at it like it was actually Jasper and in a way it was and in a way it wasn't. It was the closest thing she had to a picture of him (that she looked at). Kat did bring a few dozen pictures with her but they had yet to leave the trunk of the car. Even though his picture was burnt in her mind almost every second of every day, she couldn't get the courage to look at real pictures. It was too hard. She could deal with her memories but to look at a snapshot of him would be like a knife going through her heart. Or at least she was afraid it would be like that. It was just like her father. After her mother died he didn't, couldn't, look a picture of his lost wife. Now that she thought about it, her father had taken that death a lot harder than she'd taken Jasper's. It got to the point that he couldn't be in the house anymore. He stayed in a cheap motel for months. You would think after a death of a loved one you would try to be closer to your daughter. But not Jim, he pushed her away more and more every day. One day, just like that he up and vanished. After four months of not knowing where he was she got a letter. He apologized and said he couldn't deal with seeing anything from her mother. It was either run away or die. He chose to run. Kat had only seen him three times since he'd left. Miraculously he made it to her graduation and her wedding. She wasn't positive but she thought the third time was at Jasper's funeral. If he was there, he never came up to her.

Laying in bed missing her father, mother, Jasper and hell, anyone who ever meant anything to her, Kat heard a knock. It was almost ten. Who could it be? She walked to the door stretching and yawning. Once again she pulled back the old curtain and peaked outside. There was Billy, sporting a nervous smile and his black cowboy hat. Kat couldn't help but grin as she unbolted the door and opened it.

"Terrible sorry to bother you Mrs. Kitty but I was wondering if you would like to go for a walk…err I know you need to get up early and I…I'm sorry I'll just let you be."

Billy turned to walk away.

"Don't be silly cowboy!" Kat stuck her hand outside and waved it around. Billy couldn't figure out what she was doing.

"Just checking the air to see if I need a coat."

221

"Not at all. Not tonight." Kat pocketed the key that was hanging on the eyehook next to the door and headed out. She was going to get some fresh air after all.

The two walked in no particular direction. The pace was slow and lazy. Not many people were out. There wasn't much to do at the ranch at night. Most of the cabins had a few lights on but even more had the blue flicker of the television. Billy noticed her looking at the houses.

"Crazy how people choose to watch TV instead of taking in the air and beauty." Kat responded with a smile. A faint burning wood smell was in the air (unlike the horrible smell from last night's fiasco). Looking up the mountain she could see a tiny glow of orange through the trees. Some of the guests must have decided to rough it for the night.

Without noticing it they headed to the path that led to the lunch grove. Once in the clearing Billy asked if she'd like to sit. Kat nodded and they sat on top of a picnic table with their feet on the seat. The area was empty of people and pretty dark. From where they sat they had a decent view of the hills. Billy cautiously put some space between them. They talked about the camp for some time. Kat told him about Johnny and how she was nervous he was being abused. Billy was seriously upset about it and volunteered to help her in anyway he could. He was so enthusiastic about helping, Kat thought he might have been trying too hard to play hero again.

Soon the topics ran short and silence was upon them again. Kat thought he seemed a bit nervous. She wondered if it was because he now knew her secret.

"Mrs. Kitty?" Kat had been staring at a bug that was climbing over the blades of grass with some difficulty. She found it so interesting that she didn't want to look away. But she did.

"I lied to you. Well…not lied, I just didn't tell you the whole truth about why I came out here."

That certainly got her attention. She was expecting for him to finally ask questions but he wasn't.

"I told you I came out here because I couldn't take the city anymore. And that's partly true. But…well I had a messed up family. Mom was the most wonderful person…, still is. My dad was a drunk though. I lived with his beatings all through school. I thought it was normal. I mean it wasn't horrible stuff, just the occasional punch here and there." Billy took a deep breath and looked out to the black featureless mounds in the distance.

"Sorry…I've never told anyone this." This time Kat was the one to offer a hand as she rubbed his back for encouragement. Kat knew whatever he was going to say was hard. Real hard. It was the first time he wasn't staring at her as he talked.

"Well anyway, when I was seventeen I met a girl named Yalitza, she was Puerto Rican. We fell in love like in the movies. It was that first time ever in love sort of feeling, you know? Where you're so excited to finally be in love. Dad was prejudiced…VERY. I tried to hide it from him but he found out I was in love and teased me about it. For a while though he never met her and didn't know she was Puerto Rican. Mom did and she thought it was fine."

Kat was the one staring now. Only one of his smoky eyes was visible to her. The other was turned away to the mountains. He couldn't face her. Kat left her arm on his back. He needed the support.

"Well Yaly…that's what I called her, didn't want to hide it anymore. She came to my apartment to introduce herself to them while I was at work. She had no clue how bad he really was. She…would never have gone… Should have never gone over." Tears started to fill the corner of his eye. He tilted his head back hoping the tears would go back in.

"It was welfare check day. Dad always sold the checks for cash and used the money to buy more booze for himself. When Yaly got there, Mom was out shopping for food with the little money he would give her. He was…drunk…I can't imagine…what…she…" Billy's head dropped to his knees. Kat scooted closer to hug him with one arm.

"When I got home from work the street was blocked off. I pushed my way through the crowd and saw a white sheet. It was slowly turning red. I had no clue it was Yaly until I got a bit closer and saw a wrist poking out form under it and the bracelet I bought her for our anniversary."

Billy sat up and wiped the tears away. He took his hat off and placed it next to him.

"He raped her…When he was done she tried to get away, run out the door, but he blocked it and threatened to kill her. She was tough though. She could put up a fight. She threw things at my dad cutting him up pretty bad. He still has a scar on his forehead… Anyways he cornered her by the window. Knife in hand he was going to give it to her, cut her up. But Yaly refused she climbed out the window and shimmied a few feet away." Three deep breaths and the tears came back. He seemed to try and fight them.

"There was nowhere to go on the ledge. Either way was a window for our apartment. I guess she was up there for ten minutes. The cops were there before she fell. So was the crowd. Dad tried to act like he was saving her. He hung his fat ass out as far as he could and grabbed her ankle. He screamed, "don't do it" and yanked. He finally looked at Kat, her eyes were slightly wet with tears too.

"I left town the next week. Dad almost got away with it too. He made up a story, said I dumped her and she came over to kill herself over me. They believed him until the autopsy found his semen and evidence of rape. He finally confessed to get a lesser sentence. He should be out in a year or so."

Kat had no clue what to say. She moved her arm from his back and scooped up his hand. She held it with one and caressed it with the other. He squeezed it.

"You never get over something like that. You learn to live with it though. One day at a time." Billy said that more to himself than to Kat.

"Billy…I'm so…" He cut her off. "No…don't say anything. It's fine. I'm not looking for sympathy. I actually told it to try and help you." Kat's hand stopped rubbing his as she thought about the statement.

"Buck told me what happened to you. How you lost your husband. In a way I've gone through the same thing. I was young but it doesn't make it hurt any less. For years I haven't told anyone. I find it easier that way. Having to tell a story that hurts over and over is the worst thing. I guess for some it helps. But not for me. That's why I haven't asked you anything. I know how much it bothered me when people kept asking what happened…'How are you?'…'I'm so sorry"… I'd have to thank them and act like it meant the world to have them pity me." His tone seemed a bit angry but Kat had felt the same things and understood where he was coming from.

"I know what you're going through Mrs. Kitty. I want you to know I'm here for you. If you ever need to talk. Or not talk at all, I'm here for you. I know I hardly know you but…I…just get this feeling from you."

Kat looked at him long and hard. He looked nervous. Kind of like a kid waiting to get a review of his oral speech he just gave in History class. Kat felt she understood him so much better. She felt close to him.

"Well, cowboy Billy...Thank you." They smiled at each other. No other words were needed. She knew he could talk to her and vice versa. And talk they did.

Before they knew it three whole hours had slipped into the past. A few times they would get up and stretch and rub their sore butts from sitting on the hard wood. Kat was amazed at how much she opened up to him. She told him everything. Even things she hadn't told Val.

Kat was happy to know that other people had lived through such horrible things and made it out just fine. She actually thought what happened to Billy was worse. On one level he didn't have marriage or a long relationship to grieve over, but the nature of the incident was much worse.

Billy walked Kat back. The two hugged and said good night. Kat went to bed feeling more positive on her future than ever before. Billy went to bed feeling positive of a future with Mrs. Kitty.

14

It was like the punch line in a bad joke - a one-runway airport. Kat couldn't believe it wasn't dirt. It was so small she was even allowed to wait on the tarmac. She looked to the sky waiting to see a plane with one propeller, chicken feathers falling out of it and smoke bellowing out of the back. But when it arrived it wasn't nearly as bad.

It was old and had two propellers but both were working. It made a smooth landing and stopped a few yards from Kat. Moments later Val emerged. She was pale as an eggshell.

Val never minded flying, but when it was in a ten seater she did. Kat couldn't help but laugh as Val's legs wobbled on her way over. Val just scowled and pointed at her.

"So you're staying in Hicksville huh?" The two hugged and grabbed the luggage. Two suitcases for three days. The one Kat took felt like a hundred pounds.

"You do realize you're only here for the weekend, right?" Val didn't answer. She looked like she was still trying to get used to the ground, loving the ground was more like it.

The whole ride back Val made hick jokes. At first they were funny but quickly they became annoying. Kat begged her not to make any tonight when she'd meet Margaret, Buck and Billy. Val knew enough not to tease her about Billy.

Back at the ranch Val went overboard on the *oh my gods* and *isn't this adorable,* not to mention, *this is breath taking!* Val must have said those three sentences five times each. Kat knew she wasn't doing it to be fake or funny, she meant it. She just didn't express it correctly.

Kat felt bitter around Val lately. She couldn't explain it but she felt anger towards her. She just couldn't put a finger on it. The only explanation she could think of was the fact that she was the last and only link to her past. Maybe she felt like Val was the only thing holding her back. But that was ridiculous. Or was it? Maybe this was how her father felt. For the first time she started to understand him leaving. She still couldn't fathom it, but a tiny piece started to understand.

"Wow you're right. They did a good job cleaning this sucker! I can't tell at all there was a fire." Val examined the ceiling above the stove. Kat dragged the suitcase to the bedroom. Val followed. The two flopped on the bed and exhaled.

"What time is it?" Val checked her watch.

"Seven fifteen."

"Well that doesn't give us much time to get ready. The dance is at eight!" Kat got up almost as if panicked. She started to lay out her dress. She really had to dig for her make-up bag. She practically hadn't used it the whole trip. Val propped herself up on her elbows. Silently she watched Kat. She was frantic. Acting like she was late for her Broadway premier.

"You think Dad will let us stay out past midnight!"

Val said in her best Valley Girl interpretation with wide blinking eyes. Kat stopped, realizing how she must look. Glaring at Val, she squinted her eyes. Val squinted back. Almost at the same instant they dove for pillows. It was an all out pillow fight. Val landed the first major blow to Kat's side knocking her dramatically to the bed as if shot with a bazooka. As Val lunged over her for the kill, Kat shot her legs up and pushed her aside. Swinging with fake power she nailed Val in the face. She burst out laughing. Out of breath they laughed. Val could always make her laugh. As much as Kat wanted to get rid of the past this was one piece she was going to keep.

Arm and arm they walked through the field in high heels trying not to fall. Val's were much pointier than Kat's. They kept piercing through the grass making her slant to one side or the other. She looked like she'd had a few to many. They giggled each time one of them almost fell. In the distance they could see the twinkling of lights in the dinner hall.

For a small ranch they sure did a nice job on their bi-weekly dance. The hall looked beautiful. White lights were hung up throughout the entire area. Powder blue bows and ribbons flowed in and out of the beams. Each table had a flower arrangement and candles. Even the disco ball that was always hanging there had been polished. A young DJ was in the corner trying to look smooth in a tux. Some new dance song from Beyoncé was playing a bit too loudly. Only thirty or so people were there but it was still early. Even fewer dared to dance just yet. Most needed liquid courage from the makeshift bar that was set up out of a few tables before being able to get down and boogie.

Seeing them approach, Billy briskly headed to the entrance. He stopped when he got a full view of Kat. She was gorgeous. Her hair was pinned up with Baby's Breath mixed in it and makeup complimented her cheekbones and lips. The dress made her look stunning. Billy knew she was beautiful but he never knew she had such a nice body. The sundress clung to her breasts making them look much bigger than the B cups they were. The spaghetti straps showed off her delicate shoulders. Billy wanted to kiss them. Especially the nape of her neck. Her legs. Her legs were so nice. He could see from mid-thigh down. They were toned and smooth, he wanted to touch them. She was smiling at him. Her lady friend looked like she was about to laugh. Billy took off his hat to welcome them.

Kat felt fat, pale and ugly. The whole time getting dressed she complained about not wanting to go, saying she had a farmers tan and she'd gained fifteen pounds. It was horrible, Val tried to comfort her but no such luck. Walking toward Billy she thought he must think she looked disgusting. He on the other hand…Well, he just looked handsome as hell. He had on a nice black suit with cowboy boots, belt, one of those string tie thingies all the rich old oil men wear and the hat (of course) to match.

Val saw Billy and knew why Kat wanted to stay here so long. He was the epitome of a man, the type that women have had fantasies about. Val herself wanted him. Out of nowhere Billy produced a single beautiful rose for Kat. She blushed, accepting it. Then she introduced Val.

"You're one hunk of a man!" Kat's mouth dropped and it was Billy's turn to blush.

"Gee, thanks ma'am. You're very purdy yourself." He over-played the accent to go along with the comment then kissed her hand.

They walked into the hall and immediately Margaret hobbled over, pulling Buck behind. Margaret wore a brown pant suit (Kat wondered if Val would ever notice she had a fake leg) and Buck wore a tweed suit that looked forty years past retirement. Val was again introduced. Margaret hugged her. Val was taken back by it and tried not to laugh.

The ladies took a seat while Buck and Billy got drinks. For the first hour or so they chatted about different things while letting the crowd grow. By nine, there were around sixty people.

"There can't be this many guests in the ranch?"

Kat asked while looking around.

"No, no dear. We open it up to the town folk. They love it! If we didn't there would only be twenty people here. Now that's not a party!"

Margaret said with pride of being the party maker. The DJ went from playing the modern hip-hop songs to the classic party songs. "Love Shack" began to play. Val and Kat rolled their eyes. Buck got up and offered a hand to his wife. She got up with a giddy bounce.

"Ta Ta!" The couple worked their way into the center of the dance floor and started dancing like they were twenty. Having seen this a million times, Billy watched Kat and Val's expressions of shock.

"He might be a burly lug but he sure loves to dance!" They all laughed. Billy got up and walked into the girls' view.

"Now you ain't going to let a bunch of old folks show you up now, are you?" He offered a hand to each of them. They walked arm and arm to the floor. Strategically Billy got them a space near the old couple, who were already working up a sweat. Buck loosened his tie. He looked like he meant business as he swung his hips from side to side.

After four fast get-down-and-boogie-songs, a slow song was much welcomed. Elvis started to croon about a river flowing gently. Buck embraced Margaret with lust in his eyes. There was more to that man than she'd imagined, Kat thought. Billy politely asked Kat to have this dance. Nervously she choked out a yes. Val started to head back to the table but another cowboy stopped her. He wasn't gorgeous like Billy but good-looking enough that Val didn't turn him down.

Billy could feel the warmth of Kat's skin through the thin dress. He placed his left hand on her lower back. He wanted to rub it up and down, but didn't dare. The other hand held hers. Their fingers interlocked. Sweat started to form in between their palms. Billy's heart began to race with excitement. Kat's began to race with fear.

Val had to fight back the guy's hands a bit. He was playful but nice at the same time. She was concentrating on watching Kat more than anything. What was she getting herself into? He seemed like an amazing man but…she couldn't be ready. Not yet. The urge to run over and push the two apart was hard to resist. Val couldn't tell if it was fear of losing her to Arkansas or actual fear of her getting hurt.

Kat had only looked up at Billy twice. He was beaming a smile so big it made the Cheshire cat look upset. She smiled back politely, but all she could think of was the cookie jar with her husband in it, cracked, alone and in the dark. She wanted to push Billy away, run back to her room, grab the jar and hug it, but the jar wasn't going to hug back. The plastic chef wasn't going to talk to her. Billy would talk to her. Despite her fears, it was nice to be dancing though. It was nice to be held, even if there was a foot of space in between their bodies. It was only one dance.

One dance turned to five. Billy didn't miss a chance to dance with Kat. She protested once or twice, saying she was tired but he egged her on (nicely though) and then Kat would dance. Hell the man pretty much risked his life for her the other day, least she could do was give him a few dances. By the end of the night, they were all exhausted. But it was well worth it.

Back at the table once again they watched the crowd thin out. Most stopped and said thank you to the owners before heading out. Margaret was actually sitting on Buck's lap. Buck was nibbling on her but stopped each time someone approached. The man Val was dancing with also stayed. Billy seemed to know him. Kat never caught his name. She couldn't help but wonder if Val wasn't going to come back to the cottage tonight. Good for her, it had been a long time since she had any. Then again it had been for her too. But that was different.

Buck whispered something in his fifty-nine-year-old wife's ear, she squealed like a fifteen-year old. In an instant they were on their feet, biding the rest of the table a good night. They scurried off like a young couple still experimenting with sex.

"Well, someone is going to have fun tonight!"

Val scoffed. Her mystery man asked if she wanted to go for a walk. Politely she asked Kat for permission. Kat laughed a fake laugh and said she wasn't her mother. She really didn't want to be left alone with Billy.

"Well what would you like to do Mrs. Kitty? Is the night over for you? Would you like to go for a walk?"

Kat scrunched up her face to show she was thinking. *Leave, go back to your room and grab your husband!* That played through her mind over and over again.

"I'm fine right here. It's kind of nice actually."

The DJ was gone and the florescent lights were on. Billy held up a finger, telling her to wait a second. He jogged over to the wall control panel. With a few flicks of the circuit breaker, the lights went out and the disco ball starting spinning again, spreading spectacular streaks of light everywhere. With another flick the radio came on. He scanned through several stations before finding *Love Songs After Dark*, the nightly radio show. He was nervous and thought it might be too straightforward, but so far he felt like he was playing his cards right. And besides it wasn't like he was trying to get some. He didn't care about that. He just wanted to be in the same room with her. That was enough for him. For now.

Kat watched in horror as Billy strolled back to the table. Was he trying to seduce her? No way! He was way too much of a gentleman for that. Her heart was beating so fast she felt like she had just drunk three espressos. She didn't want to look at him. Couldn't look at him. She knew if she did it would be all over. The setting was too perfect. It was like a cheesy romance novel with two sexually frustrated people alone in an empty dance hall, Barry White begging them to hold each other, and the disco ball spinning just fast enough to be hypnotizing.

233

She was afraid to look over. He had to be staring. He always did. But it was never creepy. It was nice. For the first time Kat faced the fact that she wanted him. Deep down she'd known it all along but refused to admit it to herself. *I'm a married woman, it's wrong to want someone. Was... was a married woman.* She thought to herself. Out of all the withdrawal cravings for her silk now was probably the worst. She started to rub the fabric of her dress under her nails.

Billy wasn't sure what to do. Kat looked awkward. The music was a smidge too loud to have a conversation. Should he turn it down? Maybe ask for one last dance? Just sit here? The Barry White song faded out. "Hero" by Maria Cary started to come on. Hearing it, Kat finally looked at him.

Look at him but not in the eye...damn it. Kat looked at him right in the eyes. She couldn't look away. Finally she let the feeling of desire wash over her. It was wonderful. It was a bubbly, tingly sensation over her whole body almost like taking a bath in Alka Seltzer. She hadn't had this feeling since first falling in love with Jasper, but she couldn't remember it being this strong. Or was that just because it was so long ago?

Without saying a word he offered his hand one last time. They got up and started to dance once again, only this time there was no space between them and instead of holding hands their arms were wrapped around each other. Their stomachs touched flush. Their eyes didn't look away and hardly a blink was taken. Their smiles faded away to serious looks, the kind you get when you really want someone.

Kat's mind had gone blank. Nothing was going through it. Just this moment. Hearing the song coming to an end, Billy leaned in for a kiss. He wasn't nervous. It felt right. Seeing him approach Kat closed her eyes and anticipated his lips. It was so soft, gentle, amazing. It only lasted six seconds and their tongues barley touched. He pulled back lightly. Both of their eyes remained shut.

No fireworks exploded but they both expected them to. Kat found herself not breathing. Billy was shaking. The song faded out. For a split second it was silent. Then a commercial for KFC blurted on to the airwaves jolting both of them out of the moment. Billy smiled with a giggle. Kat looked around as if not knowing where she was.

What did I do? OH MY GOD! No, I...I shouldn't ... Jesus...I've got to get out of here. Billy looked like a man who had just won an Olympic Gold Medal. He was beaming. Kat looked like she was just in a car accident. She started to hyperventilate. Carefully, then hard, she pushed herself out of Billy's arms. Not with anger, but with disgust for what she'd just done. She backed away from him slowly. Billy's face dropped to sheer terror.

"Kitty. I'm...sorry" He wasn't sorry, it was the best six seconds of his life, but he was sorry she was upset. Kat tried to talk but she couldn't. A low mumble just poured out of her. She turned and ran. After a few steps, she stopped, kicked off her shoes and started to sprint. Billy felt like a shotgun was put to his heart and fired. By the time he got the courage to go to her cabin it would be empty. Mrs. Kitty Cutter checked out at two in the morning.

PART FIVE
RUN, HIDE, FIND

1

Before realizing it Kat had driven an hour in no particular direction. Matter of fact she had no clue where she was. All she did know was that she had to get away. She'd done a horrible thing. Cheated on her husband. Her stomach was sore from churning non-stop. A sign read: *Rest area one mile*. Pulling over and getting her bearings was a must.

After the kiss she had run to the cabin and stuffed every piece of clothing in her suitcases like a madman fleeing the country on a murder rap. She stormed out, threw the luggage in the car and took off. She only stopped the car for a few seconds to drop her keys in the mail slot of the office. She thought she heard Buck and Margaret still up making love. She got back into the car and hadn't stopped until now.

The radio remained off, she never broke the speed limit and tears did not flow. Kat was too sick and disgusted with herself to cry. She did her best to try and keep her mind blank over the past hour. Jasper's cookie jar rocked gently with the movement of the car in the seat next to her.

The rest stop was dark and creepy being it was three a.m. It was one of the "park and pee" ones with no restaurants and just parking spots and a small hut with a few johns in it. Two of the lights on the hut were out and only one flickered with an orange glow. She did have to pee after finally digesting all the drinks from the dance. There was one other car in the parking lot but it had one of those orange *move your car or else* stickers on it.

Kat decided to pee in front of her car. More likely than not she would be fine in the bathroom, but she figured it would really suck to get killed in a scummy crapper after all she'd been through. She'd rather fall off a cliff. Looking around she popped a squat in front of the car. She had a handful of tissue from the glove box. Finished, she stood up, relieved to not have gotten caught.

Back in the car she decided to put the top down to look at the stars while figuring out why the hell she'd over-reacted. A few branches spoiled what could have been a good view. But that was fine, the icy air was refreshing.

Deep breath after deep breath she tried not to think about the kiss. *What's the big deal? It was only a kiss. I mean it was quick even, nothing special. Well...it was...I can't be thinking this with Jasper right next to me. God I need help. He's dead. There I said it. He doesn't know that I kissed someone and enjoyed it. Did I just say I enjoyed it? Shit. Why the hell did I run like that? They are going to think I'm an idiot and Val is going to be so pissed at me. Oh fuck! I didn't even leave her a key.*

Do I go back? Face what has happened? I can't, I'll look like I'm crazy. And I can't be around Billy anymore. I...I actually want him. God that is horrible. How could I have such feelings when my husband has only been dead for...for too long. If I go back I know more will end up happening with Billy, I won't be able to help myself. I mean that kiss...that kiss!

Chills ran through her body as she replayed the moment over and over again in her head. She felt warm and wonderful picturing his face come at hers. She tried to stay in the moment as long as she could since she knew the second the thought of Jasper came back it would be over.

Of course the thought did come back. It was like slamming into a brick wall. But this time she was angry with him. Kat turned in her seat to face the cookie jar with a pout on her face. She crossed her arms looking for comfort.

"Why huh? Why did you have to go snooping? I was going to keep the damn baby you know!" She was yelling at the plastic chef as if it was really Jasper sitting in the seat next to her. He might as well have been.

"It wasn't even your day to run... I just... I miss you so much. Why did you do this? Why the fuck did you have to get killed? I need to know. I have to know if it was an accident or not." Tears wanted to come out but she wouldn't let them. She had cried enough. She was past shock, grief and now on to bitterness.

"If you hadn't gone for that run we'd be in our second trimester right now." The ring hanging from the rearview mirror swung lightly in the breeze. With her finger she batted it around.

"I'm going to finish my promise to you. But when that is over...when I'm done...I'm going to have to move on."

That was the hardest thing to say. She meant it but at the same time couldn't imagine it. If a little kiss sent her fleeing from a place she was enjoying then how the hell was she going to have a relationship someday? She didn't want to think about it. Too bad she hadn't met Billy in a year from now.

Kat talked to the wind for a little while longer and decided to keep moving, not to go back. It would be too hard to go back and face Billy. As bad as it was going to make her look she wanted to just push on and finish what she'd set out to do. Using her journal she wrote a five page letter addressed to Val, Billy, Margaret and Buck.

Val and Billy hardly slept that night. When Val returned, Billy was sitting on the doorstep crying. He explained the whole situation. Val called her cell at least twenty times that night before taking a quick nap. At breakfast Margaret and Buck had joined in with their concern. But what could they do? Driving around was hopeless. They could only wait. It wasn't a long wait. Hearing the low rumble of a diesel engine, Buck turned to see an eighteen-wheel Mac truck struggling its way up the drive. He excused himself to see what the guy was up to. No one seemed to pay much attention to Buck's departure but when he arrived back at the table he had everyone's undivided attention.

"Well...this is weird. The truck driver said a woman flagged him down and offered him two-hundred bucks to deliver a letter here." Buck held the paper, knowing he shouldn't be the one to read it. Glancing around the table he automatically wanted to give it to his wife but figured the proper thing to do was to let Val read it first. She accepted it with her hand shaking just as much as his.

Unfolding it, she looked at everyone for reassurance. There seemed to be a silent agreement that it might be a suicide note. The letter was addressed to everyone at the table. Val read the first line in her head, *I apologize for my abrupt departure but after last night I realized that I must continue my journey before I can move on in life.* Val breathed a bit easier knowing she was going to be fine. She began to read again but this time out loud.

After it was read Val placed the paper in the middle of the table next to the coffee urn in case anyone wanted to re-read it. There was silence all around. No one seemed to want to eat any more. The letter was extremely apologetic. Everyone seemed to understand why Kat did what she did but no one seemed to like it. Billy excused himself with a smile. Val felt horribly awkward being left with strangers for another few days. Yet strangely she wasn't mad at Kat. She wanted to be though, but couldn't bring herself to it.

"Well dear…you can stay in Kat's cabin…there are a lot of activities going on this weekend. I'm sure you'll enjoy yourself." Margaret was feeling like her daughter had moved away. But then again she always got too attached to people. Buck stared at her knowing he was going to have to comfort her later. But he felt worse about Billy. Poor kid finally falls in love, just with the wrong person.

Billy walked to the barn and hopped on his favorite horse. The same horse he rode the day he met Kat. He rode Gary fast and recklessly up to the ledge where they first sat and talked. He was trying to get to the spot so fast you would have thought he'd left pills there that he desperately needed to live.

He practically jumped down into the sitting position. A spray of tiny pebbles flew off the ledge and landed far enough down that they couldn't be heard. Crossing his arms he leaned back. The cowboy hat tipped up a bit when it touched the cold rock behind him. Three lines kept playing over and over in his head. *Billy, another time, another place, another life…if only. I thank you for opening up to me, it meant more than you know. Take care of Johnny for me.* That's what Kat had written to him. There was something

241

addressed to each person in it. Billy felt cheated. She left because of him and he got the least amount of lines. He figured (more of hoped) it was because she was in love with him and it hurt too much to think about it, let alone write it.

Thinking about the first line he scooped up some small rocks and threw one by one as if to skip them on an imaginary lake. He would watch each one arch then fall before throwing the next. In a way he felt like them. Once up so high on the mountain, comfortable sitting there for years, until someone comes along, scoops you up and throws you. Then it's just a long way down. Billy figured that was what was ahead of him, a long way down.

Val lay in bed, wishing Kat would just come back. She was depressed. This was another failure in her mission to get Kat back. Things had been so much better lately. She was petrified Kat wouldn't want to have the visits anymore. Hell she was already cheated out of this one. Another two weeks were going to go by until she could see her again? That wasn't fair. For a while Val started to really think about why she was doing this. Couldn't she find another best friend? Someone who she wouldn't have to chase after? She tried talking herself into trying to be social and finding someone else, but she knew she wouldn't. What about a new man? It has been such a long time since she had dated anyone seriously. Actually last night was the first time she'd felt something for a man in ages.

His name was Trevor Tanner or Turner, she couldn't remember but that wasn't important. They had fun dancing but the walk afterward was much better. They held hands and Val got to experience the view at night for the first time. They talked for several hours and Val was impressed that he didn't put the moves on her. In fact she kissed him when they said good-bye. He wanted to make plans for the weekend but she declined saying she would be busy with Kat. Trevor gave her his business card (he owned a security system company) just in case she wanted to call him. She took it, sadly knowing she would probably never talk to him again.

Bored, and alone Val pulled out the card. Why not? She had two days and two nights to do nothing. Val dialed the number thinking she must be crazy.

2

By three o'clock the next day Kat had already scattered ashes in Oklahoma, Kansas and now Missouri. Her eyes were stinging from the lack of sleep. Originally she was going to spend at least a day in each state and see what it had to offer. But right now she didn't give a damn. She'd just knocked off three states in one day! It was odd to her to be in the middle of the country and still being able to go to so many states within a few hours.

Kat didn't even feel bad when she pulled over in North Miami, Oklahoma to just dump the ash out the window. It was the first time she was so careless in doing so. Kat did get a kick looking out the window at brown farms thinking *Wow, Miami doesn't look anything like I thought it would!* It was the only fun she had all day. She could have at least gotten out of the car. But then again Jasper wouldn't get the hint that she was pissed at him. Besides she was tired and cranky.

It was then on to Kansas. Like anyone who didn't live in the middle of the country, her first thought was of *The*

Wizard of OZ. She got excited entering the state just so she could leave it and utter the famous line to no one. She raced through a few small towns following signs to Missouri. Finally she stopped in a town called Coffey to get some food. Passing the sign she thought of the movie *Green Mile* (*John Coffee like the drink only spelled different*. She recited the Michael Dunkin Clark line a few dozen times in her head). She'd fallen asleep during the movie, when she woke Jasper was crying. He didn't try to hide the tears. After that she would tease him now and then by putting on a deep voice and saying *"Like the drink only spelled different"*.

It was just another forgettable diner that was actually just called "Diner". One waitress had dozens of pins on her apron. Though twenty years younger than Patty she reminded Kat of her. She wanted so badly to call her. It was amazing how you could know someone for only a few hours and yet they can change your life. She wanted to call and tell her thank you for saving her. She wanted to ask her if she ever hated her husband for dying. Maybe she would call her tonight.

Behind, next to and pretty much all around the diner was a soybean farm. Kat never liked soybeans but Jasper used to make special dishes at the restaurant for the earthy crunchy people. Knowing he would like seeing where they grew (and feeling a bit guilty about Oklahoma) she walked through the field. Normally she would have been nervous about being caught. Normally she would have constantly looked over her shoulder and done it in a hurry. But it was amazing what the lack of sleep could do. About fifty yards in to the field she stopped. Without a word she took out the baggie and emptied it. Like she'd done many times before she raised her arm high to let the wind take it as far as it could. She had been accustomed to saying something or at least thinking of something nice at these moments, but she'd been raised with the old saying *if you have nothing good to say don't say anything*, so she kept her mouth shut and mind blank.

She got back to the parking lot without anyone pestering her about trespassing. Grumpy, she thought maybe she should be more daring in life. Kat then climbed into the car and tuned in a rock song on the radio. She didn't know what it was and didn't care. It served a purpose. It kept her awake and cleared her mind.

Firing up the engine she backed out and drove faster than usual. The fatigue fueled her need to get to a hotel. With any luck she would get to Missouri in an hour or two. Heading northeast she had only two more towns to go. Franklin, that went by in what seemed to be seconds, then there was another…Miami. It made Kat laugh so hard she slowed the car down a bit. She never knew there were more than one Miami, let alone three in the world. The laughing was so hard that tears started to blur her vision. It was one of those overtired laughing fits during which everything is hysterical. Kat knew that, but didn't care. It felt good to laugh even if it was at a highway sign.

Crossing into Missouri and leaving Kansas the laughing had finally stopped but it left a small smile on her face. Sleep was close and that made her happy (it wouldn't be until tomorrow, that Kat would realize she forgot to say *I don't think we're in Kansas anymore Toto!*). About five miles into a town called Vernon, she saw one of the most beautiful sights she had ever seen: a bright glowing sign that read "Vacancy" at the High Water Inn. Kat was waiting to hear the angels start to sing *Hallelujah!* She got a room, grabbed her overnight bag (which was crammed with so much stuff she didn't know what was going to be in it) and Jasper (but reluctantly). The room was dark (not in a good way) but Kat didn't care. She dropped her bags on the floor and hit the bed like a car falling off a cliff. She was sound asleep in less than three minutes.

Five hours later she woke up to undress and get under the covers (which she saw in the morning were crunchy with some sort of dried fluid that she didn't want to think about). Sleeping away, Kat had no clue that thirty miles south was another town named Jasper. The name wasn't the interesting part that night though. The man pulling birds out of thin air in a dingy lounge was.

3

Kyle Winterbourne had just finished his third show this week where less than ten people attended. He was pissed, angry, disgruntled and in need of a drink. The two beautiful assistants helped him load up the small U-Haul. He always made the assistants drive it and stay in a different hotel than him. The two twenty-one year olds hardly knew the man they'd spent the last few months traveling with. He would show up an hour before the show to set up with them, do the show, pack up and leave them on their own.

Kyle never even talked to them unless it was a show note. They were too beautiful, young and tempting for him to spend any more time then he had to with them. That was why they had to stay in different hotels. He was afraid he would come on to them, maybe even attack them. After the last case was in the truck, Kyle grunted a good bye and took off in a separate direction.

Kyle always liked to drive to the next gig the night before, that way he could get plastered and not have to worry about getting up early and having to drive hung over. The girls would usually do the opposite. Luckily tonight it was only a short drive. Thirty miles or so. He arrived in St. Clair around midnight and checked into his hotel. The overweight lady at the front desk gave him a dirty look when he asked if any bars around here had easy women in them. Biting back rude comments and trying to be a good concierge, she suggested a bar called Sally's Shot Spot in Vernon, it was a town over but worth the drive she said.

Kyle dumped off his night bag and pulled back the blankets on the bed. He always got the bed ready before going out, not in case he brought a woman back but because usually he was so drunk he would just pass out. A quick check in the mirror and a vigorous spray of *Polo Sport for Men* and he was ready. He arrived at the Shot Spot around one and was surprised that the prude at the front desk had suggested a strip club.

Kyle had always been smart in life, sometimes too smart. He used his brains to manipulate woman and even to get him out of five rape charges (not to mention the countless others he was never formally accused of). Kyle never looked at himself as a rapist. Then again most rapists probably didn't either. He would never hide and jump out at a woman. That wasn't his style. He would schmooze and flirt. He figured once a girl flirted a little, she owed him. Amazingly with his aging ugly face and giant nose he would get laid most nights without being violent. He did have a way with woman.

In the bar he immediately requested a private room and several dancers. Though his career had failed and he was doing dive bars for nickels, he was still pretty well off. He had managed to save a lot from when he was on his way up. There was no use for material things when you had no real home. Woman and booze were his only expenses. Three women came in and Kyle felt like a king, for twenty minutes until he was thrown out with force by a short but unbelievably muscular man for excessive groping and trying to pay the woman for sex.

It wasn't the first time of course, but nonetheless it pissed him off. Sitting in the gravel he checked his suit for rips, none. He wanted to kick the muscular midget's ass for making sure he hit the ground on the way out, but he knew he would be the one getting the ass kicking so he opted to flick off the building while getting his car instead.

It was hardly two and Kyle wasn't even drunk. That made him madder than being kicked out. The fact that he was sober made his body shake. Liquor stores were closed by now, he had to drive around and find a bar quickly or else he was out of luck. Then again he did keep an emergency bottle of Parrot's Bay Rum in the trunk, but that was for real emergencies, like having to clean up blood off his suit. Kyle had never killed a woman but he had made a lot of them bleed. He had a weak stomach when it came to blood so usually he roughed them up as little as possible. Hell, he didn't like raping woman but if he didn't get his rocks off every now and then he would go nuts. It was a woman's job to servicemen anyways, if they didn't want to do their job then they deserved a black eye.

Aimlessly he drove around, getting more and more nervous about finding a bar. That's when he saw it. The bitch that punched him on stage, her car was in a motel parking lot. Kyle didn't have to search his brain and wonder if it was hers or not. He always had a superb memory to go along with his intellectual skills. He never forgot a face, name or detail. In the past year or so the alcohol had lessened it but it was still sharp as a tack. He knew instantly since it was the only car with a Massachusetts license plate. He pulled into the parking lot, not believing his luck.

There was a spot available three down from Kat's. Kyle climbed into the back seat, put his finger though the plastic loop by the back window, pulled the seat down and reached into the trunk for his rum. This was definitely worthy of using the emergency stash. He sipped it, trying to work out a plan in his head. Nothing came at first but he knew half way through the bottle he would come up with something brilliant. Something worthy of revenge.

4

Kat woke up when something scratched her face. Groggily she checked to see what it was. Realizing it was most likely dried love juice she threw the sheet off her. That woke her up fast. Getting up her body ached from too long of a sleep. She spent a minute stretching then ran to the bathroom. She'd been asleep for almost fourteen hours and couldn't remember peeing once. The bathroom, like the rest of the place, was disgusting. She did her best not to sit on the seat.

She craved a nice hot shower but thought twice about it after looking at the thick muck on the tile. There was no way she was going in there without flip-flops on. She couldn't believe she was so tired she'd pulled into this place. She couldn't believe she'd slept in such a filthy bed. The sheets weren't even fresh. This was definitely the worst place yet.

With the speed of a teen dressing from fear of getting caught having sex, Kat tossed on a comfy outfit of sweats and a t-shirt, grabbed her bag and headed out. The man at the checkout counter was greasy and missing one tooth.

"How was your stay…sexy?"

Kat tossed the key at him and left without a word. She really was changing! The old Kat would have lied and said fine before talking about the nice weather.

Relieved to be in her immaculately clean car (compared to the room), Kat sighed. She looked through a few bags in the back seat before finding some breakfast bars. No need for a sit down breakfast today. Get on the road, hit the next state, probably Nebraska or Iowa, and find a clean room with a nice shower. Maybe she would even splurge on a suite tonight to make up for this hellhole.

The checkout grease ball was now standing in the door watching her. He seemed to be laughing. Kat felt a bit creeped out. She plunged the key in and turn the ignition… nothing, not even a sputter. Again she tried…nothing. The third time she turned the key harder, thinking that might do something…nope. The man watching her just went from slimy to scary. Instantly she was accusing him in her mind of doing this. What else could it be? The car was practically new, yeah she'd put a few miles on it, but hell it shouldn't have troubles for years. To have it be completely dead, impossible.

She turned her head, the man was grinning ear to ear. Kat had no clue what to do. She should look at the engine but what good was that? She wasn't going to figure anything out under there (even with the lessons her macho first boyfriend gave her when she was fifteen). Asking the man for help wasn't an option, it had to be a trap he'd set up. The only feasible option was calling *Triple A*, but then she might have to sit there with the missing tooth man staring at her for an hour. Shit.

Rummaging through her glove compartment for the number she couldn't believe she'd been up for less than thirty minutes and already having a shitty day. *Knock, Knock, Knock.* Kat's heart jumped so hard she thought it might have bruised her chest. She didn't want to look at the window. She didn't want to see the greasy man smiling. Trying not to show it, she discreetly put her hand into her pocketbook turned her phone on (in case she needed to call for help) and grabbed the can of pepper spray (or *magician be gone* as Val had called it).

With the fakest smile possible Kat turned to the man. His face was so close to the glass his breath was leaving patches of steam. Kat made a mental note to get the car washed. Muffled she could hear him ask.

"Trouble?" She cracked the window just enough so that a piece of paper would get jammed going through it.

"Yeah…car won't start." *Like you don't know that you piece of shit.*

"Pop the hoody." Hesitating, she realized the doors were locked and she had a can of pepper spray. Why not? With a loud clunk the hood unlocked. The man finally took his beady eyes off her and lugged the hood open disappearing behind it. Even more muffle, she heard the man say.

"Well would you look at that?" Definitely a trap, the bastard is trying to get me out of the car she thought. She lowered the window some more. A notebook might fit through now.

"What's the problem?" He came back around with a pink sticky note in his hand.

"Someone done unhooked your battery is all, left you a note. I'll hook it back for you…" Kat suddenly had tunnel vision, the note seemed so far away even though the man had put it half through the window. She was afraid to touch

251

it even though it was a harmless piece of paper. It terrified her.

"Lady yous goanna takes this or what?…You in some kind of trouble?" Her hand was shaking harder then ever before. Taking the paper it made a slight rattling noise from her shaking hand. The grease ball that now seemed like a Good Samaritan waited for an answer. Not getting one, he went back to the engine.

Kat shut her eyes not wanting to read the note. Not wanting this to be real. She would give anything to just be back under the come covered sheets and have this be a nightmare. But it wasn't, this was real. Opening her eyes she read the note. *Boo! I found you! Whatever will you do?*

Burn it, rip it up, feed it to a dog, flush it and a hundred other ideas of what to do with the small piece of pink paper ran through her mind. But she knew better. She knew it would serve as crucial evidence if anything ever came of it. SLAM! The hood was shut. Kat's muscles in her arms tightened so hard it took a full five seconds to massage them back. She wondered how much more of this her heart could take. She was young, but come on.

"Looks gay to me." Kat finally looked away from the note to the man. Rolling the window all the way down she said.

"What?"

"The paper…it's a gay color. Anyways it's hooked back up, no biggie, it should be fine."

Kat thanked him. He asked if he could help with anything else, she politely declined. *That's the last time I judge a book by its cover, Kat* thought as the man walked back to the office.

What to do? Going to the cops would do nothing. The best bet was to not let the pepper spray leave her hand and just put the pedal to the metal. With a loud roar the engine fired up like it had been slumbering for ages, just as she put the car in reverse her phone rang.

5

Kat wanted nothing more than to see Val's number on the caller ID. Nope. It was a number she'd never seen before. Instinct told her not to answer but the new Kat that was growing inside her answered. She didn't bother to say hello.

"Well hello Kat! It's your old friend. You know the magician you shot down then assaulted on stage? You're lucky I didn't press charges!" Kat was fuming. Realizing he called the exact second she started the car she knew he must be near. Watching, waiting.

"What do you want?" Kat said. A second later it occurred to her that the line she just said must have been used in a million movie situations like this. Well it did fit. Kyle chuckled like you would expect a sinister magician to do.

"Just wanted to say hi my dear. That's all."

Kat hung up the phone and pealed out of the spot. The greasy man inside ran out to see if everything was all right. Kat knew hanging up on Kyle would piss him off even more. But she didn't care. She had a plan. It wasn't a good one but a plan. Drive. Drive fast. Supposedly he hadn't missed a show ever. Kat figured if she drove far enough away from where ever his gig was tonight she would be able to lose him.

She headed down the street not knowing where she was going, but knowing a car would pull out and follow her regardless. Her phone was ringing again. She shut off the ringer. Seconds later a car pulled out. She recognized it. The pedal was getting closer to the floor than it had ever been. The speed was climbing higher and higher yet he stuck right behind her. In an odd reversal, but Kat was actually hoping to get pulled over. But she didn't count on it, when you want things to happen like that they never did.

In the wavy lines of the heat up ahead Kat saw the road was blocked. It couldn't be, could it? Sure enough a train was crossing. Slowly. Kat started to reduce her speed about a hundred yards away. Was Kyle crazy enough to jump out of his car and attack? Kat didn't think so but she wasn't going to risk it. She double checked her locks and prepared the *Magician Be Gone*. Full stop. No sign of the caboose.

Kat sat breathing steadily, wishing there was another car ahead of her. She kept her eyes fixed on the mirror. It looked like he was searching for something. What ever it was he found it, then opened his door. Seeing his hooknose and sweaty face (Why was he sweating?) Kat finally learned the meaning of loath.

Casually, Kyle walked towards Kat's car but stopped at the rear. From behind his back he pulled out a two-foot sword that shone like a light. He must polish it daily. Her heart sank. *This is it.* Kat thought. He looked at the sword for a second then plunged it hard and fast down towards the ground. It snapped through the rubber tire so easily it could have been a balloon. Kat tried to think of something to do while the loud hiss buzzed in her ear. Anything that involved getting out of the car was too risky.

Kyle pulled out the sword and examined it for damage. None. Carefully he wiped it with his disheveled shirt, cleaning it as if it were covered in blood. Then calmly he went back to the car and sat down. Kat stared shaking. She was also confused, why would he go back in his car? The thought of backing the car into his and driving back to the hotel on the rim tempted her but she knew the car wouldn't make it. Or would it? Ten more train-cars until the caboose. She could wait until it passed, jump out and stop any cars on the other side for help. If she was going to do that why not call the police? Wait! That was it, he'd finally broken a law and she could prove it!

Kat grabbed her phone, it was vibrating. Incoming call from Kyle. She looked up to the mirror. His arm was hanging out of the car with the cell phone, he pointed at it. *Fuck me,* she thought, there was no way to call out with an incoming call. She answered, ready to give him an earful.

"Listen you rat faced loser, I'm calling the cops you finally screwed up you…" Her scream died down at the sound of the noise he was making.

"Tsk tsk tsk." Kat heard on the other end repeatedly. It was so cold and calm she forgot what she was going to say next. It was going to be a zinger too.

"Now listen Katharine. I know you want to call the cops but I must warn you. I also tampered with your trunk a bit too." Kat didn't speak, Kyle had control again. That wasn't good. For a minute she'd thought he was screwed, that she had him. But now he was the one teasing her.

"Speechless ah? Well if you must know there is a significant amount of marijuana in your trunk. To be more specific, let's say ten to twenty hard years worth. You call the cops screaming and accusing and they will search your car. Then just guess who will be going to jail? Hmmm…I'm not sure but I have a strong feeling I will be performing tonight." Now Kat was screwed. She could still run though.

The train was just about to pass, the rim would hold out long enough to get her somewhere where she could toss the drugs.

"Ahh the train is almost gone. Now if you try to run I just might have to make an anonymous phone call reporting a car I saw dealing drugs." Kat was furious. He had her every which way.

"FINE. What do you want you sick bastard?" Again Kat felt like she was delivering a cheesy movie line. She wondered if it was delivered well. He giggled his evil magician laugh again.

"This is what you are going to do. Pull your car over and park it on the side. You will then get in my car and put the handcuffs on that are on the backseat."

Kat's arm was going numb. For a minute she thought she was having a heart attack but it was her right arm from clenching the pepper spray can so hard, she eased up on it a bit. Getting in his car would be a death sentence but what could she do? Maybe she should get in and just spray him, punch a few times, throw the pot in his car and call the cops. It would work, but only if she was Angelina Jolie and this was an action movie. She was trembling so hard that she knew attacking someone stronger would be impossible.

"What will you do with me then?" Kyle must have been really enjoying this since he giggled at her question. Kat knew whatever the answer was it would be a lie.

"Let me assure you my dear no harm will be done to you. All I want is to get what is rightfully mine. What you teased but didn't come through on. Then I will drop you off back here and that will be that."

Kat believed him but didn't at the same time. The records she read on him had no violence. One case the woman said she fell and started to bleed from her nose. It also said when

Kyle saw the blood he started to dry heave. Maybe he wasn't lying? Or maybe he had changed, for the worse.

"That's all you want? How do I know you won't kill me?" Another goddamn giggle. Kat wanted to kill him for the giggle alone.

"Well for one I don't think you are in any position to ask questions. But on the other hand I am a gentleman, You have my word, and if you are really concerned about it I'll let you send a postcard to a friend first, saying you're spending the weekend with me." That blew Kat away. Was he kidding or just stupid? She didn't know what to say or ask so Kyle spoke again.

"You see my love you're in quite a pickle. For one you can't get away right now, and you'll never be able to prove rape because the letter will say you're having a wonderful time with a gorgeous magician. Second you will go along with having intercourse with me because I truly hate to force someone…takes the fun out of it. You see I'm merely blackmailing you. That's all. And do feel free to tell someone I was blackmailing you. I think they might get a kick out of you having drugs in your car. Oh and the pot will be yours to keep. I know you'll throw it away which is a shame, so I've taken the liberty of rubbing it into as many fibers as possible in your car. I do hope no drug sniffing dogs come by you."

Kat felt like he was talking forever. He must have planned this for weeks. The train passed, Kat didn't drive on or speak. Three cars and a trailer truck where waiting on the other side. She wanted to jump out and scream for help, she'd be safe in a matter of a few seconds. But then Kyle would just drive off and she would be a lunatic with a lot of drugs in her car and no proof that they weren't hers. She let out a big sigh as the small group of vehicles passed by, leaving her alone with Kyle.

"Well, what will it be my dear? I call the cops and you try to talk your way out of a felony or an hour with me in bed. You know more likely than not you will enjoy it. It might brighten your day. Besides you look like you need to get laid."

If Kat had a gun she would have gotten out of the car and shot him six times, reloaded and shot him six more times. But she didn't, she only had a can of pepper spray and zero guts.

She did believe him now. In two hours it could be all over. She could be on the way to Iowa, leaving the fear of the nasty magician behind forever. But the thought of his naked boney body on her sweating and pumping in her made her want to gag. There was no way she could let that happen. She fled three states away because of a kiss, there was no way she was going to sleep with someone even if he did have a gun to her head. Jail or rape? Jail or rape?

"I'm getting impatient my dear. Shall I just call the cops?" Kat thought it was amazing that no cars were passing by.

"No… no cops." She could tell Kyle must be grinning ear to ear.

"Wise choice. Now be a good little girl and pull over." Kat did as she was told. She was going to go along with it, but not go through with it. She would die fighting if she had too. Hell, yesterday she was ready to jump off a cliff, so what if she died now. Once on the shoulder, Kat thought of something brilliant. It would work! It had too!

"I must warn you. I've got my period…and it's pretty heavy today." There was silence on he other end for a few seconds.

"The more lube the better…ugghhmm…my dear." Kat could tell he was hoping she was lying. It sounded like he gagged in mid-sentence. She was lying but she thought pushing it more might work. "No really…it's embarrassing…it's all the heavy brown gook right now. It's ically disgusting." She heard Kyle cough. He must have held the phone away from his face to do so, For the first time she felt a bit of hope, but if he got her in the car it was over. He would make her strip and prove it.

"Just get going!" He hung up sounding angry. Perfect.

Kat desperately started to search the back seat to find something to put on her underwear. Something that would fool him. She only hoped to have enough time to get it down there. The phone rang again. On the third ring she answered.

"SO HELP ME GOD! I don't want to hurt you but you're really getting on my nerves! You have five seconds to get out of your car! I want your hands up as you walk over here." Shit. Kat was out of luck. She found nothing that could pass for blood. She stuffed the small pepper spray bottle in her sweatpants pocket hoping it didn't bulge too much. She opened the door, put one foot on the ground and stopped. She didn't want to leave Jasper. But she knew taking the whole thing would be impossible. One baggie would have to do. She stuffed it in her other pocket. At least Jasper would be with her if she died.

Out of the car she alarmed it and shut the door. The keys dangled from her hands as she held them up. She raised them way above her head hoping a car would drive by and think it was suspicious. No such luck. Amazingly, she stopped shaking and could walk fine. Slowly, but fine. She refused to look at him, keeping her eyes fixed on the empty road and the waves of heat rising from it. Today was definitely the hottest of the trip so far.

Opening the back seat door felt like opening her own coffin. She wondered if people got this same feeling when picking their own final resting box. Probably not. Val had picked out Jasper's, did she feel odd? Oak, plain, simple, she wished she'd been there, it would have been so much nicer. The cuffs were on the seat, Kyle turned completely around to greet her with a sweaty smile. She moved them out of her way before sitting. The back was clustered with stale clothing that stank of old alcohol. Some props were strewn around. Kat wondered where he put the sword. It had to be under the seat. She sat holding the cuffs, the door open still.

"Shut the door and cuff yourself to it!"

Kyle schmoozed like it was a sexy pick up line. Kat hesitated. *Do It! Spray his ugly ass face, reach under the seat, find the sword and stab his ass!* Kat thought and wanted to, but found herself doing just what he said. It was amazing how easily fear could take control.

With Kat completely locked in, Kyle looked pleased as a kid finally getting candy. His lips. They reminded her of Don Knott's: big, stuck out and always wet with saliva. They were disgusting at best. She couldn't take her eyes off them - probably because she dreaded them being on her more than anything else. Kyle started to drive. Her car got smaller and smaller until it disappeared into the waves of heat. Not being able to see it anymore, she turned back around and looked out the side window to avoid eye contact. Kat now knew what being arrested felt like, only now she was being taken to Hell, not jail. She felt numb, not scared anymore. Her mind felt like it was floating in a bowl of Jell-O. It was an odd sensation and that was the only way she could think of explaining it. Jell-O. Her thoughts were cloudy, but she tried to concentrate on the cuffs. She hadn't put them on tight. Most likely she could squeeze out of them, spray him in the face, and go through with the original plan. But she didn't. She sat there like a convict being driven to her execution. All hope gone, not knowing what to do. Instead of getting angry with Kyle, she was furious with herself. Why couldn't she just attack him, take charge? They do it in the movies, why couldn't she? That was when the poor victim thinking started to set in. The "Why me?" and "How could such a thing like this happen?". She pitied herself and it didn't feel good.

Kyle could not believe his genius. It had only taken him a quarter of the bottle to come up with this plan and so far it had worked like a charm. He looked at her now sitting in the back feeling sorry for herself. Hell, she should be feeling lucky. She was about to ride the magic bullet (a penis name he had come up with in his magic heyday, he thought it was so clever). That was an honor.

This was going to be a treat. He wasn't going to have to rape her. He would still have her hands cuffed to the bed so she couldn't attack but he wasn't worried about her doing that. He had mentally defeated her. Kyle always felt good doing that. Overpowering someone mentally was a thrill for him (a product of his older brother doing it to him). The best part of this whole plan was going to be at the end, when he turned on the TV after they were done to show her the video. That was the revenge! Not just humiliating her and sleeping with her, having a tape of it was the kicker! Maybe he would put it on the Internet later (most likely not, but that would be fun to scare her with).

Seeing the hotel come into view Kyle felt himself getting hard with anticipation. It wasn't the same hotel he was staying at, in fact he had never made it back there last night. He had stayed up working this plan out. At five AM he got a new room and prepared it for the events, took a two-hour nap then headed back to Kat's hotel. He parked across the street waiting and watching. Yeah, he'd be tired for the show tonight but if things went well he'd have time for a nap before hand.

In the designated parking spot Kyle shut off the engine, he was fully erect now and had to adjust himself before getting out. He glanced back. Kat was looking more like a zombie, white with no emotion on her face. He opened her door, her hands followed it and she was pulled into the harsh sun. He grabbed her arm, standing her up. Her skin felt smooth and he felt the magic bullet twitch. With the quickness of an escape artist he had the cuffs off and back on her. A little old lady was getting in her car a few away. She could only see the tops of their heads. Kyle waved, she nodded politely.

His hands were rough. They felt like dry scales scratching her under arm as he led her to the door. *Why hadn't anyone noticed a man taking a woman with handcuffs into a room?* Kat thought. But by the looks of the place no one would care anyway.

Inside she couldn't see a thing until the lights were flicked on. She almost laughed at the room (laughing was an emotion, good maybe the Jell-O was starting to melt). It was almost completely lit by green rope lights, only one dull orange bulb in the ceiling offered any contrast. It was one of those places Kat had always heard of - a themed room sex motel. This must be the jungle room. And if so Kyle must think he was the king of it.

Kyle left her side and strolled into the center of the room. Kat figured he was going to do a magic trick. In fact he did say *"ta da"!* But it was no magic trick.

"Is this not great?" Kat gave the most sarcastic smile possible. He came over and pinched her cheeks as if they were old boyfriend and girlfriend. She squirmed away but only slightly.

"Now is Kat going to be a good girl?" She just stared at him. He nodded as if answering for her. Again he took the cuffs off her but this time he put them on a table that was made out of a tree trunk next to a postcard and pen.

"There is your postcard my dear! Write away. Write away!" Kat stood there refusing. This time he did do a magic trick. One that actually impressed her. Out of thin air he produced the sword he'd popped the tire with. With great glee he twirled it and pointed at the post card. Kat picked up the pen and sat down out of fear of the sword and respect of the trick.

Kyle jumped on the bed and it swung from side to side. Kat hadn't noticed it was hanging on chains wrapped with fake vines. The room was covered in vines. Fake monkeys and parrots were hanging from them here and there. It was quite cheesy and definitely tacky. There was one giant ceramic lamp in the shape of a tree with a black panther wrapped around it. It looked like something out of a sixties hunting lodge. There were a dozen other stupid jungle items strewn about but Kat stopped looking and turned her attention to the card.

Short and sweet, she wrote: *Val having a fantastic time in a cheesy sex hotel with the over-the-hill David Copperfield wanna-be we saw in D.C. See ya soon! Love Kat.* She knew it would piss him off, but the longer she was with him the more she was ready to do something. As she gathered the courage do something, she remembered the pepper spray. He hadn't checked her pockets! She even had her keys, always a good weapon (so she'd learned in a woman's self defense class that Jasper had made her take a few years ago).

Kyle got up, noticing she had put the pen down. Spray now? No…she needed to wait until he put the sword down, wait until he was defenseless. If she sprayed him with the sword in hand he could throw it and cut her. He picked it up and read it. His already loose face went slack and twitched a bit. His knuckles went white around the sword. She prepared to move in case he swung. He put it back down.

"Fine…it doesn't matter anyway. It just makes you look like a whore not caring who you sleep with. See that? You try to harm me and instead you damage your own image… tsk tsk."

Kyle once again felt smart for turning it around to make her look bad. It didn't matter anyway. It was time to have fun now. He went over to the bureau that had an assortment of toys, oils and candles on it. Most of the stuff was his, some the hotel's. He lit several candles and discreetly hit the record button to the camera that was hiding behind a big plush giraffe. One of the candles he lit was under a glass bowl of scented oil. He always loved incense and smells. This scent was *Jungle Passion* or so said the man at the desk. It was one of the non-included items, Kyle had had to pay five dollars extra for it. He had filled it to the rim earlier. Liking the smell so much he put an extra candle under it in hopes to double the pleasing aroma. He turned back to Kat, penis again hard.

"It's time my love! Strip for me!"

"I need to take out my tampon first." Kyle felt his stomach bubble a little at the thought. But he calmed it by telling himself she was lying.

"Be my guest. The bathroom is there. Oh and if you think you're smart you're not. I nailed the window shut earlier today." He gave her a sinister smile.

Kat got up and backed into the bathroom. The florescent light burnt her eyes. They had been adjusted to the dim green-orange glow. With the door shut she checked the window. She wasn't even thinking about trying to escape, she just wanted to see if he was lying or not. He wasn't.

She ran the water and splashed her face. *I can do this. I can do this,* played over and over in her mind. She shut off the water and wiped off her face with a towel that felt as fresh as the sheets this morning, and then she looked in the mirror. She didn't see herself looking back. She saw a woman who had matured, a woman who had gone through a lot and had become stronger because of it. She saw a woman who was about to kick the shit out of a sick bastard. Kat smiled at the new her in the mirror.

She pulled out the small baggie of Jasper's ashes and gave it a gentle kiss. She wasn't mad at him anymore. Back in her pocket she made sure she could feel it against her thigh for comfort. Next she took out the pepper spray and shook it long and hard. Carefully, she placed her index finger on the trigger and put her hand back in her pocket ready to spring into action. She flushed the empty toilet and put her free hand on the cold knob. *I can do this.*

6

The door opened to the dull green-orange glow of the fake jungle. It took her eyes several seconds to adjust and see that Kyle was naked except for boxers. For a second she was surprised he wore boxers but then she saw that they had stars and moons on them. It went with the theme of his show. The show she hoped she would be missing tonight.

Kyle's hand went to his face to block the severe light from the bathroom. Kat was hardly recognizable in the glare. She could tell he had been stroking himself by the way he jumped up and half heartily pulled the blanket on him. The bed swung silently from his movement.

"Shut the damn light off!" That was the last thing she wanted to do. First she had to get a visual of the sword first. Her head panned back and forth like a spectator watching a tennis match, searching. On the night stand. Opposite night stand! Perfect. Kat took a step forward.

"Shut the GOD DAMN light off!" The last drop of fear in Kat made her turn and flick it off with her free hand. She could now see Kyle smiling, it seemed a bet green, probably from the light reflecting off his teeth.

"Strip. Don't worry you don't have to do anything fancy. Just get naked right there. I like to watch."

Kat felt a bit of panic start to well up from deep down. She wasn't going to go through with it! She had to. The hand around the pepper spray started to sweat. She worried it might slip or he might notice she hadn't moved it from her pocket. Still not ready to attack Kat placed her free hand on the bottom of her shirt. Slowly she pulled it up. The air felt sticky hitting her stomach. Maybe it was all the damn oil incense. It was so strong Kat felt like she was sniffing lines of powdered pineapple.

Kyle couldn't help but touch himself at the site of her tummy. It wasn't the flattest he'd seen and far from the tannest but he'd been dreaming about it all night. While waiting this morning he had touched himself twice in the car picturing these very events. Both times he'd used an empty coffee cup to catch the load. He snickered to himself when he made a comparison between the coffee cup and Kat in his mind. Man he was a genius!

Rubbing himself over his lucky boxers that an old assistant had given him years ago to celebrate their two-hundredth show together, he throbbed from wanting to see more of Kat. But she was taking too long. The shirt had stopped going up soon as he saw a centimeter of her blue bra. He wasn't expecting it to be blue. What a pleasant surprise. While enjoying the surprise he realized Kat hadn't moved her other hand. She wouldn't be trying to cross him now would she?

Wanting to vomit at the site of Kyle stroking himself with just the tips as if he was petting the head of a cat, she was ready again. The disgust fueled her. She took a small step and whipped out the can. Just as fast she pushed down on the spray button hard as possible. A hard tiny stream squirted out with a big mist following it. It had enough force to hit the other side of the room but didn't. Within a second her nostrils weren't filled with powdery pineapple anymore.

Kat had thought it would be perfect aim. Hell as long as it came within two feet it should do a number on him. That was the problem. It sprayed five feet to the left of him hitting the fake vine and dispersing into a fine mist. Kyle froze in confusion, staring at the mist wondering what the hell it was. But he didn't stay still long enough for Kat to re-aim. By the time Kat had adjusted the spray to hit Kyle, his boney shoulder was deep into her stomach.

Kat felt the air knocked out of her the same time as the can slipped from her wet hands. On the quick painful backwards journey to the wall Kat watched the can land and roll under the nightstand. Her eyes were glued to it until pain forced them shut. Kyle had tackled her into the wall. She could feel his still hard penis hitting her thigh.

Kyle had acted out of rage. The same time Kat hit the wall so did his head. A bright flash accompanied it. Thankfully it was only the top of the head and not his beautiful face. His heart started to pound. He had never had to attack a woman so brutally. Occasionally he hit one or two but usually he was prepared for it. He could tell she wasn't going to stop either. Her hands were already grabbing his sides.

Kat wrapped her hands around his torso. Thankfully his head was under her armpit. She tried to give it a few whacks with her elbow. Kyle tried to claw at her but kept hitting the wall. With all her might Kat threw him aside. It wasn't much of a throw but enough to cause him to tumble to the ground. For less than a second he was sprawled in front of the bathroom door. Kat was caught in the corner, she needed to get by him. Frantically she looked for a weapon, but too late. Kyle was already up. The two faced off like a pair of scared children about to fight for the first time.

Kat decided to make a dash over the bed to the sword. She jumped on the bed, landing on her knees. The blanket tangled her up just enough to allow Kyle to jump feet first on the bed and right past her. The bed swung like a violent pendulum threatening to take them both out, but Kyle was still able too pick up the sword. The scared boy that was there a second ago was gone, he now felt like a pirate on the turbulent sea brandishing his sword over his attacker. Kat clumsily backed off the swaying bed.

Kyle held the weapon high ready to claim what was his. He gestured for her to go to the table where the cuffs lay. Kat sidestepped the whole way to keep him in view.

"Put them on! And don't even think about heading for the door." Kat had thought about it, but knew it would take much longer for her to unlock the deadbolt and slide chain than it would for him to take three steps forward. She looked at the cuffs, not wanting her first ever stand to be over. That was when she felt it. A two-inch patch on her thigh was burning. It felt like one of those hot packs you put in your gloves in the winter when you're out shoveling for a long time. It was itching and she could think of nothing but it. She reached down to extinguish whatever it was. It was Jasper's ashes.

But that couldn't be, she must be crazy! She had too much to worry about right now…she was about to ignore it when she suddenly came up with a plan for her escape. She could think about the logic of why it was burning later. Casually, she sunk her hand into the pocket and itched hard to make it look like that was all she was doing. At the same time she reached for the cuffs to distract from what she was really doing. Taking her thumbnail she punctured the baggie, releasing the ash. She cupped her hand below it and emptied as much as she could into her palm. Satisfied she had enough, she was ready.

Kat turned to Kyle, who was grinning and doing his stupid giggle. She held the cuffs out toward him.

"Should I cuff my hands to the bed posts?"

She gestured to the fake vine in the back. Kyle, who hadn't thought about it turned to look. Kat pulled her hand out of her pocket. Soon as his head started to turn back to her she flung the ash at his face. Her aim had been much better this time.

It covered his face in an even spray. Tiny and not so tiny chunks flew into his eyes. He had no time to close them. Kyle felt a handful of sharp sand smacking him. He blinked instantly but wished he hadn't. As his lids closed the jagged pieces of ash scraped his corneas and burned like acid. That wasn't his only problem. He had also inhaled a fair amount in through his mouth and nose. He felt like he was suddenly stuck in a sandstorm. He screamed for air as the pellets bounced around inside and stuck into the soft lining of his lungs. A coughing fit followed to no help. His bony hands instinctively flew to his eyes but instead of helping, it dug the shards in farther. He wanted nothing more than to stick his head in a bucket of water to flush them out.

Kat saw the damage it was doing to him but knew it wouldn't last long enough. With both palms she shoved his hairy sweaty chest hard. He gasped for more air as he flew back onto the bed. Not even realizing it, Kat wiped her hands off on her pants. Not wanting to touch him again but knowing she had to, Kat grabbed his wrist away from his eye and cuffed it. She yanked him up closer to the vine-covered headboard. He was half-heartedly trying to fight her but trying to breathe and clean his eyes was more important. She swung the cuffs around the pole, glad it was steel and not wood. Without a hitch she snapped the cuff on his right wrist and jumped back from him. He was an escape artist but hopefully not prepared for this little trick.

Kat stood, breathing hard and looking down at the mostly naked, boney, sweaty man who was finally starting to breath again in between coughing fits. She felt a sudden wave of pride fill her body, until she realized she had no clue what to do now. If she just left him here, someone would find him soon and he would be pissed and wanting revenge more than anything. She needed to do something, but what? Exhaustion and shaking soon replaced the pride. This was the most intense thing to ever happen to her. She couldn't stop shaking. Needing support, she leaned against the dresser. She leaned a bit too hard and knocked over a stuffed giraffe.

Kat turned to pick it up and noticed a camcorder was hiding between its legs. She hadn't seen it before. Looking closer she saw the red record light was flashing. The bastard was going to film this! He had filmed this! Wait! That was it. She turned to see if Kyle had opened his eyes yet. Nope. Streaks of pain-induced tears were flowing down his head and into his ears. Kyle was starting to make some grunting noises, his voice would be back soon. She angled the camera to get a better view of him.

In the bathroom Kat took one of the sanitary plastic cups that didn't look too sanitary and filled it with cold water. She went to Kyle with it and sat on the edge of the bed. From a foot above his mouth she poured it in. He jumped at first then raised his head as high as he could to suck it down. She stopped the stream.

"Plu...plea...se...eyes...eyes...!" Kat dumped the rest on his face. He let out a moan and blinked profusely. He opened his eyes to no success. All he could see was spots of green.

"More! God please more! I can't fucking see!"

Kat got up from the bed and out of the camera's view.

"NO! Not until you tell me why you tried to BLACK MAIL ME into having sex!" She raised her voice on black mail so the camera would be sure to get it. Kyle already looked like he was in pain but his face contorted more at the question.

"Because no woman flirts with this magic man without putting out! I get what I want."

"So since I accidentally looked at you I owe you sex?"

"Oh you wanted it and you know it! All whores do. That's what women are! Some just need a little help when it comes to giving it up!"

The shaking had stopped and rage was taking over. She had never wanted to harm someone before but the thought of this boney bastard raping God knows how many women made her see red.

"How many woman have you raped? Don't lie to me either, you're not in a position to lie!" Kat picked up the sword that had fallen from his hands during the ash storm and put it to his face then slid it down s she could press the cold metal against his stomach. He flinched. She slid it farther along his torso until the point was pushing into the ribs on his side. Kat couldn't believe what she saw. Something in his boxer shorts started to rise.

"I've never raped a woman! I've had to help many realize they wanted me though!"

The thought that she was turning him on made the anger rise. She took the flat part of the sword and slapped it hard against his chest. It left an immediate red line. He winced once again with pain.

"HOW MANY?" Kat found herself screaming. For a minute she was worried someone would hear her screaming, then she realized they were in a sleazy sex motel. She could scream all she wanted.

"How the fuck do I know? Few dozen, maybe less?"

Kyle at first couldn't believe this was happening. The fact that it aroused him being dominated, was shocking, he never knew he would like that. Then she started asking too much about others. That made him nervous. His penis immediately went limp. His throat tasted like he'd chewed on an ashtray and his eyes felt like cigarettes were put out in them.

How could this be happening? She couldn't out smart him. Kyle was a genius. Not one woman had ever gotten him. Even the five that cried about it. He had won the trials.

He would win this. Or so he thought. She wouldn't have the balls to hurt him seriously. She would leave soon and he would have time to get ready for her again. Thank God she didn't know about the camera.

Kat knew she couldn't let this man go on raping women. The video would be great evidence but from what she could gather from all the *Law and Order* episodes she'd seen, it wouldn't be usable in court. Killing him would work but that thought never crossed her mind. Well not seriously. And as much as she thought it was funny that Kyle was squeamish at blood, she was pretty much the same. Something had to be done though. She took a deep breath to clear her mind. Instead of clearing her mind the deep breath burned her nostrils. Damn pineapple smell, she realized she was standing right over the almost boiling decorative bowl of scented oil. Wait a minute...

Kyle had kept his mouth and eyes shut since it stung too much to open them. He was nervous wondering what the hell she was going to do and what he could do to fight it. If he had his damn lock pick he would be out of this in a flash, damn it. He heard a light switch flick again and hoped she was getting him another glass of water. The last one felt like a cup of Heaven being poured onto him. With another cup he thought maybe his eyes would improve, allowing him to at least see a little bit. The switch clicked again. He wished it wasn't such a soft carpet so he could hear her footsteps better. Then the bed started to gently swing. She must be climbing on it. Something cold touched his hips on both sides. Must be her fingers. He tried not to get excited, it got him a whack last time. But then the fingers were gone. What the hell is she doing?

Kat was going to remove his boxers for this but decided against it when she saw it flinch. She'd already seen enough of this man anyway. She especially didn't want that image stuck in her head. Knowing he was going to scream she lightly placed a pillow over his face. He tried to fight it off but it only moved a bit. It wouldn't do much but it might help a bit.

With the towel she took from the bathroom she carefully lifted the bowl of slightly bubbling pink oil. The heat went through the towel. Good, it would burn. She turned around ever so slowly, trying not to spill it on her hands. She stood above him, his legs were spread apart just enough. Second thoughts started to jump her mind, but before they could win over she dumped it.

Kyle's body arched off the bed, legs flaring up, arms fighting the cuffs. Kat thought that he looked more like he was getting electrocuted than burned. The scream was awful. The pillow hadn't done much. After a solid minute of kicking and yelling he settled down enough for her to look at the damage a bit closer. A low constant hum came from under the pillow. Kat wondered if he was in shock. It has done more damage than she'd thought it would. From his knees to just below his belly button was scarlet red. Steam was coming off his shorts, she wondered how that was possible. But the worst part was the skin that was falling off his muscle. White globs of skin were being pulled down right before where his shorts started. When she leaned closer a big chunk actually fell to the bedspread, Kat fought off a gag. The moaning stopped, as did his movement. Jesus, he'd passed out! Kat couldn't imagine what under the shorts looked like. It had to be worse, it was a direct hit. For a second she pictured him peeling the shorts off and all the skin going with it.

Starting to feel guilty, she told herself to think of the revenge she had taken for so many woman and how many

274